T0355029

THETIS

THETIS

THE DEEP SKY SAGA

BOOK TWO

GREG BOOSE

DIVERSION
BOOKS

Diversion Books
A Division of Diversion Publishing Corp.
443 Park Avenue South, Suite 1004
New York, New York 10016
www.DiversionBooks.com

For more information, email info@diversionbooks.com

First Diversion Books edition October 2018.
Paperback ISBN: 978-1-63576-458-1
eBook ISBN: 978-1-63576-457-4

LSIDB/1810

To Veronica and Juliette,
my two moons.

CHAPTER ONE

As the ship rumbles and roars and lifts off the beach, Jonah squeezes his armrests like a man dangling over a cliff. The plastic in his grip bends inwards, creaking and then popping until it finally cracks, and the sharp shards cut into his skin. The pain feels good. The pain distracts him. His fingernails pull back on the plastic until he feels warm blood covering his cuticles. He shouldn't be on this ship. He needs to get off this ship. Before he screams. Before he sobs. Before the voices from the beach come back in his head and tell him to do things he doesn't want to do.

The seatbelts crisscrossing his chest are the only things stopping Jonah from barreling into the flight deck and screaming at the pilot to let him out. He tries to undo the clasps, but his bloody fingertips slip and slide over the cold metal. Even if he could get a solid grip, the man who smells like lavender, who pulled him onto this ship and pushed him into this seat, locked his belts by typing in a long code near Jonah's shoulder. It's not fair; only he and Brooklyn—the two blind kids on the verge of death—have locks on their belts. The lavender man and a woman with a gruff voice and a terrible cough who says she's a doctor must think they're either contagious or dangerous, or both. He *is* dangerous, Jonah thinks. But in different ways. The voices on the beach say he's been chosen for something. And he knows it's not to be saved by these people from Thetis and then to live a happy, simple life in the Athens colony. They've chosen him for something bigger, something he can feel will hurt himself and others.

Even with the belts pinning him to his seat, Jonah lunges forward and tries to stand. Next to him, Vespa Bolivar gasps as if he's just woken her from a bad dream.

"Listen to me," Jonah whispers. "We need to get off this ship. Right now."

Vespa sighs and pats his chest right where his heart pounds. "We'll get off on Thetis, okay? Just try to relax. We're getting saved, Firstie. Things…I think things are finally starting to work out for us. Screw Achilles. It's over."

A thousand pinpricks run over Jonah's skin. *It's over? It's just beginning.* His belts finally give some slack, and he doubles over in his seat, bouncing there for a few seconds before shouting, "Let me out of here! Somebody let me up!"

"*Jesus, cadet.*" Vespa grabs his bicep with both hands. "Just sit still. You're going to rip out your tubes. You seriously need to chill the fuck out."

The ship banks right and the rubber tube sticking out of Jonah's arm brushes against his cheek. He instantly panics, swinging his hands in the air like he just walked into a spider web. A bag hangs somewhere over his head, pumping him full of what the doctor on board says is the cure to his Sepsis Bimorphyria disease. He can only take her word for it. He has to. If he could see, if this disease from the wormhole hadn't turned his eyeballs blue and eventually blinded him, then he wouldn't have to. He also wouldn't need to ask Vespa so many questions.

"What's the medicine look like?" Jonah asks. "How much are they giving me? Is it too much? How much is left in there? What color is it?"

"It's clear, I guess," she says. "Looks like medicine."

"But how much are they giving me? Is it a lot? Is it too much, you think?"

"I don't know, Jonah. A bag's worth?"

"But how big is the bag?"

Vespa stops answering. Her body heat disappears as she shifts toward the window, so he reaches for her hand, leg, anything, but she blocks him, softly pushing his hand away each time.

The ship stops and then bounces gently, hovering in one spot, and Jonah pictures the island below glowing with fire. He pictures the waves lapping at the beach, pulling and pushing blood and ash through the gray sand, leaving faint red and black lines all along the shore. Somewhere down there a herd of giant white spiders floats over the waves, their hairy arms intertwined, drifting along like a lost blanket. Jonah wishes he was with them, sitting on their backs, heading anywhere but Thetis.

The ship's boosters chug and wheeze for a moment, and Jonah can't help but think that at any second the engines will fail, and they'll go down in flames like the *Mayflower 2* did just a week ago. The ship's going to tear through the jungle and rip apart, shedding bodies in every direction. They're all going to die. Everyone, except maybe him. He'll survive just long enough to blindly starve over a day or two. That's been his luck. That's been his life. But then the boosters get louder, the wheezes turn to roars, and the ship shoots forward like an arrow. Not up toward Thetis and the rest of the Silver Foot Galaxy, but straight ahead.

Jonah again reaches his hand out for Vespa and this time she takes it. "It's okay; I think we're headed for the crash site. I told them where it is. They need to see if there's anything salvageable to bring back to Thetis. They were counting on a lot of our supplies, you know. I think us crashing really screwed them over."

He's both relieved and terrified to learn they're not leaving Achilles just yet. Maybe there's still time to abandon ship. Maybe when they land, they'll let him out and he can somehow find his sheaf with his parents' photo on it. Maybe he's already had enough medicine, and his sight will return long enough for him to wander off into the jungle and die staring at it with his back against a tree and the sun on his face. Maybe he'll eat some weird plant and he'll be magically cured, and he can live here alone without anyone hunting him down. And maybe the voices will never come back.

"What's it look like out there?" He asks.

"It looks like hell, Jonah. Just how we left it."

He knows the valley below is charred and black, that they're flying over dead bodies, some with symbols carved into their skin. Tunick and Sean carved those symbols, a warning to him and anyone else who survived the crash. That's after the brothers tortured and killed two adults and wrote *Run* and *Kids are free now* on their shirts. He wants to run. He wants to land and the doors to open so he can run away and be free.

Jonah leans back and feels every bruise and cut on his body. He clenches his eyes and then opens them with a shot, testing the medicine dripping into his arm, hoping that if it actually does work it will be instantaneous. Still, he sees nothing but blackness and horrific, broken images from the past few days. He listens to the whirs and hums and beeps of the ship, the boosters that blast them forward. He listens to his friend Brooklyn groaning several feet away and to the lavender man mumbling coordinates before someone closes a door between them.

He wipes a bloody hand on his leg and fumbles his fingers over Vespa's bare arm. He pulls her in and whispers as quietly as he can: "These people from Thetis flying the ship—you think they're going to kill us? I think they're going to kill us. Remember, Tunick and the Splitters said that Thetis was a very bad place to be. They said—"

Vespa pulls away again. "*Jesus.* It's over, Jonah. It's over. Please just shut up and stop asking me everything. I need a moment, okay? I need a second to relax. I need time, too, you know. You're not the only one going through some shit in their head right now."

Jonah opens his mouth to speak, but instead holds his breath and focuses on his own thoughts, preparing to fight any alien voices that may be trying to speak to him. They came to him on the beach just before being "rescued," the upside-down numbers and symbols racing through his brain, the lights crashing into his skull. He thinks about the dazzling display of colors the symbols brought, and then he thinks about the demonic voices that came immediately after:

"It's you now."

"We need you, you need us."

"Eat the seeds."

"We are Zion."

Over his shoulder, Jonah calls out for the pink-haired hacker who disappeared in the portal days ago. "Kip? Kip, I need you."

No one answers.

"Kip? Where are you? I need your help up here. *Please.*"

Vespa growls and then balls Jonah's ripped collar in her fist. "Stop it. Just…stop it. Please. And you need to stop calling for Kip. Something's…there's something wrong with him. He looks weird. He looks…he looks messed up, Jonah. Like he's older now and taller somehow and his clothes are all torn up. Even his hair isn't pink anymore. When we get to Thetis and we've got a chance to settle down, we need to ask him what the hell happened when he went through that portal. Find out where he went and what he knows and what he saw."

A door opens, and Jonah instantly smells the lavender man. Jonah leans his head into the aisle and waves his hands blindly in the air. "Where are we going? I can't see what's going on or where you're taking us."

The smell of lavender grows stronger, and he can suddenly feel the man's presence right next to him. The man's voice is low and wheezing and filled with sadness: "We're looking for survivors, kid. Just like you."

"Did Kip bring you here? The kid back there who's not talking? How did you find him?"

"We found him on the other side of the island," he says. "Surprised as you are to find him there, especially after everything we've been through with him. He was just standing there on the beach like an idiot with a wall of fire coming right at him. Hasn't said a damn word."

"Everything you've been through with him?" Jonah asks.

Vespa leans over Jonah. "Well, if Kip didn't bring you to us, then how did you find us?"

"We picked up a signal from one of the homing devices from your ship—from one of the rovers—and we headed that way. Then we saw the fire and smoke on the island, and like I said, Kip was just standing there on the beach. We picked him up, and then we immediately saw you three, so now we're going to comb the wreckage and look for survivors and the supplies you guys were bringing us. So, you all up to speed now? Can you shut up now so I can go back to doing my job?"

Hopper's homing device, Jonah thinks. It still works. When it fell overboard while they were fighting the airplane fish, they all thought it sealed their fate. Now, if only Jonah knew if it has saved them, or if it has somehow dug their graves.

The ship slows down and begins to lower with a series of whirs and clicks. The air pressure changes in Jonah's ears. When the door opens, he's running and never coming back. He's going to be free. But before Jonah can even ask for someone to loosen his seatbelts, the man gasps and then falls into a horrible coughing fit. When he finally catches his breath, he whispers, "Holy…*Jesus Christ*. What the hell is that? Who would…"

Jonah pictures the man with his nose to the window, staring at the half-mile stretch of wreckage. He replays the crash in his head, the way the ship slammed into the ground and how the huge modules spun off in different directions. He remembers the cadet Daniel being split into two by the black boulder tearing through his module's wall, and then he thinks about Manny falling out of his seat and onto the porcupine tree. He thinks about his lost sheaf and his parents' photo. He thinks about the snouts racing through the site and the demic sent sailing into the darkness after being hit. He thinks about all the dead kids. And he thinks about the cook hanging from the tree, twirling in the air like a lost toy. For the first time, Jonah is happy he can't see.

"I said, *What the hell is that*?"

"We crashed," Jonah mumbles.

"Shut the…*I know that, kid.* But I want to know what the hell it is you guys have been up to here. Because holy shit."

Jonah's ears pop as the ship lowers to the ground and the outer door opens. There's a sound of an LZR-rifle coming to life. He finds Vespa's hand and squeezes it, but she quickly pulls away and undoes her seatbelts.

"Wait. I'm coming with you," she yells. Then, her hand finds Jonah's shoulder, and she whispers into his ear, "Stay here. Do *not* go out there, Firstie. I'll be right back."

"No! Let me out! I'm coming with you! Please!"

"You want to stay here. Believe me."

Sickness suddenly rushes through Jonah's body; his stomach shrinks and twists, his limbs go stiff and unresponsive. He tries to grab Vespa as she squeezes past, to force her to unlock his belts and take him by the hand, but instead all he can do is bite the flesh of his shoulder and try to work past the panic. An image of Portis pops into his mind, the cadet who couldn't stop biting his own skin after the wormhole. He's on his way to the other side of Achilles right now with the Splitters and his friends. Or, he's on his way to Peleus, the other moon, to find more verve. Or, he's dead.

There's yelling outside. Vespa and the man argue, and then new voices join in. Cheering voices. Angry voices. Jonah stops biting his shoulder long enough to yell, "Kip? Come here, come here. What happened to you in that portal? What did you see? Where did you go, man? Are they going to kill us on Thetis? Talk to me!"

No answer. There's more shouting outside. Jonah recognizes one of the voices, but he can't place it with the dozens of faces from the *Mayflower 2* bouncing around inside his head. Then Jonah hears a pair of feet pounding up the metal incline and into the ship.

"Well, *shit*. Little Firstie here made it out alive, I see," a boy says as he falls into a nearby seat. "Guess the weak survived, too."

"Who is that?" Jonah asks.

"Cadet Griffin Bishop, Third Year. Total motherfucking badass. But you knew that."

Jonah can't help but smile. The cadet with the lion shaved into the side of his hair. He made it. He will know what's going on.

"What's happening out there? How many of you are left? How many people are still alive?"

"Christ, man, I don't know. There's just four of us. Me and three brave-ass demics. But there are...others who are still alive. Sort of."

"What does that mean?"

"Firstie, I just got saved from a fucking nightmare, okay? Give me a tick." Griffin then takes a deep breath before yelling: "Let's go already! Let's not just sit around here! More of them could still be coming! You all have *no* fucking clue what's happening! None!"

Jonah painfully turns his body toward the boy's voice. "More of who could be coming?"

"*Fuck me.* Your eyes, dude. Your eyes are totally blue. What the..."

"I know," he says. "I'm sick. I'm sick, and I'm dying. So, just tell me what happened after we left. Please."

"After you left? *Jesus*, man. That feels like so long ago, I don't even know. That first night you left, we were sabotaged, man. Straight up trapped. Shit was just blowing up everywhere. We were getting shot at from all these different angles, from all over. Things were blowing up like bombs, everything was on fire, people were dying. I should have gone with you guys. We *all* should have left that night. I ended up running away with a big group of kids, and then we got separated, and then I just kept running. I've been hiding inside the jungle for days, man, with these three demics right here... Guys, right over here. Sit down. Hurry up. Sit down so we can go."

More footsteps. More smells. More bodies falling into seats around Jonah. Then there is sobbing. Uncontrollable sobbing.

"Then what happened?" Jonah asks.

Griffin lets out a laugh. "Then a couple hours ago, some spooky, messed-up kids from Module Eight showed up. Remember that module that went missing during the crash?"

"I forgot about that."

"Yeah, well, they just showed up a little while ago, and they didn't say anything, and then they just started digging...and..." His voice rises, directed toward the front of the ship. "We have to go! Let's go already!"

Before Jonah can ask another question, can say he remembers how angry Paul was when he found out Module Eight was still missing after the crash, he smells Vespa then feels her scoot past his long legs. She drops into the seat next to him and grabs his arm and gives it a quick, intense squeeze.

"What's going on?" he asks.

Vespa takes a breath and then clears her throat: "There are some survivors. But, Jonah...I don't know if it was Tunick or Sean or someone else, but someone dug up the bodies from the crash that we all buried, and they...they laid them out on the ground. In a pattern."

"What kind of pattern?"

Vespa sighs. "A big crescent moon with three bodies balled up inside it. The same symbol from the caves."

Jonah's insides go cold. That's the symbol Malix found carved into the adults he found on the beach. That's the symbol that sent Kip through the portal.

"And," Vespa continues with a shaky voice, "they took more of the dead bodies and lined them up and spelled out the words, 'Don't leave' on the ground. It's pretty messed up. It's *really* messed up."

"'Don't leave?'"

"It wasn't us," Griffin yells. "It wasn't us, I swear to god. It was those asshole Module Eight kids who did that. I couldn't stop them. I tried. I swear, I tried. I was yanking on their shoulders and punching them in their faces. They're like zombies, though. There's nothing we could do."

Vespa leans closer to Jonah: "They carved the same moon-

and-circle symbol into all the dead bodies. They're covered with them. Absolutely covered."

Jonah almost vomits; he pictures the mangled corpses of his classmates and teachers and engineers lying head to toe, their skin covered in alien hieroglyphics, their bodies spelling out another warning. *Don't leave.* He didn't want to leave for Thetis, and now he doesn't want to stay on Achilles. What are his other options? Back to Earth? Can this ship get them home?

"There's more," Vespa says. "There's..."

Feet march past with strong, sour odors close behind. The tube running out of his skin bounces up and down as an arm bumps against Jonah's. And then another and another bump past. No one says a word, though.

"No! *Hell no,* man. Get out of here! You're not coming with us!" Griffin shouts. "Get the hell out! All of you, get out!"

The lavender man's voice suddenly booms inside the ship, echoing up from the open door: "All the way to the back! Get to the back! Keep moving!"

"They're from Module Eight," Vespa whispers. "They look like how Kip looks. And Jonah, listen, something else: Dr. Z is here, too. She's alive. But she's—"

Dr. Z is alive? He immediately sits up straight. She's the one who diagnosed his disease after the crash. She's the one who knows how to save him. And Brooklyn. "Dr. Z! Dr. Zarembo, where are you? Dr. Z? It's me, Jonah Lincoln! I'm right—"

Vespa digs her nails into Jonah's wrist. "No, stop. She's like Kip and the others; she's not talking. She's totally messed up, too."

Griffin's mouth appears next to Jonah's ear: "The doctor helped the zombie kids with the bodies. She's...she's the one who cut the things in their skins."

Jonah doesn't believe it. "Dr. Z! Please! I need your help! My eyes are totally blue now! And so are Brooklyn's! We're both blind!"

A hand clamps hard over Jonah's mouth. "Shut up, Firstie," Griffin says. Then, to the front of the ship: "Kick the lady and these zombie kids off the ship before they kill us all, and let's go already!"

Jonah yanks Griffin's hand away. "No, Dr. Z is—"

Then Vespa's palm quickly covers his lips. "Not right now, Jonah. Not right now."

He grits his teeth, leans back. Griffin isn't telling the truth, he thinks. He knows Dr. Z; she's one of the few people on this moon he can trust. There's no way she dug up dead bodies and spelled out some sick warning. There's no way she carved symbols into their skin.

"Where is she?" Jonah asks Vespa.

"She's in the back. She keeps opening and closing her mouth like she's talking, but she's not saying anything."

"I'm telling you guys," Griffin says. "Stay the hell away from her."

Jonah smells the lavender man. He takes a long wheezing inhale before shouting, "Okay, listen up! I know you all want to get to Thetis as soon as possible. I do, too. Especially after seeing some of this shit. But we're going to fly back and forth for a bit and look for some important things that were on your ship. Now, has anyone seen something that looks like a satellite anywhere? I need to know that immediately. It's green and looks like...like a satellite, I guess."

No one responds. Jonah thinks back to the crash. He never saw anything that looked like a satellite.

"We need that thing, people. You have no idea how much we need that thing."

"Let's just go already!" Griffin yells.

The man grumbles. "Everybody lock in and shut up. We're going to fly around looking for it."

The outside door closes, and the ship pressurizes. Jonah hears Griffin sigh and click his belts together. No one behind him makes a noise. The kids from Module Eight and Dr. Z can dig up fifty dead bodies and lay them out in a pattern, but they can't put on their safety belts? The engine roars to life, and Jonah feels the ship begin to lift off.

"Wait!" Vespa yells. "Oh my god, wait! Look! Stop! Go back down! Open up the doors!"

"Yeah, yeah, I see him. Lower it back down!" the man yells.

"Holy shit. It's Cadet Sigg!" Griffin laughs. "Paul, you sly motherfucker."

Vespa's voice is suddenly full of hope. "How can...I can't believe it. We saw him..."

"Die," Jonah says. "He died."

The ship sets back down, and after a symphony of noises, the door opens, and a pair of feet immediately sprint over metal. They stop just a few yards from where Jonah sits.

"Vespa?" Paul's voice cracks and wavers: "You're alive."

"I thought you were dead, that you died on the beach," Vespa cries. "I can't believe you're here."

"Yo, cadet. Hell yeah. Good to see you, man," Griffin says. "Sweet scars. Lots of blood, though."

Paul's voice suddenly lowers. "*Shit.* Shit, shit, shit. Those kids from Module Eight...shit. They shouldn't be on here. They need to get off. Right now."

"Sit down!" the man shouts. "We're leaving! Now!"

"Sir, you don't understand!" Paul yells back.

"Sit! Down! We're not leaving anyone behind. Those are my orders, cadet. I don't give a shit what they look like. As long as they're breathing, we're bringing them home."

Without another word, Paul drops down into the seat in front of Jonah. The backrest leans into the boy's long legs, pushing them into the aisle. Vespa's body shakes next to Jonah, bouncing with held-in cries. He doesn't know if it's because Paul survived, or if it's because they're finally leaving this god-awful moon. The door closes, and the ship starts to rise again.

Jonah leans forward and whispers, "Were you just pretending to be dead on the beach? Why? And why were you out there hunting me down?"

Paul shifts away from him.

"Why were you hunting me? What happened to you out there?"

The cadet still doesn't answer him.

Jonah breaks; he reaches over the seat and grabs the top of Paul's shaved head and yanks it backward. "Why were you trying to kill me?"

"That's it," the doctor with the gruff voice says as she charges toward him with a series of coughs. "No more out of you."

Before Jonah can shout again, an icy coolness runs from the tube into his veins, and a second later, his eyes close and he's asleep.

CHAPTER TWO

HOT, SOGGY AIR BLOWS UP AND OVER JONAH'S SKIN, WAKING him with a jolt. He tries to jump away from it, to escape the soaked pillow under his neck and the damp sheet pulled up to his chest, but straps across his forehead and upper arms hold him to whatever it is he lies on. It takes a moment for him to realize that he's moving; wheels squeak below him, struggling to maintain a straight line to wherever it is he's going. Jonah opens his eyes to see blobs of whites and grays and browns. Something dark blue slowly crawls from left to right, a blurry glacier going in the opposite direction.

"Jonah? Are you awake?" Vespa asks somewhere behind him. He hears footsteps now. Naked feet slap dirt all around him. Someone nearby cries for her mom and dad. A boy—is it Griffin?—says he can't believe he made it here, after all this time.

It feels like hours pass as Jonah struggles to turn his head from left to right. A fuzzy black shadow quickly moves toward his face. A second later, he feels Vespa's hand on his. "We're on Thetis. We're here."

We're on Thetis. Another dark blue blob crawls by in the distance. Everything reeks of salt and sulfur. The air is thick and suffocating; sweat drips into his ears and eyes and mouth. *We're here.* Vespa releases his hand, and Jonah watches her shadow get smaller as her words bounce back and forth inside his head. When her words finally stop and settle, and Jonah can focus on them, two things hit him at once: They made it to Thetis—their final destination—and Jonah can see more than blackness. He can see colors. He can see shapes and movements. The medicine works.

The combined revelations cause the cadet to struggle wildly against the straps; he grabs the edges of the bed and wrenches his shoulders back and forth. Someone pushes down on his chest, a woman shouts for him to calm down and relax and just lie back, but Jonah sees more blobs of whites and grays and browns, and the excitement is too much. He screams and rocks his body. He screams for Dr. Z and for Vespa and for his dead parents. The bed shifts sharply to his right and the wheels squeal and grind, and then Jonah feels his world tip over. For a moment, he's suspended in the air, floating, stuck back up on the wall of his broken module after the crash with Manny and the Third Year with half his face torn off, and then a second later, his cheek bounces against the ground. Vespa shouts his name, Griffin laughs somewhere on his left, and then he falls back asleep with dozens of blurry shadows charging toward him.

• • •

The lights in the room are weak, but they buzz loudly, flickering on and off, on and off. With half-opened eyes, Jonah stares at a bulb above the door of his small room, its pattern hypnotizing him into a drooling stupor. He can't see the details of the bulb—his sight isn't completely restored—but more colors have begun to distinguish themselves. The bulb is yellow. Next to the door, hanging on the wall, are green rectangles. The door is brown with a dark square at the top, perhaps a window. Jonah rolls his head to the side and sees black squares just inches from his face, lit up with moving white lines. Thick white tubes descend from the squares and end in his wrist and chest.

He closes his eyes and instantly sees Tunick sitting cross-legged in his cave, purple flames spreading out behind the man like wings. He watches Tunick lean forward and shove a verve seed toward his face. Behind him, Hopper and Michael laugh and dance. Aussie's face appears on his leg. He watches quietly as her vomit drips over his pants. Jonah then sees himself leaping through the fire, running and escaping, and then there's Bidson grabbing Tunick's wrist and not letting go.

"Bidson," he mumbles. "Thank you so much. I never got to—"

There's a click and Jonah opens his eyes to watch the brown, blurry door slowly open. A large figure quietly enters the room and walks directly up to Jonah's face, bending down to eye level, covering Jonah with mint breath. The cadet sees a long gray beard and tanned cheeks, wide shoulders under a dark green shirt. Two green dots stare at him for ten seconds before blinking. Before Jonah can ask who the man is, or how long he's been lying there hooked up to all these machines, his right eyelid is pulled up and to the side. A tiny red light then blocks any vision he has, blinding him, and the cadet wrenches his face away from the man's fingers. Jonah tries to shield his eyes with his hands but can't; his wrists are strapped to the bed.

"I know it hurts like hell," the man says with a chuckle. "But I'll tell you what: It's a good thing it hurts, kid. Tells us that the medication is working. Looks like you just may see again. How about that?"

A tear slides down Jonah's face, and he tries hard to keep his lip from quivering, but there's no controlling it. Back on that beach, before the ship from Thetis roared over his head, he thought he had days to live. Maybe just hours. And those final moments would be behind a cloak of darkness. And now he's being told that he's going to see again?

"What about Brooklyn?" he asks.

"The girl going through the same shit as you? She's improving," the man says. He lets out a string of dry coughs before adding, "But not like you, cadet. Not yet. But let's give her time. See what happens."

"Is she going to live, though?"

"She should. I think we got to you guys just in time. *What a fucking disaster.* You guys really screwed up. Fucked us all over. But yeah, it looks like you and the girl should be okay. Lucky sons of bitches."

Jonah lets out a quick, guttural sob, and then he laughs a laugh so loud he thinks anyone still on Achilles could hear him. His tears flow freely. He allows his jaw to tremble. He lets snot run out of his nose. He doesn't care what this man thinks of him; all he cares about is his friend. As the cadet tries to catch his breath, his fear that Thetis is a bad place is momentarily gone; even if Thetis is a bad place, it's a bad place where he and Brooklyn will be able to see. That gives him more of a chance.

"Where is she?"

"She's a few doors down, sleeping, totally out of it. But, I'm going to be honest with you, cadet, she—"

The door clicks and opens again, and then a tiny woman framed with long, dark hair glides into the room. As soon as she clears her throat, Jonah instantly knows it's the same doctor from the rescue ship.

"And how is this one doing?" she asks.

"Ask him yourself," the man says. "He's awake. And crying like a little baby."

Jonah laughs again and then sucks up any snot still dripping out of his nose. It hurts. It's still broken, the shards of bone sticking into his cheeks. It's then that he feels the stitches struggling to keep the skin on his back together. He feels another set somewhere on his left shoulder. The rest of his body is numb, though. He can only imagine how much medicine pumps through him, how many stitches are holding him together. It doesn't even bother him, though; he only cares that these shadows have colors, and that these shadows are growing outlines.

"Crying is a good enough sign, I suppose," the woman says. She sits on a stool and pushes herself over to Jonah's face to exam his eyes. The lights above the door continue to flicker on and off, on and off, and the woman's face goes from white to black every other second. "Amazing. Your pupils are coming back to your eyes. It's like they're growing back. I can see a faded outline of your iris. And even the blueness of your sclera—that's the white parts of your eye, if you didn't know—they're getting less blue. I'd say we got to you just in time."

"When?" Jonah whispers. "When can I see everything?"

The woman stands and is immediately caught in a coughing fit that sends her stumbling into the wall. When she's done, she apologizes and makes her way back to Jonah's bed where she flicks a finger at one of the tubes sticking out of his wrist. "I guess we'll find that out together, huh? Don't strain those eyes too hard, though. Let's not get ahead of ourselves and waste what we've already accomplished."

Jonah smiles and closes his eyes, but then immediately opens them back up. He's suddenly worried that if he closes them for too long, if he falls back asleep, that his sight will somehow disappear again.

The man clears his throat. "Thank you very much, Dr. Kinney. That will be all for now. I know you have a lot more patients to get to."

The cadet watches the blurry woman make her way back toward the door, her shadow getting smaller and smaller. "More than I would ever like, sir. I still can't figure out what's wrong with most of them or how to get them to snap out of it just yet. Their eyes are…there's just nothing behind them."

"Is it…" the man starts to say.

"Verve? No. No traces in their systems."

"And what about Kip Kurtz? What's the story there?"

Dr. Kinney pauses. "I really don't know. He's not talking."

"That will be all, thank you."

It takes a moment for Jonah to remember they picked up the kids from the missing Module Eight. How they're like zombies.

How Dr. Zarembo and Kip are like zombies, too. How they dug up the dead and laid them out to spell "Don't leave." And then, of course, they all went and left Achilles. Jonah wonders what the repercussions will be.

Once the door closes, the man begins to pace back and forth, grumbling like a grizzly bear. Finally, he sits on the doctor's stool and takes a deep, strained breath.

"My name is Commander Stennis Mirker, and I'm in charge here at the Athens colony. I know you're in a lot of pain, kid, and that you've got a hell of a lot of medicine pumping through you right now, and that your eyes aren't exactly the best, but I need to ask you a few questions."

Jonah trusts the man's voice, the way it seems to go up and down with empathy. A second later, though, he remembers that the name of the person in charge of the Athens colony is Captain Julia Tejas. She was all over the news for years leading up to the voyage to Thetis. He can picture her curly black hair pulled back over her thick shoulders, the way her hands flew around her head as she talked about the dangers that laid in front of her and her crew. Jonah remembers her first video sent to Earth from Thetis, how big her smile shined as she showed off their first working water well.

"What about Captain Tejas?" Jonah asks. "I thought she was in charge."

The man takes another deep breath before standing back up. "Captain Tejas...is no longer with us. She disappeared. She cracked. Left us to fend for ourselves. Between you and me, cadet, she was never the same after the accident with all those kids a year ago. We haven't seen her in a while."

"But...there *was* no accident with all those kids, right? We know that those kids didn't actually die. They stole your ship and flew to Achilles. I met some of them. We all did. They...they tried to kill us. They tried to kill me."

Commander Mirker's bearded shadow gets closer and soon a cloud of mint envelopes Jonah's face. The man gently places his hand on top of Jonah's as he asks, "Who exactly was there, kid? Who tried to kill you? What were their names?"

The cadet pauses. Something keeps him from telling the truth. At least, for now. "I don't know. They never said their names. But they chased us and attacked our camp."

"Do you remember what they looked like?"

Jonah pictures Sean stumbling toward him in the canyon, blond curls stuck to his forehead, his arm dangling at his side by a thread of flesh. "I...I was blind. I couldn't see anyone after the first day. I only saw the crash."

Commander Mirker puts his head in his hands. "That must have been pretty awful. All those people dying. Friends of mine died on your ship, you know. More than friends. People I had been waiting a long, long time to see."

"I'm sorry," Jonah whispers.

It takes a moment for the man to compose himself. "Me, too. Thank you, cadet. But I feel like I need to personally apologize to you and to all the other survivors. For what happened. For not getting to you quicker. For taking so long, for taking way too long. As soon as we lost contact with the *Mayflower 2*, we scrambled to get our ship in good enough shape to go after you, because, well, we think someone sabotaged it. That's another mystery maybe you could help us solve."

New tears slide down Jonah's cheeks. If they would have gotten there sooner, Garrett would still be alive. The cook and the professor down in the jungle may never have been killed by Tunick and Sean. Brian wouldn't have been eaten by those fish with the airplane fins. Rosa wouldn't have jumped overboard. Bidson wouldn't have...

"Even if you couldn't see anything, maybe you heard what went on. Do you want to tell me what you heard?" the man asks.

"I do," Jonah says. "But I can't yet. My head, it really hurts. I can't really remember things right."

Commander Mirker pushes the stool away from Jonah's bed and slumps over, his fuzzy shadow becoming a fuzzy ball. After a moment, he stands with a sad grunt and says, "Well, when you're ready, I'm ready."

"Can I ask one thing?"

"Of course, cadet," the man says.

"Why did you tell Earth all those kids died on that field trip when they actually didn't? They stole your ship and went to Achilles. Why not tell people on Earth that instead of saying they died?"

Commander Mirker opens the door halfway. Before slipping out, he says, "Those kids, they *were* lost. To us. They *were* dead, cadet. They decided to take a goddamn drug and they wouldn't stop and their minds went to hell. They were dead to us. Wasn't exactly the truth, but it sure felt that way around here."

And then the door clicks shut, and he's gone, and Jonah is left alone to think about Hess and Lark and Camilla. They said Thetis was a bad place to be, and that they were almost murdered by the adults here, if it wasn't for Tunick saving them, but it sounds more like they were out of control, slaves to the verve. He witnessed that firsthand. He should have told Mirker the truth. He will the next time he comes to visit.

As soon as the thought crosses his mind, the door reopens, and Jonah decides it's his chance to come clean, to tell Commander Mirker about Tunick and the verve and what they said was happening on Thetis, but it's a smaller shadow that enters the room. A yellow blob slowly makes its way toward Jonah's bed, stopping at his feet.

"Hello," Jonah says. "I'm really starting to feel better. I could use some water, though."

The yellow blob silently rounds the bed and comes closer to Jonah's face where details start to appear. The person has reddish hair and pale skin. The yellowness comes from the person's jacket. A second later, a sour stench reaches Jonah's broken nose. It smells like…Achilles.

"Hello?" Jonah asks.

Dr. Z's blurry face is suddenly inches away from Jonah's, her breath putrid and hot. In a slow, emotionless voice, she says, "You weren't supposed to leave."

Jonah's body goes still. "W-w-why?"

Dr. Z presses her forehead into Jonah's, slowly smashing him down into his damp pillow. Spit shoots from her mouth onto his lips as she says, "Because the old boy chose you. *They* chose you."

He can't speak. He can't move. *The old boy chose him? They chose him?* That's what the voices on the beach said. He watches helplessly as the doctor raises her arm over his chest and opens her hand. Dozens of what feel like rocks bounce all over his body. Then, in a voice so loud that it rattles Jonah's teeth, she screams, "EAT THE SEEDS!"

Like a spider approaching a fly caught in its web, Dr. Z slowly climbs on top of Jonah and bobs her head up and down over his, her hair sweeping back and forth over Jonah's face. It falls into his mouth and he can taste its crispy, burnt ends. She slams a hand onto his chest and grabs a handful of the verve seeds from the bed. The lights continue to flicker on and off over her shoulders.

"Enter the exit," she whispers. "Exit the entrance."

Jonah's shoulders pop as he tries to wrench his wrists from their straps. He attempts to buck her off of him, wildly twisting left and right, and then he rockets his knees into the woman's back. He strikes her right in the spine—hard—over and over and over, but she doesn't move. She doesn't make a sound.

"Help!" Jonah screams. "Someone!"

Dr. Z drops a hand over his nose and mouth, smothering him. He again slams his knees into her back with all his strength, but she just giggles. Jonah's teeth find two of her fingers, and he bites down until he tastes her blood. She finally takes her hand away, and he lets out a short scream before the doctor puts a hand on his neck, squeezing, crushing his larynx. Her other hand scoops up the seeds all around him. As soon as Jonah opens his mouth to try to catch a breath, Dr. Z drops several seeds inside.

"EAT THE SEEDS!"

The seeds hit the back of his throat and clog his airway. He chokes and coughs and starts to suffocate, but still he refuses to bite down on the verve. He knows what will happen. The hallucinations. The confusion and hysteria. Most of all, though, he knows the voices in his head will come back. The room flickers and dims; he's losing consciousness. The seeds find their way into the spaces between his gums and cheeks, and he spits a few out. They land on his cheeks and forehead and then clink against the floor.

Jonah begins to black out. He stops resisting, instead focusing on the sounds of his own gurgles and Dr. Z's giggling and the humming of the medical machines near his head. He can hear the light bulb near the door buzzing and flickering. Then he hears the click of the door and quick footsteps. Just as his eyes roll back into his skull and begin to shut off, a shadow rams into the doctor, knocking her onto the floor. The doctor crashes into the machines hooked up to Jonah, and she gets tangled in his tubes, yanking them from Jonah's skin, and it feels like tiny fires are ignited all over his body. Jonah raises his head and spits all over himself—a mess of vomit and blood and seeds—and that's when he sees Mirker's blurry outline stand over Dr. Z as she scrambles back and forth on her hands and knees in the corner.

"We need him to eat," she whispers.

Mirker looks over at Jonah, his face nothing more than blocks of white and gray in the cadet's eyes. "The kid eats when we say he eats."

Dr. Z gets to her feet. Humming a quiet, haunting song, she begins to circle Mirker. The boy watches helplessly from his bed, his wrists rubbed raw from the straps. Mirker circles along with her, quietly breathing through his nose while stifling a coughing attack. He steps on a seed, crunching it loudly under his boot. He looks down at the ground for a second and then he raises his head to Dr. Z. "Are you...are you *fucking* kidding me? You brought this stuff in here? Do you have any idea what this shit has done to this—"

Dr. Z shrieks and dives for his waist, but Mirker squats and catches her in his armpit. He swings a fist into her gut and screams, "Do you have any idea what this shit does?"

He keeps punching her. There's a snapping sound, and Jonah doesn't know if someone smashed another seed, or if Dr. Z's ribs just broke. Mirker doesn't let up; he just keeps swinging, delivering blow after blow. The man is vicious, relentless, a wild beast protecting its offspring, instantly reminding Jonah of his time spent living under a bridge in Cleveland with the mentally ill and addicts, where there were no rules. And definitely no mercy.

Dr. Z somehow gets loose and falls onto her back. She immediately jumps to her feet, seemingly unfazed by the brutal beating, squaring off again with the man who is practically twice her size.

"That didn't hurt, huh? I don't know what's wrong with you," Mirker says, "but I'm about to make it worse."

Dr. Z points at Jonah. "The old boy wants him. *We* want him."

Mirker stands between Jonah and the doctor and opens his arms out wide. "Yeah? Well, we want him more. But you can go ahead and try to take him."

Dr. Z charges ahead, screaming, "We are Zion!" She grabs Mirker around his neck, and they spin around and around until Mirker leans over and launches her across the room. Jonah hears the wall splinter from the impact, and then he watches Mirker's blurry shape stalk over to the woman and pick her up by her red hair. He holds her at arm's length, avoiding the woman's swinging arms and legs.

"If you think we're going to put up with bullshit like this again, you're dead wrong," Mirker says to her. "Or, you're just dead."

The door opens and in rushes the tiny Dr. Kinney and another figure. It takes him less than a second to recognize it's Vespa.

"Jonah!" Vespa runs to his side.

"Untie me!" Jonah yells. "Hurry!"

"No, stop! Leave him there!" Mirker shouts over his shoulder.

"Why not?" Vespa asks.

Dr. Kinney throws her hands in the air. "What the hell is going on?"

"She was attacking the patient," Mirker growls.

"He saved me," Jonah says. "Dr. Z…she was on top of me and trying to get me to eat…she wanted me to eat verve."

Dr. Kinney's small shadow picks something off the floor. She holds her fingers up to the flashing lights, and then a second later she turns and whips her hands toward the door; a seed pings against the wood. She stalks over to Dr. Z, who dangles from Mirker's hand and asks, "What are you doing in here? Why would you bring this stuff back to Athens?"

The doctor's yellow shape bounces with quiet laughter before it falls limp in the man's grasp. It's as if she's suddenly been turned off, or just fell asleep. Or died. Mirker lifts Dr. Z up to his face. "Does someone need to take a little ride to the Polaris Mons?'"

Dr. Z remains silent. Mirker shakes her back and forth and then drops her onto the ground like a bag of trash. "You stay there." The man then turns to Jonah. "You eat any of those? Tell me now. Tell me right now and we'll pump your stomach."

"No, I swear. I spit them all out."

He looks at Vespa. "What about you? You take any?"

"No," she says.

Mirker grabs Dr. Z again, holding her up by the back of her jacket like a cat holds her kitten by its scruff. "Good. You're good kids. I'm glad to hear you know not to eat that shit. Because if you did..." He stops and slowly inhales what sounds like a painful lungful of air. "Doctor?"

Dr. Kinney steps forward, the lights flashing onto her back. "Yes, sir?"

"Do me a favor and make sure these two are okay, and then pick up all these seeds and burn them in the pit. And make sure you get them all. Check twice."

"Of course, sir."

The woman circles Jonah's bed and places a quick hand on his forearm, giving him a gentle, reaffirming squeeze. The simple, protective touch has an amazing effect on Jonah. He leans back into his pillow. Adrenaline drains from his body, and his fists uncurl and relax. The doctor then pulls Jonah's machines back into place and reattaches the tubes to his skin, igniting the tiny fires all over again.

"Okay. What else can I do for you?" Dr. Kinney asks Jonah.

Vespa sets a cool hand on Jonah's forehead. "For starters, you can take these straps off his wrists. They almost got him killed."

The doctor raises her head to look at Mirker, and the man hesitates before nodding. Jonah's straps are undone, and he immediately touches his neck, fingering the circle of bruised skin.

"But don't go anywhere yet," Mirker says with Dr. Z dangling from his hand. "You need to stay hooked up to these machines for a few more hours or you're going to go right back to being blind. You hear me?"

Jonah drops his hands from his neck and nods.

"And," Dr. Kinney says, "after that, you need to come back in here every day for treatment, for at least a week. Just for an hour. Because if you don't, none of this is going to work."

"Okay," Jonah agrees.

"Don't forget to get every single seed, doctor," Mirker says. "Feel better, cadet. We'll put someone outside your door so you can rest in peace. This kind of bullshit, I guarantee you, won't happen again. We'll talk about what happened on Achilles when you're ready." He then opens the door and disappears, dragging Dr. Z behind him.

As the doctor crawls back and forth on the floor to collect the verve, Vespa stands guard at the door. Even though Jonah barely sees her blurry shape, he can tell she's prepared for battle. With anyone. With everyone. A few minutes later, when she's sure she's checked every corner and under every machine twice, Dr. Kinney comes back to Jonah's bed.

"I'm very sorry that happened," she says with a strained sigh. "These stupid seeds have undone so much progress we've made here. You have no idea."

"Forget apologizing. Just make him better. Make him *and* Brooklyn better," Vespa says.

"We're doing our best."

"Your best almost got Jonah killed," Vespa says.

The doctor pats Jonah's arm again and then walks over to the door where she stops to whisper something to Vespa. The cadet brings a hand to her face, and her body slumps. As soon as the doctor leaves the room, Jonah asks what was said.

"Brooklyn's not doing as well as you are," Vespa says. "She may not make it."

He closes his eyes, sending slow tears down his temples. A second later, though, his eyes pop open, and he sits up with a gasp.

"You have to go check on her! You have to make sure no one is going after her like they went after me. The kids from Module Eight, they're messed up like Dr. Z."

"Shit," Vespa whispers. "You're right. What about you, though? I need to stay here until someone else—"

There's a knock on the door. A second later, a large pale head with short black hair appears inside the room.

"Hey, hello. The commander asked me to watch the door and guard you so you can get some rest. My name's Freeman. And nobody gets past Freeman."

"Freeman?" Jonah asks. "Where's Brooklyn at? The blind girl they rescued from Achilles with us?"

The man pauses.

"We just need to make sure she's okay," Vespa adds. "Jonah was just attacked in here, and we need to make sure she's safe."

"She's just down the hall. At the end. Number three."

Vespa jogs over to Jonah and gives him a quick hug. The smell of her hair and skin is reassuring, even if it does instantly remind him of the beach on Achilles.

"You should take a shower," Jonah says.

"Yeah, I know," she whispers in his ear. "Right after I make sure you guys are okay. I'll watch this Freeman guy from the door. Nobody's going to mess with you guys. I promise. So, get some rest. And then we'll get cleaned up and figure out our place here."

A moment later, she's gone, and Jonah's alone in the room with the flickering lights and the hums of his machines and the pain circling his neck. After five minutes, his eyes close and he's asleep.

• • •

Jonah sits up as if someone turns him on with a button. Adrenaline shoots through his body like lightning, practically sizzling his skin in the pool of sweat beneath him. It takes him a few seconds to shake off the dream he was having: he was in a dark, endless tunnel with a flashlight when he came across a line of rocks sticking out of the walls, circling the floor and ceiling like a mouth full of teeth. He thought maybe it was a portal he had to jump through, but once he got closer, he saw that the rocks were the stone heads of people from the *Mayflower 2*: Manny, Garrett, Rosa, Portis, Griffin, Paul, plus demics whose names he never knew, the flight crew. They had their mouths open in permanent, horrific screams. Their eye sockets were empty, but tears flowed down their stone cheeks. Terrified, Jonah ran in the other direction, only to immediately trip and lose his flashlight. When he grabbed it and shined the light at his feet, he saw that he fell over the stone head of Tunick. Tunick's mouth was stuck with a giant grin, his sharp teeth holding several verve seeds. Jonah's flashlight died right then. When he hit it against his thigh to get it working again, the beam lit up Tunick's head, but it wasn't him anymore. Instead, it was his own face, frozen in a look of agony with the seeds sitting on his tongue. While everything else in the cave was brown and gray, his stone eyes were a bright, bright blue.

The dream flashes behind his eyes like the light above the door of his hospital room. Jonah hits his temples with his fists and blinks hard. He's safe; still in the bed, still hooked up to machines with tape and tubes. He scans the walls, relieved to see it's not covered with faces of the dead. No Manny or Rosa. No grinning Tunick. Jonah stretches his neck to see a bag of clear liquid dripping into a rubber tube, and then he looks down to see his naked feet sticking out from the end of the off-white sheets like two hibernating animals checking out the winter landscape. His feet are dirty, caked with grains of gray sand and smudged with black and red marks. The nails are scuffed and chipped. A bandage covers the top of his left foot, its edges frayed and uneven.

As Jonah surveys the room, noticing the slight patterns in the cement floor and the narrow shadows running down the black, wooden walls, it slowly hits him that his vision is…it's crystal clear. He can see patterns. He can see that the walls are made of some kind of fuzzy, black wood, and his bandages are frayed, and that there's sand sticking to his feet. The medicine works. He can see again. He can't believe it.

The door opens, and Jonah watches a man's weathered face stick through the opening. It's dark and covered with white stubble. Under a large forehead, his eyes are brown and sharp and sad. But they seem kind and concerned.

The man enters the room and closes the door behind him. Jonah sees he's thick with muscles under his tan jumpsuit, built like a bull. "You awake in here?"

As soon as he hears his voice, Jonah realizes this is Freeman, the man asked to guard his room.

"Yeah," Jonah says. "Thanks."

Freeman turns and cracks the door back open and looks up and down the hall before closing it again. He moves quickly into the room and sits on a stool at Jonah's feet. The man clasps his hands and opens his mouth to speak, but then he reconsiders it. The sadness in his eyes fills the room.

"How are you doing?" Jonah asks.

The question brings a quick smile across the man's face, and he leans back and laughs at the ceiling. "When was the last time someone actually asked me that?"

"I don't know," Jonah says, pushing himself up on the mattress. "When?"

"It's been a long-ass time, I know that. I'm okay, kid. I'm okay. Considering everything. Now, how are *you*? By the way you're staring right at me, it looks like you can see better, am I right?"

It's Jonah's turn to smile and let out a quick laugh. "I honestly can't believe it. I can see almost perfectly, like my disease somehow never happened. I can see your face and your eyes and my feet and pretty much everything. I don't know how long I've been asleep for, but just a little while ago, all I could see were blobs and shapes and some colors and shadows and stuff. Now, it's like…it's like Achilles was all a bad dream, and it never happened, and hey, here I am. I can see."

Freeman stands and leans over Jonah to take a closer look at the machines beeping and humming on the other side of the bed. "Oh, it happened all right. It happened so much that all the good stuff you guys were supposed to bring us… But you're lucky, you know. Really lucky. Lucky not only that you survived the whole crash and that our ship found you, but also that…" He sits back down and takes a long, labored breath. "Let's just say, thank God for Commander Mirker, kid. Because just a month or so ago, things around here got pretty scary."

Jonah sits up completely. "Pretty scary how?"

"I'm sure someone will tell you all about it when you're feeling better and you're out of here. It's not my story to tell, really."

"I'm feeling better, Freeman. Tell me. Please."

Freeman stares at him for a few seconds, and then he looks down at his own shaking hands and mumbles something Jonah can't understand.

"What?" Jonah asks.

"I said, 'We're all going to die here.'"

Jonah's skin goes cold. He rips the covers off his bruised legs and attempts to scoot to the edge of the bed, but the tubes attached to him pull the machines clanking into the metal frame. *They're all going to die here?* Jonah wraps his fingers around the rubber tubes, knowing that they're keeping him alive, but at the same time, they're keeping him prisoner. He needs to find Vespa and Brooklyn and hide.

"Whoa, whoa," Freeman says, placing a giant hand over Jonah's wrist. "You're not cleared yet. Don't take those out. Please don't. Of course, we're all going to die here, kid. That's what I'm saying. Thetis is our home forever now. Where else would we die, right? Just don't take those out."

The cadet raises his elbow like he's about to yank the tubes out. "Then tell me what happened a month ago that was so scary."

"Fine. Sit back and stop pulling on things, and I'll tell you. Christ, kid."

Jonah slowly falls back against his pillows. He closes his eyes for a second and then tests them again. He can still see.

"About a month ago, the captain, Captain Tejas, she went out and left for a bit on a simple survey mission. Heading southwest, she said, looking for new plants and species and whatnot, just seeing what else was out there, you know? No big deal. We all go out and do that. You're *supposed* to go out and do that. You will, too, you know what I mean? But when she came back later that day, she was acting really strange and wasn't talking right and seemed really off or something, like she went down to check on the construction of the...road or whatever in the valley. Later on, she stood in the middle of the village and was just staring at everyone like she had never seen us before. We'd try to talk to her, but nobody could get a clear answer out of her. Then the next morning, she's back out there ranting and raving about how we were all doomed and this and that and how we were an infestation on Thetis and that we were killing the planet and stuff like that. And *then*, for the rest of the day, she was saying that our only hope for survival here was that somebody needed to sacrifice himself for all our sins."

"Like who, Jesus? She thought Jesus was coming to Thetis?" Jonah asked.

"That's what we asked her, and she kept saying no, but she wouldn't say who it was supposed to be. Then, that night, Mirker caught her putting explosives all over the village, the ones we use for excavating, and thank God he stopped her before she blew anything up."

The lights in the room begin to flicker again, and Jonah stares at the man, watching his face fall further with every sentence.

"She got away, though," Freeman continues. "And she ran off into the trees, and now we're all a little freaked out that she's still out there somewhere, planning something again. When you get out of here, keep your eyes open for explosives or mysterious things around the village and stuff like that, okay?"

"Everything is going to be mysterious to me here," Jonah says.

The door flies open and in walks Commander Mirker. He's huge, and for the first time, Jonah sees the details of his face: Sharp green eyes surrounded by deep wrinkles, a gray beard that reaches high up his tan cheeks and down past his collar. The moment he sees Freeman sitting at Jonah's feet, he lets out a grumble of disapproval.

"Thought I ordered you to stand outside and make sure he was safe?"

Freeman stands with a cough and nods at Mirker with respect. "Sir. Thought he could use some company."

"I could," Jonah adds. "I mean, I did. And he was watching the door the whole time. He only just sat down because I asked him to. Him just standing out there the whole time was making me nervous."

Freeman gives Jonah a quick smile and walks toward the door. "Feel better, kid."

When the door shuts, Mirker leans against it in exhaustion, his huge biceps straining against his olive-green uniform. "You ready to get out of here?"

"Out of here?"

"Yeah," Mirker says. "We've been monitoring your progress on the machines, and it looks like you're done in here for the day. You can see, right?"

"I can. And I can't thank you enough. I mean, I thought I would never—"

"So, it's time you assimilated into the colony and make yourself at home. I want to sit down and talk about your time on Achilles very soon, and I mean *very soon*, but for now, you should get acclimated. Welcome to your new home."

Jonah swings his feet over the side of the bed and starts picking at the tubes in his arm. "First, I want to see Brooklyn."

CHAPTER THREE

THE CADET SLOWLY WALKS OUT OF HIS HOSPITAL ROOM ON sore legs, the soles of his feet thick and callused from running through the jungle on Achilles.

"Turn left," Mirker says behind him. "She's right there."

Jonah shuffles down the hallway of black wood, his hands running along its soft, almost furry texture. He finds a door marked with the number three and takes a deep breath. Before going inside, he looks back down the hall for reassurance. Mirker and Freeman both nod at him, and then they immediately begin a heated, muffled conversation between the two of them, one that must have previously ended too soon.

The room is brighter than Jonah's, spot lit with steady lamps circling the one bed inside. It's so bright, in fact, that Jonah has to cover his eyes, which is something he thought he'd never have to do again. He squints into the whiteness and sees his friend Brooklyn unconscious and wiped clean, her face and arms covered with tubes, a threadbare sheet pulled up to her chest. A shadow suddenly moves in the corner on the opposite side of the room, causing Jonah to jump and ball his hands into fists.

"Relax, Firstie," Vespa says as she steps into the light.

He unconsciously follows her orders and uncurls his hands, relieved to see the cadet standing guard over their friend. "How is she?" he asks as he steps up to the bed. The smell of chemicals and sweat and sulfur hit him, and he has to momentarily turn away and cover his face with the collar of his shirt. Did his room smell like this?

"The same, I guess. Hasn't woken up yet," Vespa says. It takes her a moment to realize that not only is Jonah standing there, but it looks like… "Wait, your eyes. Can you see? Can you see me?"

Jonah nods and a single tear barely makes it onto his cheek before he wipes it away.

Vespa practically leaps over Brooklyn's bed to hug him. Her embrace is suffocating, but entirely welcome, and Jonah wraps his long arms around her back. He buries his nose into her black hair, which has been shampooed and stripped of smoke and death. The two stand like that for thirty seconds, both of them squeezing each other so hard that they begin to cough, and then they laugh. And then they fall silent. Vespa pulls away, struggling to stiffen her quivering lips. She bounces on the soles of her new shoes and then suddenly reaches up to touch the corners of his eyes with her thumbs.

"It's good to see you," Jonah manages. "Like, *really* good to see you. You look…you look really nice. You look beautiful, Vespa."

"This ugly mug?" She blushes and then takes a few steps backward before collapsing into a chair next to the bed. "I bet you say that to all the girls right after regaining your eyesight. I bet it's good just to see anything."

"It's definitely good to see her, too." Jonah reaches for Brooklyn's small hand and holds it gently between his giant palms. He stares at the demic's long face covered with bandages and thick ointment. Scratches and bruises crisscross and stretch from her cheeks down into her collar like a warped chess board. He presses his hands together, flattening the girl's warm fingers, trying to give her some of his good luck. The last time he saw her was on the top of the ridge before he and Vespa slid down the canyon to stop Tunick and the Splitters from leaving with the ship. He doesn't know how, but he knew she'd somehow survive up there all alone. But now, staring down at her small body wrapped up in this large bed, he isn't so sure she'll survive all this, even when she's surrounded by her friends.

"Brooklyn," he says. "It's me, Jonah. And Vespa's here, too. We made it. We're on Thetis. So, wake up already so you can boss people around up here."

No response.

"Jonah's here," Vespa tries. "Squeeze his hands, Brooklyn, if you can hear us. Move something. Wake up and make fun of Jonah's big ears."

The girl doesn't move a muscle, and Jonah slowly releases her hand. He shuffles past Vespa and stands over Brooklyn's face, and without thinking, he places his fingers on the girl's eyelids and pulls them back.

The blue underneath is so solid and so bright that it startles Jonah. There are no corneas and no pupils and no white parts. Nothing is growing back. He releases her eyelids and a breath he didn't know he held.

"I thought she was doing better. Why...why isn't it working for her like it worked for me?" he asks.

"It is," Mirker says in the doorway. "She's stabilized right now. She's doing okay. Or at least better than she was when we found you. Unfortunately, she was further along than you were. But we're hoping to see some real progress soon. Keep giving her the meds. Keep hoping. Keep trying."

Jonah grabs Brooklyn's hand again. "Please get better. Please."

Mirker walks up to the bed with a sad, forced smile. "She will. She'll get better, I promise."

"Thank you," Jonah says to him. It could be from all the emotions he has for his friend right then, or the fact that Mirker saved him from Dr. Z earlier, but Jonah feels a fatherly sense from the man. It's impossible to ignore; half of Jonah wants to yell at him and blame him for all his problems, and the other half of him wants to hug the man and be taken care of and praised for what Jonah was able to do on Achilles. "Thank you for everything. For helping her and for helping me and Vespa and everyone else. We thought we were dead. You saved us."

Mirker puts a hand on Brooklyn's damp forehead and sighs. "You don't need to thank me, cadet. We're just happy you're here. We're happy you guys made it. We thought we lost everyone."

"Barely. We barely made it," Vespa whispers.

"Hey cadet, why don't you get some air and show Jonah around a bit," Mirker says to her. "You've seen the place already. Maybe you can help Jonah find his yurt. Number thirty-one."

"Sure."

They stand and say goodbye to Brooklyn and promise to be back in a couple hours. After passing through a maze of soft black wood, Vespa opens a door and steps aside.

The moment Jonah walks out of the building and onto the soil of Thetis, he can sense the difference between this planet and its moon. There's less humidity. There's more salt or something in the air. More sunlight hits his face with more warmth. Also, there's more gravity here, much closer to that on Earth. No more fifty-foot leaps or slow-motion falls, he thinks. No more acting like a comic book hero. Which is for the best; he doesn't want to be a comic book hero. He just wants to live the life of a quiet, secondary character who never gets in anyone's way. One whose friends get better and share this quiet, once-in-a-lifetime adventure with him. And who knows, maybe in five or ten years he'll start a family with someone. Someone like Vespa.

Vespa grabs Jonah's upper arm and gives him a slight pull to the left: "This way, Firstie."

The Athens colony looks much less futuristic than Jonah had imagined; with its tall wooden fence topped with spikes dominating the horizon and the dozens of dark green tents and yurts, Athens looks more like a temporary military base than an interstellar space colony. Everything is olive-colored and nondescript and lined up with precision, creating long alleyways and predictable turns. He had seen photos and videos of the colony on his sheaf and on the news but figured that the tents would have been replaced with concrete buildings by now. He pictured gleaming white towers with shining windows and alien birds with villagers riding them, circling around their tops. He pictured paved roads with strange flowers lining their edges. He wanted a futuristic town square with a futuristic gazebo. A water fountain. A pool with a high dive. Instead, he finds this? A glorified campsite behind a huge wall? What has everyone been working on for the past year?

Jonah follows Vespa left and right, passing several colonists who stop whatever work they're doing to look the two over. No one makes a move to introduce themselves or asks to show them around. The cadets quietly wave at each person they encounter, and all they get back are shaking heads and stiff shoulders. Jonah can't tell if it's his eyes still adjusting to the sunlight or adjusting to just being able to see in general, but everyone to him looks a little pale and sickly, moving slowly with heavy feet.

"Do they hate us or something?" Jonah asks.

"Something like that," she says. "Seems like everyone was counting on us to bring a bunch of stuff here to help. And then when we crashed..."

"And that's *our* fault somehow?"

"It's someone's fault, in their eyes, and now we're here to use up even more of what little resources they have left."

When they get to the center of the village, a long black building emerges with several open doors running along its side. Short fences and tall cages surround each opening, but that doesn't stop the animal noises within. Jonah's mood picks up instantly; he forgot about the farm building. He forgot about the videos and photos of the Athens scientists collecting animals and plants and anything else they could bring safely into the village. He walks faster and faster, and then finally he breaks out into a full-on sprint toward the first open door.

"I thought you were sick!" Vespa yells after him.

Jonah reaches a six-foot tall fence and easily peers over it, his heart in his throat, his cracked fingernails digging into the fuzzy wood. On Achilles, every creature was a mystery, a potential killer, capable of anything. The hoppers, the glowing beetles, the white spiders and snouts and airplane fish. Jonah had no idea what to expect. No one did. This, though, is like a zoo, with a safe barrier between him and the unknown.

There's movement in the open door, and out of the shadows come three green round creatures cautiously hopping into the sunlight on one thick leg, their long thin tails leaving lines in the dirt. Jonah laughs; he recognizes them immediately from his sheaf's *Thetis Bible*, the living document of the planet updated by the people in the village.

"Vespa, look," he calls. "They have frosties!"

"Well, that's a dumb name for some green puffballs," she says as she looks through the fence slats.

"Just wait," Jonah says. "They might do it..."

Within seconds, the creatures hop in a tight circle in the far corner of their pen. One of them tucks its leg under its body and sits still in the black dirt, and immediately another jumps on top of it and pulls its leg under itself. And then the third frosty leaps onto the top one.

"Okay, now I get it," Vespa says. "They stack up like Frosty the Snowman. Clever."

The smile on Jonah's face feels like the first genuine smile he's had in years. He watches in awe as the bottom frosty stands and starts to hop along the fence line. The other two balance perfectly on top, and then both stand and balance on their single legs, and soon the green snowman is twice its height from moments ago.

"Now, like, imagine a hundred of them doing this, all on top of each other," Jonah says. "Because that's what they do. It's so they can eat certain insects living in the top of trees."

Vespa puts her hand through the fence slats, reaching out to pet the top one. "I think I remember those photos from the *Thetis*

Bible now. They can keep hopping and none of them ever fall off somehow."

"They can do that because," a woman says as she steps out from the doorway's shadows and into the sunlight. She's a tall, broad woman, dressed in a blue jumpsuit with long brown and gray hair pulled up into a messy bun. Her face is kind, framed with long wrinkles, dotted with soft brown eyes. Dry sweat glazes her cheeks. A short black stick hangs from her one hand while a bucket swings from her other. "Their claws dig deep into the top layer of the other one's skin until they hit the skull, and from there, their claws can find these tiny, perfect little indentations in the bone to slide into, locking themselves in. It's really quite spectacular. Now, young lady, I would suggest pulling your hand back inside the fence before the top one bites it off."

Vespa yanks her hand back out of the pen and shoves it into her pocket.

The woman turns the bucket onto its side, and with a winded breath, she tosses its contents into the middle of the enclosure with a resounding *thwap*. A dozen white sluglike things slide off each other and begin to crawl in every direction, changing colors as they move. Immediately, the woman jerks her black stick over her head, extending its tip, and then she corrals the slimy things into a three-foot-long line. The bottom frosty bounces over to the slugs and tips toward the ground to eat the closest creatures. The other two hold on, tipping toward the ground to get their fill, too.

"I'm Francesca," the woman says as she continues to line up the slugs that try to get away. "Welcome to Thetis. I'm really, truly sorry for what happened to you guys, for the crash—I'm sure you lost a lot of loved ones and it was a horrific experience—but we're happy you're here. We're thrilled you made it."

"Thank you. I'm Vespa, and this is Jonah. And you're like the first person to actually welcome us. Everyone seems to…hate our guts?"

Francesca bends down to cautiously pet the top frosty before walking back toward the door. "Don't take it personally, dear. There were just...things that we needed that were on the ship. Has anyone told you about... Tell me, how are you feeling? Having any difficulty breathing?"

Vespa and Jonah look at each other and then shake their heads at Francesca.

"That makes sense. You just got here. Commander Mirker wants to be the one who explains everything. But, we'll all be fine. Humans always find a way to survive."

Jonah finds himself monitoring his breathing. When everything feels normal, he says, "But I want to do more than just survive."

Francesca smiles at him. "Well, now. That's a nice attitude to have. Thrive, don't survive. Why don't you two stop by sometime when it isn't the feeding hours, and I'll show you around in here? Lots of *very* neat stuff to see."

"Definitely," Vespa says.

"But what does the commander have to explain to us?" Jonah asks. He looks at Vespa, but she's busy studying the frosties attacking their lunch.

"Oh, I'd get into a lot of trouble for speaking out of turn. Just ask him the next time you see him." Francesca disappears into the shadows, the empty bucket bouncing off her leg with hollow thuds, and eventually Jonah and Vespa pull themselves away from the frosties to see what else feeds along the farm building. In one cage, they see dozens of creatures that look like large squirrels with wet, pebbled frog skin, leaping from branch to branch of a fallen tree. Jonah can't remember their names but recalls seeing photos of them. The creatures pair up on the branches, standing on their back legs and holding each other's front paws, practically waltzing for a few seconds before separating and pairing up with someone else. All at once, though, they stop dancing and freeze, save for the tiny wet ears rotating on their heads, and then they scurry into the building in a tight pack.

"Lunch time," Jonah says under his breath.

Behind another fence, Jonah recognizes the two bright yellow animals as capstones: sheep-sized, bird-like beasts covered in feathers. Instead of wings, though, they have extra-long arms that drag limply behind them as they sprint back and forth on their spindly legs. They stop moving only long enough to pick up the flat rocks scattered around the ground with their long arms, and they carefully set them on top of their tiny heads like caps. As soon as they start running again, though, the rocks fall off, and the beasts jump up and down in frustration. The capstones repeat this over and over, grunting in approval when they put the rocks on their heads, growling and hopping mad when they fall off.

"What's the point of all that?" Jonah wonders out loud.

"I'm sure there's a good explanation, but who knows, maybe they just want to feel pretty."

"Well, they're going to need to do more than put rocks on their heads," Jonah says.

"Firstie, come on. Look at these things. They *are* beautiful. I mean, we're on a new planet staring at an actual alien right now. Think about that. These are aliens. And they're weird and goofy and strange, and they probably smell like ass, but I don't know. I guess I just can't believe we actually made it here. I honestly can't believe we're standing on Thetis. So, it's all pretty beautiful to me. Even these guys."

Her words hover over Jonah like an umbrella, momentarily blocking the constant downpour of fear that follows him everywhere. He hasn't taken a moment of gratitude yet, to sit and be thankful that he's here. That he's...special. That millions and millions of people will never see what he's seeing right now. There's a war going on back home. There's a draft and no end to the fighting in sight, and kids his age are being gunned down by the thousands. But he's here and not hiding in the bathroom of some terrible new foster home, watching these goofy—no, these *beautiful*—animals run back and forth and doing something that must have a purpose. Maybe he'll get a chance to study them himself and figure it out.

But he also remembers Vespa's story about her dad. He remembers the faint crucifix tattoo on her chest, a symbol of her father's mission to control her and her sister and bring them closer to his

God at whatever cost. The discovery of Thetis eventually drove him insane, and now here Vespa is, breathing Thetis air, walking on Thetis soil, proving her father wrong that his God didn't create everything in the universe. He had forgotten what a big deal this is for her.

The cadets watch the capstones for another minute before the beasts scurry inside to eat, their long feathery arms trailing seconds behind their bodies, and Jonah turns to Vespa. "I'm really happy you're here with me. I wouldn't be here if it weren't for you."

Vespa blinks her big green eyes and shrugs. "And I wouldn't have made it this far without you, Firstie. I wouldn't have gone west with everyone else if it weren't for you."

"And *I* wouldn't have gone west if it weren't for Brooklyn."

They hang their heads for a moment before turning away from the farm building. The cadets silently walk north, passing more yurts and tents and groups of sullen people trudging along. A pair of white drones zip by overhead, disappearing over the spiked fence a few seconds later. They pass by a couple of acres turned into a thriving garden, thick with green leafy vegetables and tall corn stalks. Two men walk through the tight rows with sheafs in their hands, dictating into the microphones and taking photos of the produce.

"I could go for some lunch, too," Vespa says. "How about I get you to your new place, you get settled for a bit and check your shit out, and then we get some food in the dining tent?"

"Sounds good to me."

As they walk past the garden, Jonah notices two things: off on his right, in the far northwest corner of the village, a long black tube sticks out of a white roof like a giant spoon sitting in a bowl. The tube must be fifty-feet long, pointed high over his head. The Woesner Telescope. It's the reason Jonah ran west; his mission was to get himself in the lens of that thing and signal for help. His life had depended on it. Jonah shakes his head; he's so close to it now he could hit it with a football. And then on his left, far beyond the fence, gathered in an uneven huddle at the bottom of some distant hills, three towering white modules stand straight up. Giant marshmallows in the hot sun. Unlike his ship, the first *Mayflower* vessel worked as planned. The metal structure opened up, and the modules drifted down under enormous parachutes. And then the passengers got to work setting up the Athens colony.

Vespa steers them toward a row of small yurts and they find a faded "31" stenciled onto a windowless door.

"Fancy stuff, huh?" Vespa says.

"Fancy enough for me." Jonah has lived in far worse conditions; he's slept under bridges and in the doorways of shuttered stores. He's lived in foster homes with angry men and sadistic teenagers. He'll take a small yurt with a door any day of the week.

Before Jonah can reach the doorknob, a voice calls out over his shoulder. The cadets turn to see a man marching toward them in a tan jumpsuit, his cheeks covered in a thick black beard, his shoulders flared and pulled back. As he gets closer, Jonah sees he's no older than nineteen or twenty.

"So, what the hell happened up there, huh?" the man barks. "How the *hell* did you get all this way and then crash on the moon and screw everything up?"

Vespa and Jonah are speechless as the man's hands tighten into fists. He looks ready to explode. Jonah instinctively tries to push Vespa behind him, but she shoves his hands away and puffs out her chest.

"Where is it? What happened to it?" the man seethes.

"Back off," Vespa says. "Now."

He keeps marching ahead, keeps tightening his fists. "Don't tell me what to do, girl."

Vespa takes a step toward him. "Dude, leave us alone. You have no idea what we've just been through."

The man reaches behind his back and pulls out a small blue handgun. He aims it at Vespa's head and shouts, "Screw you! You have no idea what *we're* going through."

Vespa stands motionless, but Jonah puts his hands up and shuffles in a circle until he's standing on the man's left. The gun wavers up and down in the man's trembling hand. Jonah needs him to drop it for just one second. Then this guy is done for.

Vespa laughs. "You're going to shoot me? For what? For being asleep on a ship and then waking up in the middle of a crash landing? Yeah, asshole. This is all my fault. Us sleeping passengers in the rear modules are to blame."

The man takes a step closer to Vespa. "Where's Tunick? He with you? And Kip is back, too? They all come back? Where are they?"

"Kip is back, too?" Vespa repeats.

A woman's voice comes from inside a nearby yurt: "Louis, put that gun down! Now!"

It's all the distraction that Jonah needs. He rushes at the man with his shoulders like a linebacker. He connects with his ribs, plowing him completely sideways. In the same motion, Jonah grabs the man's wrist, twisting it until the gun bounces on the ground. The man spins out of control then falls onto his chest. A second later Vespa is on his back. She locks her fingers over the man's forehead and pulls back, a move she learned from Brooklyn the first time they met. Into his ear, as sweetly as possible, she says, "Nice to meet you, Louis. I'm Vespa Bolivar. Where can I get some fresh towels for my friend here?"

Jonah grabs the gun and sticks it into his pocket just as a woman with a shaved head stumbles out of her yurt with a rag over her mouth.

"Hey! Get off of him!" she shouts through the rag.

Vespa and Jonah look at each other, and then Vespa pulls back a little farther. The man howls and spits, begging for mercy.

More colonists come out of yurts and tents and running down alleys, all of them yelling for Vespa to get off of the man's back, all of them looking thin and exhausted. A few men and women raise handguns, shouting for Vespa to let him go. *Or else.* Jonah pulls his gun out of his pocket but keeps it flat against his thigh. A short woman wearing a blue and yellow headscarf sees this and points at Jonah and shakes her head, warning him not to get involved. Not exactly the welcome he had been dreaming about for over a year.

"Whoa," Freeman says as he breaks through the circle.

"Everybody, put your weapons down! Everybody! And you," he points at Vespa. "Get off of him. *Now.*"

Vespa releases the man's head and then casually stands up and brushes the dirt from her clothes. "Asshole pulled a gun on us for no reason."

"For no reason?" Louis shouts as he struggles to get to his hands and knees. "Are you kidding me? You guys crashing up on Achilles... You have no idea, do you? You don't. We're not going to make it now. We're dead. We're all doomed."

"What? Why? What does that mean?" Jonah asks.

"Nobody's *doomed*," Freeman says as he helps Louis to his feet. "Louis is just being dramatic, that's all. Aren't you, Louis?"

Louis grits his teeth and then spits over his shoulder. Jonah can tell he wants to start the fight all over again, but instead he takes a deep breath. "I want my gun back."

Everyone looks at Jonah, who studies the weapon in his sweating hand. He pushes a small button to release its cartridge, and then pulls back on the chamber—sending a bullet helplessly to the ground. Instead of handing it over, though, he presses the weapon back against his thigh.

"Tell me why we're doomed," Jonah says to Louis.

Louis looks to Freeman and then connects eyes with a couple more people in the circle. He shrugs. "Talk to Mirker. There were... there were just a lot of personal items aboard the ship and other stuff, and now they're all gone."

"Yeah, well, there were a lot of *people* onboard, and now they're all gone, too, so," Vespa says. She slowly takes the gun out of Jonah's hand, flips it around, and gives it to Freeman. "I'm sorry if any of your shit got ruined, but *none* of you have any idea what happened up on Achilles, so stop treating us like we're some kind of enemy or that we had anything to do with the ship going down, and start treating us like survivors who just went through a very traumatic event. And just, I don't know, stop being such fucking dickheads. Because that'd be pretty cool."

The woman with the headscarf walks forward with her hands

clasped. Tears run down her cheeks. "Did you know my daughter? Ariel Abbasi? She was on the ship. She was coming to be with me. She's fourteen and very short, and she looks like me. Just like me. Did you know her? Did you see what happened to her?"

Vespa's answer sticks in her throat, her grief instant and palpable. "I don't know who that is, I'm sorry. I didn't know her."

"Me neither," Jonah says with his head hung low; he doesn't want to look into Ariel's mom's eyes while he's lying. He remembers Ariel well from the dining module. He randomly sat at her table on numerous occasions, often listening to her talk about an application she was building on her sheaf to show evolution in real time, but mostly he remembers her talking about her goal to explore Thetis and discover more animals on the planet than anyone else, and then she would go on and on about what she would name them. She was sweet and liked to drum on the table with her index fingers and always wore a beautiful headscarf just like her mom's. The last time Jonah saw Ariel, she was lying face up and covered with burns, dead. A huge gash ran above her eyes from ear to ear. Jonah jumped right over her as he ran to help Garrett and Paul with the trapped girls. But he can't tell her mother that. He doesn't *want* to tell her mother that. He also doesn't want to give her false hope, but this seems like the better alternative.

"Maybe she's still alive then?" Ariel's mom asks.

"Maybe," Vespa says. "Lots of kids got lost up there."

"That's true," Jonah whispers.

"Then we have to go back. We have to go back right now," Ariel's mom says. She then grabs another woman's hand, and they run toward the hospital.

The rest of the colonists stare and linger, and Jonah can see and feel and taste their misery. He always pictured entering the Athens colony as some type of champion, as an elite member of this tiny group living light years away from Earth, as someone relatable and welcome and desperately needed, a new set of hands and eyes to help build this community from the ground up into something historic and astounding, but standing there gathering the stares of all these angry people, he feels like an outsider, unwanted, another mouth to feed. Different galaxy, same story.

"Hey, tall guy. You Jonah?" a voice comes from Jonah's right. He turns to see a boy his own age standing at the open doorway of Yurt 31. He's short and skinny with skin the color of porcelain. A shaggy mop of black hair covers half his face. The boy brings a mug up to his thin lips and blows steam from its top before taking a loud, slurping sip.

Freeman hands Louis his gun and pats him on the chest. He then whispers something into his ear and pushes him into the crowd. Freeman walks toward Jonah and Vespa with shrugged shoulders and an apologetic smile. "We're happy you guys are here. Honestly. Don't get the wrong impression."

"Why could we get that?" Vespa asks.

The boy in the doorway takes another loud sip. "So, like, is this Jonah, or what?"

"Yeah," Jonah says. "I'm him."

"Cool. I'm your roommate, Matteo. Want some tea or something?"

Jonah shares a look with Vespa before asking, "What kind of tea?"

Matteo laughs and gags, spraying tea at Jonah's feet. "*Jesus Christ.* Dude, you were just blind—or, am I wrong?—and you *just* got rescued after probably thinking you were about to die up there on that moon, and here you are being picky right now about what kind of tea I have? That's the funniest shit I've ever heard. Come on in, ya psycho. Let me show you your hammock and stuff."

Matteo turns and disappears inside the yurt, leaving a cloud of steam in the doorway like a ghost.

"Go ahead," Vespa says as she gives Jonah a slight push. "Check it out. Get some rest. We'll eat soon."

Jonah crosses his arms over his chest. "*All I've been doing is resting.* What about what that Louis guy was saying about Kip or how we're all doomed? There was something on that ship we didn't know about, Vespa. Something obviously super important. And we still haven't talked about Dr. Z going crazy and spelling out 'Don't Leave' with those dead bodies on Achilles *right before we left*? And *now* we have to deal with all these…assholes looking to fight us?"

Vespa shakes her head. "I hear you, I know. Let's talk after dinner or something." She turns and starts to walk away. Over her shoulder, she calls, "Oh, and you think I can't handle some assholes and their animosity, Firstie? Because I thrive on it."

"You should rest, too!" Jonah yells after her.

Vespa raises her fist in the air and gives him a mocking thumbs-up before disappearing around the corner.

Matteo's face reappears in the doorway. "Dude, get in here before people rip you to shreds."

CHAPTER FOUR

The yurt is warm and smells like lemons mixed with body odor. On Jonah's right hang two green hammocks, frayed and a bit dusty, and Jonah immediately wonders who used to sleep in the second one. Tunick? Krev? Armitage? To his left, a small tabletop stove with a percolating tea pot sputters out a low whistle. Matteo sits down on a wooden footlocker under one of the hammocks and takes a loud sip of his tea. He closes his eyes, and a small smile crosses his lips. A moment later, he looks up at Jonah with a straight face.

"So, you meet Tunick, or what?"

"Um." Jonah still doesn't know what he should reveal about Achilles. After all the lies and backstabbing, he knows it's possible that Tunick and the Splitters have spies here. He doesn't know who here is friends with whom, or who has enemies and why. "A lot happened on Achilles with a lot of people. I'm still pretty much processing it."

"Yeah, you met him. Yeah, you did. I can see it on your face."

Jonah remains silent. Maybe there's a free yurt on the other side of the village, one where he can be by himself. He needs time to think and decompress and look over his wounds and take a nap and, and, and. What he doesn't need to do is talk about Tunick.

Matteo takes another loud sip before standing to open a cabinet under the stove. "Okay, fine. You'll talk about it when you're ready to talk about it. When the nightmares end and all that good stuff. I get it. So, what do you want to know about this place? Because I'll fill you in. Be your guide or whatever. Your seeing eye dog, not that you need one of those anymore, am I right?"

Jonah quickly walks back toward the front door and opens it an inch. The crowd is gone, as are Freeman and Louis and Vespa. He quietly closes the door and tries to lock it, but there's no lock.

"Yeah, uh, we don't exactly have locks, *per say*," Matteo says as he fills up a second mug with hot water. "With so few people here, we're supposed to be able to trust each other and whatnot."

"And do you?" Jonah asks, thinking about Captain Tejas putting explosives all over the village.

Matteo stuffs some tiny orange leaves into a metal tea ball and drops it into the second mug. He holds it up to Jonah with a wink. "Here ya go, big guy. Matteo's famous tea, made from the finest alien leaves on Thetis that I've been able to find so far."

Jonah hesitates to take the mug. "You made tea from leaves growing here? On Thetis?"

"Don't worry, dude, it's been approved by the good old FDA. You know, the Fucking Doctors in Athens. Look." He takes the tea ball out of Jonah's mug and drops it into his own, taking a sip to make a point. "It's freaking tasty, man. And safe. And it's caffeine free, which is pretty boss."

Jonah takes the mug and sniffs the pungent tea; it's sweet and citrusy. "You didn't answer my question. Do you trust the people here?"

"No, not really. I mean, after Tunick and Lark and Camilla and everyone else went a little crazy last year, it's been a bit difficult on the old trust meter. But since then, it's been relatively quiet."

"What about Captain Tejas, though? With her trying to blow things up?"

"I don't know nothing about that," Matteo says. "Didn't see it myself and doubt it even happened. More likely she just got sick of this place, went out for a walk, and fell down a hole, and then Mirker took over."

Jonah sits on the other footlocker and takes his first sip. It's weak but not bad, and the hot liquid sliding down his throat feels good, restorative even. "Did you know that on Earth, we were told that a bunch of the kids here died on a field trip? Because that's what we heard happened to Tunick and Krev and Lark and everyone. We even had a moment of silence for them, all around the world. We actually mourned them."

"How sweet are you guys?" Matteo laughs. "But, yes, we all agreed to say they died on a field trip when that shit went down. Needed to keep the community looking good and safe and all that. No need for Earth to know we had some drug addicts up here causing all these problems and stealing spaceships. We needed to be sure we still got our funding and reinforcements and supplies. Had to make sure you guys still made the trip."

"And look how well that turned out." Jonah stands and circles the room before carefully sitting on the hammock furthest from the door. He gently lies back with his mug held over his head. "Did *you* know Tunick?"

"Of course. Everyone knew everyone."

"And?"

"And the guy was a big-time goofball, but overall, pretty harmless. Made everyone laugh, helped out a lot around the colony. Dude was *strong*. He and Armitage, and I guess Krev, they were big time important in getting this place put together. Even if they were only seventeen or whatever."

Jonah tries to picture Tunick without his beard and long hair, digging trenches and erecting tents, helping others. It's difficult to imagine. His eyes drag along the sparse interior of the yurt, its canvas walls and ceiling, the one rocking chair on the opposite side of the room made of the same fuzzy black wood as the walls in the hospital and farm building. Then he looks back at the door and the white outline of the sunlight framing it. Jonah swings his feet onto the floor, sets his steaming mug on the ground, hooks his hands into his footlocker's handles, and drags it toward the entrance.

"Uh, see you later?" Matteo says.

Jonah puts the footlocker right in front of the door and then walks back over to his hammock and climbs back on. He reaches his long arm toward the ground and retrieves his tea.

Matteo pours more hot water into his mug. "And you just did that because..."

"For one, that Louis guy who just pulled a gun on us. Secondly, have you seen some of the kids we brought back from Achilles? The kids with the blank stares who don't talk?"

The boy slowly blows steam away from his mug. "Um, yeah. And I'm staying clear of that little rat pack. Hopefully, the doctors will zap them back to normal here soon."

Jonah wants to know what that means, but he's suddenly exhausted. He sets the tea on the ground again. The hammock is more comfortable than he thought it would be, and his eyelids become too heavy to stay open. A year ago, or even a week ago, there's no way Jonah could have fallen asleep with another person in the room, especially a stranger, but now... He hears Matteo walk across the room and shove the footlocker to the side, and Jonah can't even open his mouth to protest.

"Told you that shit was caffeine free. Alright then, roomie. You take a nap or whatever. Bathroom is in the next tent over, if you need to use it. I have like a hundred tasks to do and whatever. See you at dinner time. Hope you like rice and potatoes."

As soon as the door shuts, Jonah is fast asleep.

• • •

Jonah stands in front of the small stove in his yurt and drags his fingers across his tired face, picking the crust out from the corners of his eyes. He has no idea what time it is or how long he's slept. All he knows is that sunlight no longer frames the unlocked door and that Matteo has left him a note.

"Jonah, don't drink all of my tea. Other than that, go buck wild. But don't really; I like to keep this place neat. Also, that was my hammock you slept on. Get it together. ;)"

He looks at the note and then at the tea kettle and realizes he doesn't even know where to get water. Or food, for that matter. The only directions he has are to the bathroom, and that seems like a good place to start before looking for dinner.

There's a knock on the door. He groans; he's not ready for visitors and small talk. He doesn't want to talk about Achilles or Tunick or whatever supplies didn't make it to Thetis. He wants to pee, find something to eat, and crawl into his own hammock until morning.

"Jonah? You awake?"

As soon as he hears Vespa's voice, he rushes to the door and swings it open. She stands in a clean tan jumpsuit, backpack over her one shoulder, her black hair pulled up high above her head in a fountain, her green eyes darting left and right. She looks beautiful, like a flower growing in the cracks of an abandoned parking lot. Before he can say anything, she's inside and pacing between the hammocks.

"I need you to come with me. Right now," she says.

"Okay, sure. Where?"

"Outside the gates."

Jonah pauses. "Why out there?"

"Because Paul is missing. He's out there. And he's not supposed to be out there. And I need your help getting him back."

Jonah sighs and sits on a footlocker. "Paul doesn't need me out there looking for him. That guy hates me. He *hunted* me, Vespa. He hunted me down with Armitage and Ruth and wanted to kill me."

"Yeah, well, I don't care about any of that right now," Vespa says. "He's out there with Dr. Z, Jonah. Someone at the gate said they saw them leave the village about a half hour ago. They said she was dragging Paul away like he was dead or asleep or hurt. She took him, Firstie. And we have to help him."

Jonah stands up, but then sinks down into his hammock, the ropes creaking under his weight. Paul is huge, much stronger than he is. And Dr. Z was able to drag him around?

"Why didn't they stop her at the gate?"

"Someone tried," Vespa responds. "And now that guy is lying in the same hospital bed you were just in."

"But how is that even possible? Didn't Mirker lock her up after she attacked me? Shouldn't she be in some sort of jail or at the bottom of some deep pit or something?"

"That's exactly what I thought. They're going to send out a search party in about an hour, but that's too long to wait. I need to go now. And I need you to come with me."

"Me? Why not take someone like Griffin? He actually likes Paul."

"Because," she says. "Dr. Z seems to have a thing for you. You could be…like…"

"Bait?"

"Exactly."

"Gee. Thanks."

Vespa walks up to Jonah's hammock and grabs ahold of one of the rope knots. She gives it a little shake. "Sun comes up in ten. You and I are going to be outside the gates by then. You hear me?"

He can see the desperation on her face, or maybe it's heartbreak. Is she in love with Paul, or just worried about him?

"I'm hungry," he says. "It's morning time? Shit. I missed dinner last night. And lunch yesterday."

"I've got you covered," Vespa says, patting her backpack.

They speed through the alleys of the dark village as quietly as they can, setting off tiny motion-sensor lights as they dart from yurt to yurt. As they pass by the Woesner Telescope, Jonah stares at the huge tube shining in the Achilles moonlight. He wants to get inside that building and look into that telescope and see what it sees. He wants to know what it knows.

After thirty seconds, they reach the forty-foot tall gate that's flanked by the fifty-foot fence. At its base, on the right side of the gate, sits a wide building with five small windows dotting its side. It's the only structure in the village other than the observatory building made of stone and concrete. A single red bulb sits above the door.

"So, how do we..." Jonah mumbles as he looks for a button or switch to open the gate. Then he sees it: high up on the wall, maybe twenty feet up, is an emergency button. *How are they supposed to reach that in an emergency?*

The door to the building suddenly swings open, and out comes a thin man wearing a red ball cap. He reeks of sweat and something that might be alcohol, but Jonah knows that can't be right; alcohol is forbidden in Athens.

"Who is it?" the man asks with a yawn.

Vespa steps forward, entering the red glow from the bulb. "I'm Vespa Bolivar, one of the survivors from Achilles. And this is Jonah Lincoln."

She pulls Jonah into the light just as the sky overhead changes from black to dark green. The man's features come into view: long nose, furry cheeks, spidery blue veins spreading from the corners of his sleep-deprived eyes to the corners of his temples, disappearing into his cap. An LZR-rifle hangs from the strap crossing his back.

"Gate doesn't open for another hour," the man says. "Come back then. And you're going to need an escort on your first time out. Does Mirker know about this?"

Vespa quickly steps past him and peers her head into the door of the building. "A woman and a cadet got through this gate just a while ago. How'd that happen?"

The man rubs his jaw and Jonah sees it's slightly swollen. Also, his lip is cracked and lined with blood.

"*That happened* because the good doctor got the jump on us. Broke Blix's arm and maybe even his leg. And she tossed me around like I was nothing. I didn't have much of an option but to open the gate unless I wanted my brains splattered all over the ground. She had that kid with her who seemed out of it, too. But look, Mirker knows all about it. Said to just let them go and suffer out there for a bit, and that we'd go out looking for them when the sun is up."

"But," Vespa says, and before she can continue, there's a low rumbling and the ground begins to shake. Metal pulls on metal, chains roll over gears, and a second later, the gate begins to separate.

"Back up," the man says.

A pair of square headlights attached to a rover appear on the other side of the gate. Slowly, the vehicle rolls into the village, its electric engine humming. As soon as it's through, the gate begins to shut, and that's when Vespa grabs Jonah's hand. They make a break for it, but the man in the red cap raises his rifle and steps in their path.

"I don't think so," he says. "Not without an escort. You kids have trouble hearing?"

"Who here needs an escort?" asks another man's voice. It comes from an open window of the rover. "We'll take 'em out. Show them the neighborhood. Introduce them to the locals and all that. Breakfast has been delivered, my good man. Be sure to tell Mirker."

The passenger door opens, and a stocky man slides out of the rover and onto the ground, his boots crunching the dirt. A curtain of brown hair falls over his eyes, and he pulls his hand through it, brushing it over his round scalp and putting it into a ponytail. His head nods up and down, up and down, never stopping. A walkie-talkie crackles on his shoulder, and he reaches over to silence it.

With a whir, one of the back windows lowers, revealing a short Indian woman with a pencil between her teeth. She looks Vespa and Jonah over with a set of fierce brown eyes, then her cheeks harden, and she chomps through the pencil, breaking it in half. The window goes back up without her saying a word.

"Okaaaay," Vespa mumbles.

A second later, a bald man pulls himself out of the driver's side window with a hacking cough. He winks at Jonah. "You kids want to see the sights or what?" The sky lightens some more, showing a maroon scar on the man's face, crossing through his left eyebrow down to his chin.

"We're looking for someone," Jonah says. "A couple people left the village a little while ago, and she wants to find them."

"Ah, yes. The doctor and the cadet." The man with the ponytail plants his hands on his lower back and stretches, his head still nodding. "We can probably help you. As long as it's okay with the big guy."

"You can?" Vespa asks.

The back window lowers again, and the woman reaches her hand out the window. She holds Dr. Z's yellow jacket. It's covered in dirt and ripped almost beyond recognition.

"Where did you find that?" Jonah asks.

The woman throws it at Vespa who catches it in a cloud of thick dust. "About half a mile up the path. See all that orange stuff on it?"

The cadets take a closer look at the jacket; wet orange smudges lie under the layer of black dirt. It smells like death and sweat.

The bald man lowers himself back inside the rover and says, "That tells us they went through what we call the 'marble zone.' It's pretty close. Shouldn't be too hard to track."

"Not for us," the other man says, his hands now on his hips. He leans left and then right, groaning. "Plus, we have drones."

The sky overhead is now more light than dark, and Jonah can see the white modules far in the distance. He can also see that the man nodding and stretching in front of him has dark circles under his eyes, like he hasn't slept in days. Jonah knows that look.

"So, can we go right now?" Vespa asks.

"I just need to clear it with Mirker first," the man with the red cap says.

The man with the ponytail whips a small sheaf out of his chest pocket and unfurls it. His eyes scroll over the device, typing a message. A few seconds later, he shrugs and says, "Says just don't let the kids out of our sight. And to bring the doctor back alive."

"What about the cadet?" Vespa asks.

"Doesn't say anything about what shape we need him in. So, I guess we'll see what happens."

A back door pops open, and the woman scoots over without

a word. The cadets don't hesitate; after Vespa, Jonah pulls himself into the rover and reaches for the shoulder belt, but halfway through bringing it across his body, he releases it with a zip. He wants to be ready to get out—or even escape—at a moment's notice. The man with the ponytail jumps in the passenger seat and sets a hand on the bald man's shoulder as he looks over the vehicle gauges. In the middle seat, Vespa leans forward and says, "Ready when you are."

They roll backwards out of the gate, the electric engine barely making a noise. The guard gives a tired wave as he speaks into his walkie-talkie. The gate closes as soon as the hood is clear.

The inside of the rover is like a control center; there are over a dozen screens lining the ceiling, headrests, console, and windshield, showing green graphs and red sonar blips and glowing blue charts, all flanked by scrolling numbers that mean nothing to Jonah. He takes a bite of a homemade protein bar from Vespa's backpack and keeps watching. One screen appears to show the weather with little blobs of clouds moving along the eastern coastline of their small continent, while several others show live feeds of the sleepy village and alien landscape: a vast stretch of a valley bursts with thousands of geysers shooting high into the sky, while black dots—birds or huge insects—hover and then fly straight through the spouts; on another feed, fast-moving waves lap a rocky beach; and then another screen shows a mountainside covered in huge, stacked pools of water that spill and empty into each other, creating a beautiful, seemingly endless waterfall. Seeing all the water across the screens reminds Jonah why the planet was named Thetis in the first place: In Greek mythology, Thetis was known as the goddess of water. She married a half-god, half-man named Peleus. Their son: Achilles.

Jonah's eyes shift to a drone feed slowly sweeping through a group of a purplish trees. At the base of the trees, boulders surround the trunks like clumsy pyramids, some piles reaching halfway up the trunks. The camera swoops left and right until diving and landing on the ground with a slight bounce just as a herd of large shadows appears.

"Watch this," the woman whispers as she presses the screen. "Just watch."

The camera zooms in on the shadows, which quickly become turtle-like creatures with smooth, domed backs. Jonah doesn't remember these animals from the *Thetis Bible*; they must be newly discovered. They're as big as horses and move quickly, scrambling up to the boulders on tall, narrow legs with wide feet; they look like walking tables, Jonah thinks as he watches them form huddles around the different trees. While the others remain still, one from each huddle falls onto its side. The others crouch behind the fallen member and lower their heads, and then together they push the creature toward the tree trunk, bulldozing the boulders farther up the trunk.

"That's kind of…" Jonah starts, but the woman holds up her finger for him to hold his thought.

Each of the creatures being pushed by its huddle dives its feet into the cracks between the moving rocks. It doesn't take long before the shoved creatures start pulling long snakes out from between them, and it doesn't take long for Jonah to realize that they aren't snakes they're grabbing, but instead they're long tentacles or arms attached to fat, hairless animals being violently pulled to the surface. As soon as the sideways turtle-creature has a tentacled animal in each claw, the others stop using it as a plow and take the fat animals in their mouths.

The woman taps the screen and zooms in tight on one of the huddles. "And then…"

The turtle-creatures strip the animals of their tentacles and toss them into a pile where the sideways member rolls back onto its feet and dives its head into the tentacles with fervor.

"Apparently, the arms are the best parts," the woman says. "The others reward the one they use as a plow with the meatiest bits. They're the leaders of their little clans amongst the herd. There's a hierarchy. To be used is to be respected."

Jonah thinks about that phrase, to be used is to be respected. He's been used all his life, by foster parents who simply wanted the monthly government stipend for keeping him under their roofs, by older kids on the streets of Cleveland who used him and his baby face to beg for food and loose change, by the academy and by Tunick and the Splitters on Achilles, and never once has he felt respected.

"That was interesting and all," Vespa says, "but can we focus here? A crazy woman has our friend somewhere out there."

The man with the scar turns around with a smile. "You got it, captain… Captain what again? I should know my new captain's name, don't you think?"

In the passenger seat, the man with the ponytail chuckles and nods and turns a few knobs on the console between them.

With venom in her voice she reports, "My name is Vespa Bolivar, and I'm a fourth-year cadet who just survived a crash landing, a bunch of bloodthirsty animals, a sadistic group of teenagers, and three nights of sleeping on your shitty hammocks. I've earned some stripes. Now, let's—"

"We're here," the woman says matter-of-factly.

The rover comes to a stop. The first thing Jonah sees out the window is a grouping of gray, twisted trees. The same ones Armitage Blythe pulled the bark from in his infamous video shared around the Earth at lightning speed. He can still picture the cadet tearing the bark away, revealing a nest of white, bat-like creatures that took flight in a misty cloud of ink. The second thing Jonah sees is the blood smeared across several of the trunks, leading down an embankment.

"Everybody out," the bald man says.

CHAPTER FIVE

THE GRAY GRASS UNDER JONAH'S BOOTS POPS AND SHATTERS with every step. He follows the adults into the trees, stepping where they step, bracing his hands where theirs just were. It's hot and sticky, and his gray jumpsuit clings to his skin like wet tissues.

"We found the yellow jacket right over there," the woman says, pointing to the bottom of a large, twisted tree. "Showed up in our headlights while we're headed back to camp."

Jonah stares at the tree and the blood on its trunk, wondering why they didn't leave the jacket where it was for evidence, or immediately investigate once they found it. He also wonders whose blood it is. Did Paul wake up and attack Dr. Z, ripping her jacket off and then chasing her into the forest? Or did Dr. Z carve up Paul's skin with some new message to warn the others?

He stumbles past everyone, making his own path, and soon finds himself standing on the edge of a cliff. Half a mile below, thousands of geysers erupt in the valley, creating an enormous cloud of green mist that hovers overhead, blocking out the sun. The cliff Jonah stands on goes on for miles and miles, almost completely circling the valley. Way off on his right, a series of waterfalls descend the cliff into a giant pool that narrows and funnels into a twisting stream, cutting right through the geysers on the valley floor.

"You see those little black dots in all those waterfalls?" the woman asks as she comes up behind him.

Jonah thinks he might see some black specks in the water when he squints but can't be sure.

The woman holds her sheaf out in front of Jonah's face and turns on the camera. She raises her chin, triggering the zoom function, and suddenly it's as if they're hovering right above a waterfall halfway up the cliff. On her screen, small horned animals with squashed, pig-like faces bob up and down in the water above one of the falls. There are hundreds of them, maybe thousands. And they go over the falls seemingly without worry, plummeting with their short arms held above their heads. The woman zooms in even closer on a couple of the animals, following them all the way down the cliff, down waterfall after waterfall, and when they finally reach the giant pool at the bottom, they go underwater and never resurface, disappearing without a trace. Her sheaf scans the pool's surface and then follows the stream cutting through the valley. Not one of the animals floats through. Thousands keep coming down the falls, and then they're gone.

"Are they...dying? Are they killing themselves?" Jonah asks.

"Maybe," the woman answers. "But we don't know for sure because we can't find any bodies. They just," she snaps her fingers, "go away. Even with our drones, we can't figure it out. Yet."

Jonah watches for a few more seconds before his eyes are drawn to a splattering of blood near his feet. There's more to his left, and he quickly starts to follow it down a ridge that hugs the cliff's edge.

"Yo, Firstie," Vespa says behind him. "Wait up."

The man with the ponytail suddenly pushes past Vespa and then Jonah, descending the ridge in a jog with series of loud, hacking coughs, his head still nodding, his rifle bouncing on his back.

"He lives for this kind of stuff," the woman says as she drops in line behind Vespa. The bald man takes up the rear, whistling and clicking his tongue as if this is just a walk in the park.

"Does he keep nodding because of the… What's wrong?" Vespa asks.

"It's from the wormhole," the woman says. "He hasn't been able to stop moving his head ever since we went through two years ago. Even does it in his sleep, from what I've heard."

The ridge continues to descend and curve left, ending at a large, circular space dotted with cave entrances. As Jonah comes down the final steps of the ridge, he doesn't know where to look: at the half-circle of black doorways punched into the stone, or at the small sculptures all around him; rocks of all sizes and shapes are stacked on top of each other, balancing and wobbling in the swirling wind that sweeps through the area.

"Who the hell made those?" Vespa asks.

A low groan comes from one of the caves. The man with the ponytail whips his gun off his back and looks through his scope, nodding and bobbing the barrel of the rifle from cave to cave until pointing at one on the left. "He's in there."

"Who? Paul?" Jonah asks.

"Better be."

Vespa and Jonah sprint into the cave and slide to a stop when they find Paul leaning against the cold wall. His eyes are closed, and his head is down, and right below his heart, blood stains his green jumpsuit.

"Paul!" Vespa grabs his face and tips it up to hers. "Shit, shit, shit. Are you okay? What happened?"

Jonah's eyes bounce from the wound below the boy's heart to the tiny, precise cuts all over his skin, covering his neck and face and even the palms of his hands. The lines are shallow, looking as if someone carefully dragged a paperclip or needle across his skin.

"What the hell did she do to him?" the man with the ponytail asks as he approaches. He's out of breath, hands on his knees. "Looks like the doctor went to town on him. Looks like she was… designing something."

It takes Jonah a moment to realize that the scratches aren't random, but instead form patterns like a maze or a map. He immediately jumps to his feet and squints into the darkness, knowing that Dr. Z could be just out of sight and ready to attack.

"Is he breathing or what?" the bald man asks. He stands just outside the cave, his back to the group, his rifle sweeping the open space.

The woman takes a few photos of Paul with her sheaf before setting a canteen to his lips. Paul's throat pulses and swallows, his head rolls over his shoulder, and his eyes flutter open until he focuses on Vespa.

"Hey, cadet," he whispers to Vespa.

"Hey, yourself."

Paul's eyes connect with Jonah's, and then they crawl to the three adults hovering nearby. The boy plants his hands on the ground and tries to stand, but immediately clutches the wound on his side and groans.

"Where's your friend, the doctor?" the bald man asks.

Paul sets his head back against the wall. "If she's not dead, I'm going to kill her."

The woman rolls up her sheaf and sticks it into her pocket. "Come on, let's get him back to the rover."

Vespa and Jonah duck their heads under Paul's arms and gently bring him to his feet. They carry him out of the cave and sit him next to one of the wobbling stacks of rocks. In the sunlight, the scratches on Paul's skin are clearer, easier to follow. Jonah studies the lines, trying to make sense of them.

There's a noise farther up the cliff, a slow clicking and clacking of falling rocks. A few seconds later, a curtain of black dust and debris rains down into the area, blanketing each of them from head to toe before they can find cover. Stacks of rocks tumble all around them.

"Let's move him! Hurry!" Vespa shouts.

The men raise their weapons, whipping the barrels back and forth as Jonah helps Vespa pull Paul into the opening of the nearest cave, setting him against the wall. Jonah stands to leave, but Paul reaches up and catches him by the wrist. He pulls him down until they're at eye level.

"She keeps talking about you," he whispers.

Jonah looks up at Vespa standing above them with clenched fists and wet cheeks. She doesn't even look at Jonah; she's completely focused on Paul. The two cadets must have spent time together while Jonah was recovering in the hospital. It's nice to hear that Vespa's been talking about him.

"The doctor," Paul says. "The doctor keeps talking about you. Jonah, she's going to—"

More and more rock and debris rain into the open space. The rocks get bigger, breaking open and bouncing over the edge. A pumpkin-sized boulder grazes the bald man's shoulder, spinning him around, sending him close to the cliff's edge before the other man grabs his rifle strap and pulls him back. But then a rock bounces off the ground and hits the ponytail man's legs, pushing them both forward. Jonah doesn't hesitate; he dashes out of the cave and grabs each man by the arm and yanks them back. All three fall to the ground in a pile while the rockslide continues to punish the space all around them.

"Come on!" the woman shouts as she sprints into the cave with Paul and Vespa inside.

But before Jonah and the men can untangle themselves, a herd of brightly colored animals appears at the top of the cliff. They stand tall, shoulder to shoulder in silence, swaying left and right in haunting unison, their fat fluffy bodies shedding what look to be red feathers into the air. They have small, pointed heads with flat, pink faces, looking like mutant baboons who just raided a chicken coop.

"Mimics," the bald man says as he gets to his feet. "Fucking hell. What are they doing all the way over here?"

"What are they?" Jonah whispers as he pats his pockets for anything that can be used as a weapon.

"A bunch of assholes," the man with the ponytail responds as he aims his rifle upwards. His head nods faster than before, his eye bouncing against his scope.

"A bunch of assholes who can rip your body into a hundred pieces," the bald man says. "But maybe we'll get lucky and they'll just turn around and—"

The animals suddenly stop swaying, and then at the exact same time, each one drops to its knees and begins to climb down the cliff headfirst.

"Damn it," the bald man seethes.

The animals race to the bottom, crawling over each other, humming in wet, guttural voices. The humming gets stronger the lower they get, and soon it grows into a loud buzzing noise that reminds Jonah of a swarm of bees.

The bald man readjusts his rifle. "Now?"

"Just hold on. They might still just leave us alone," the other man whispers. "Let's not get them riled up any more than they already are."

When the animals reach the tops of the caves, they peek their tiny pointed heads inside to look around. Vespa gasps at the sight of them and jumps to her feet, but not before grabbing a large rock as a weapon. The woman pulls a blue pistol out of her pocket and aims it at the animals with both hands. Paul tries to get to his feet, but all he can do is roll onto his side and try to squirm farther inside the cave.

"Vespa!" Jonah calls.

In horrifying synchronicity, the animals on the cliff side rotate their heads one hundred and eighty degrees to look at Jonah. Each blinks their dark square eyes and bares a bottom row of sharp brown teeth. Then they take turns dropping to the ground where they squat and hum and wait patiently as the others rejoin the herd, one by one.

"Now?" the bald man asks again.

"Almost," says the man with the ponytail. His nodding keeps getting worse, more erratic, and Jonah is surprised he's able to hold his gun so steadily.

The animals suddenly stop humming as if a switch has been flipped, and in unison they march toward Jonah and the men until they're just ten feet away. The animals form a half circle around them, their feathery red shoulders touching so there isn't a space between them. Jonah kneels down and picks up a loose stone; he instantly remembers the black rocks on Achilles and how they turned into sharp blades. He hits it against the ground, hoping it'll break into something he can defend himself with, but all it does is create an echoing thud. In response, the animals slowly squat in unison and slam their feathery paws against the ground, mimicking Jonah's movements.

"I'm shooting in ten seconds," the bald man whispers. "So be fucking ready."

The animals don't advance, though; they stand and stare and hum. Then, high up on the cliff above the caves, three more of the animals appear. They're bigger than those circling the men on the ground, and their red feathers have dark tips, blue or purple, Jonah can't tell exactly. In less than ten seconds, the three have descended the cliff wall and leaped to the ground. The half circle separates for the three to enter.

The middle and tallest of the animals has a yellow face lined with open wounds. By the way the others give it room, it's obvious this is the leader of the pack. Its square eyes land on Jonah and stay locked on him as it rolls its tiny head back and forth. Then the animal turns its attention to the man with the ponytail, studying his nodding head that just keeps getting faster and faster. In response, the leader begins to nod its head to the same rhythm. In seconds, all the animals do the same, matching the man's movements exactly.

The man with the ponytail drips with sweat, and when he brings his one hand up to wipe his nodding face, the animals do the same thing.

"Stop moving," the bald man whispers out of the side of his mouth.

"You bloody know I can't."

Jonah looks from the men to the animals, their bright red

feathers practically glowing in the little sunlight piercing through the cloud of mist overhead. He can see tiny bits of fuzz lift off their bodies and float away in the wind.

The leader with the dark tips and yellow face takes a step toward them.

"Shoot already!" Vespa yells from the cave.

The animals turn their heads to look at her, and that's when the man with the ponytail takes his first shot, blasting the leader right in the chest. The animal flies several feet backward in a cloud of feathers and smoke. The sound of its skull hitting the rocky ground echoes all around them.

The roars that come from the other animals are deafening. The two larger mimics that entered the fray with the leader immediately leap to its side and flip it over. They shake its shoulders, and when they realize it's dead, the two grab handfuls of the leader's blue-tipped feathers from its chest and stomach and rip them out and rub them against their faces. In a matter of seconds, the others surround the leader's body and tear at its feathers, rubbing them on their own triangular faces while howling.

As the two men stand and watch in shock, Jonah begins to shuffle toward the caves, never taking his eyes off the thirty animals that strip the leader naked of its feathers, revealing a lifeless white body oozing yellow liquid from where its feathers once grew.

The mimics separate and begin to hum all over again. They solemnly watch each other until one of the fatter animals on the right begins to grunt and shake. Within seconds, the tips of his red feathers turn dark blue right before their eyes. The others squat in unison around their new leader who drops a leg over the old leader's body and sits on its stomach, pushing a large blob of yellow liquid out of the hole in its chest.

Jonah continues to shuffle toward the caves with the stone in his hand. The new mimic leader lifts its head toward the two men standing near the cliff's edge and juts out its lower jaw a few inches. Immediately, the other animals turn in perfect unison and rush the men.

Blue lasers blow through the animals' arms and legs, spinning them in different directions. The man with the ponytail screams as he fires, his head nodding so quickly that it's a blur on his neck. Three of the animals peel off from the attack when they spot Jonah near the caves, and together they sprint and jump with their feathery arms out in front of them.

Jonah throws his stone as hard as he can, hitting the middle animal in the face, knocking it to the ground where it curls into a red ball. He ducks and rolls out of the way of the other two, immediately getting to his feet and running in the opposite direction of the caves. The mimics spring off the stone wall without missing a beat, landing on either side of Jonah. One of them grabs him by the leg, yanking him to the ground. Jonah swings his fists, striking the animal twice in the face, but it doesn't even flinch. The beast raises its long feathery arm and slams it down on Jonah's right shoulder. The pain is blinding; his lungs empty of air, leaving him wheezing and immobile. He knows in another second, the other arm will fall on him and end this short battle, but he hears the sizzle of a laser cutting through the air, and he opens his eyes just in time to see the mimic tip over with a smoking wound in its chest. Red feathers float above Jonah as he rolls over to see the woman standing in the mouth of the cave with her blue handgun wavering in her hands. Jonah gets to his feet and staggers toward her, his shoulder throbbing.

The men continue to fire near the cliff's edge, blasting the mimics every which way. Some of the beasts go flying over the edge while others fall flat on their backs in a growing pile. Feathers gather and swirl like snowflakes in a storm, covering the ground with a thin layer of red.

"Come on!" Vespa shouts. "Get inside!"

The bald man screams and runs forward with his rifle blazing, blasting several mimics out of his path before diving into the cave. He lands hard on his side, and his rifle bounces at Vespa's feet. The cadet snatches it up and puts the butt of the gun against her shoulder and fires. The remaining dozen animals are picked off one by one while the man with the ponytail wrestles a small one on the ground.

Jonah is only fifty feet from the cave when a new herd of the mimics appear at the top of the ridge and immediately start to descend the wall. They're all bright orange and drop in front of him by the dozens, and to avoid charging into their feathery arms, Jonah has to change directions. He picks up another stone and sprints into a smaller cave on the right. It's from there he watches the orange herd overcome the man with the ponytail, jumping on his chest in unison before reaching down to tear at his limbs and head. They rip out his long hair and rub it all over their faces. Vespa concentrates her fire on the wall of mimics marching toward her, picking them off with ease.

In horror, Jonah watches the man get torn to shreds. But he can't just hide and wait for this man to die; he steps out of the cave and throws the stone as hard as he can, winding up like a baseball pitcher in the first inning of a game. The rock hits an orange mimic in the middle of its back. The beast straightens up and rotates its head all the way around until spotting Jonah standing in the entrance of the small cave. With a stomp, it orders several from its herd in Jonah's direction.

Jonah can't get to Vespa. He can't help the man with the ponytail. All he can do is backpedal farther inside the cave and search for a weapon. The ground beneath his feet seems to shift and lower, crumbling with every step. His hands find a large rock sticking out of the wall, and his fingers wrap around it just as three of the mimics enter the cave. He yanks at the rock and finally loosens it, but still it won't come free. The humming from the animals fills the cave. One of the mimics charges ahead and launches itself at Jonah. The rock finally breaks off the wall, and Jonah swings it upward just as the animal lands on him; the jagged edge digs into the beast's belly, and together they fall to the ground. There's a resounding crack below him, and before Jonah can roll out of the way, the ground opens up, and Jonah and the beast fall into darkness.

• • •

Jonah and the mimic cling to each other as they fall, twisting and twirling, flipping over each other for what feels like days. Jonah tries to scream, but the animal's feathers cover his face and throat. The mimic plants its feet against Jonah's chest and kicks wildly, shredding his suit and skin with its claws until the beast straightens its legs and launches itself away from him. Jonah finds its ankle, though, and grabs on. Instead of separating itself from the cadet, the mimic flips over backward and begins to descend belly-first. As soon as Jonah finds himself sitting atop the animal like a cowboy on a horse, they hit an invisible surface of a pool, sending a series of fluorescent blue lights rippling in every direction.

The cadet bounces hard off the animal's back and tips face-first into the pool; the water is hot and thick and smells like sulfur, and when he opens his eyes underwater, he's overcome by fluorescent blue lights that follow his every movement. He screams, shooting fat bubbles out of his mouth that explode inches from his nose like blue fireworks. He whips his long arms over his shoulders and kicks his feet with everything he has left, but the water is as thick as gelatin, and he rises only a few inches at a time. His lungs burn, burn, burn, and his arms lose feeling as they struggle to bring him to the surface. He reaches for the mimic's body that still somehow floats above the water, grabs its wrist, and pulls his face out of the pool with a loud, heaving breath. The dark space echoes with his gasps and the sloshing of the water around him. He can't see anything, save for the blue bacteria glowing around him.

With the mimic in the crook of his arm, Jonah paddles, first to his left until he runs into a rock wall, and then to his right until his feet start to find the bottom of the pool. Once he gets his footing, he releases the animal and trudges up an incline with a ring of blue surrounding his torso like a hula-hoop. Jonah collapses onto his hands and knees, his bloody chest heaving for air.

"Vespa!" he shouts. "Paul! Someone! Help!"

His voice echoes for five, ten, twenty seconds, bouncing back and forth in the huge sinkhole or cave or wherever he is. He shouts a few more times. No one answers but his own frantic voice.

He stumbles to his feet, and with his hands out in front of his face, he walks in circles, aware of the cruel irony of being blind once again. He bumps into a wall, and his hand leaves a bright blue print that illuminates everything in a three-foot radius. He spins on his heels and then whips his hands at the air in front of him, trying to dry them off, lighting up the air around him so that he's practically standing in a lantern's glow. All he can see are more and more rocks and the water's edge where the mimic lies facedown, but it gives him an idea. He jogs over to the dead animal and rips out several handfuls of its feathers, doing everything he can not to vomit from the stench and sickening sounds. Jonah dunks the feathers into the thick water, shoves them into his pockets, and then turns to walk farther into the darkness.

Every few feet, Jonah whips a single feather out in front of him, lighting up the air with a dense blue fog. He moves slowly through the space that narrows into a tunnel, eventually coming to a wall of boulders that blocks his way. He has no choice but to climb, hoping to find a hole in the ceiling that leads back to the surface and his group. Or, maybe on the other side of the boulders, there will be light at the end of the tunnel, and he'll stumble out right next to where they parked the rover. He'll grab whatever weapons he can find inside the vehicle and rush back to help Vespa and the others.

The wall of boulders only goes twenty feet high, nowhere near the ceiling, and to Jonah's dismay, there's nothing on the other side but more darkness. Jonah drops to the ground and shuffles forward, holding his breath. He flicks a couple feathers, and as soon as the air lights up, he screams and immediately turns to run. He hits the wall of boulders and bounces backward, knocking the wind out of him. Still, he tries to climb back over the wall, but his fingers shake too much to get a grip. Jonah twists around and shouts, "Vespa! Paul! Someone help!"

More than a minute passes before Jonah reaches back into his pocket for a feather. He takes a few steps forward, and with held breath, he flicks the air.

A skull over three feet tall lies on its side, speckled with black mud and fading blue water spray. It looks like a dinosaur fossil, but that's if dinosaurs were missing eye sockets or ear holes, and if the bones weren't wire thin and woven together like mesh. The skull's mouth is giant and juts out like a bird's beak. Before the blue fog disappears, Jonah sees that the ground below the beak is scarred and chipped away as if the animal had dug or pecked at it during its final moments.

Another whipped feather reveals a ten-foot long length of mesh bones descending from the back of the giant skull, but instead of finding the rest of the animal's body, Jonah discovers another skull at the other end. It's the same size and shape, also half-covered in dried mud. His head suddenly starts to hurt, as if someone pulled a pin in his brain that was holding everything in place, and he has to sit down. The pain intensifies, and he presses his palms into his temples, squeezing, sitting in complete darkness between the two skulls.

He feels them coming. The voices from Achilles, the ones that will tell him to eat the seeds. The ones that say he's been chosen. Symbols begin to form in his mind, racing back and forth, and just as they begin to form into letters, he hears…

"Jonah!"

His name echoes all around him. Is it in his head? Are the voices coming out of his own mouth? Are they coming from the giant skulls? The pain strengthens in between his ears, and he has to set his forehead against the cold rock floor where he rubs it back and forth, leaving a bright blue mark that hurt his eyes.

"Jonah! Where are you?"

It's Vespa's voice. He tries to scream back, but all he can do is clench his jaw and whisper. His head feels like it's going to explode into a thousand pieces. He slaps his palms on the ground, and when his right hand finds a rock, he squeezes it, trying to alleviate the pain. He hits it against the ground, sending an echoing thud all around him. He hits it again, over and over, sending a thundering wave of echoes throughout the cave.

"Jonah?" Vespa yells. "Is that you?"

He fights through the agony and hits the rock against the ground three times in response.

"Make that noise again if that's you, Jonah!"

Three more strikes against the ground.

"Okay! Hold tight. We're coming down. We have a rope, and we're coming down!"

With the last of his strength, Jonah hits the rock three more times against the ground, and then brings his hands back up to cradle his head. His brain buzzes with electricity, popping and crinkling, somehow both shrinking and expanding at the same time. The symbols begin to flash behind his eyes in neon green, zipping from left to right, right to left, flipping upside down before crashing into each other, finally melting together and mutating into words that boom in his ears.

"WE CHOOSE YOU!"

Jonah squeezes his temples in agony and begs, "Stop. Just please stop."

"You will stop them. You will save us. Or you will die."

"Who…who are you?"

An image flashes in Jonah's mind for less than a second: he sees an ocean of tall, yellow creatures with two heads marching down a giant hill full of rupturing geysers, much like those he's seen here on Thetis. A rolling cloud of black smoke comes over the other side of the hill and washes over them, turning the creatures to ash, blowing them away.

Another voice enters his head, slightly different from the one he just heard: *"Enter the exit. Exit the entrance."*

"Please!" he shouts. "I'm just a kid! Choose someone else!"

Another image flashes: It's a close-up of one of the creature's faces. No eyes. No nose. Just yellow flesh over a long sharp mouth that suddenly opens and shuts.

Jonah drags his head blindly along the rocks, whispering, "I'm just a kid. I'm just a kid, just a kid, just a kid."

Something touches his shoulder and he screams; he flips over onto his back, breaking the connection from the voices in his head. He opens his eyes to a bright white light hovering over him. Two more float on either side.

"Jonah?"

"I'm just a kid," he responds in a soft whisper. He sits up with his arms covering his face. He buries his head into his knees, his shoulders bouncing with held-in sobs, and he replays the images of the yellow creatures descending the hill before turning to ash.

"Yeah, and I'm just a man," says a gruff voice. It takes Jonah a few seconds to recognize it as the bald man with the scar on his face.

"Hey, it's me," Vespa says as she sits down next to him. "It's okay, Jonah. We found you."

Jonah carefully raises his head to see Vespa's feet lit in a circle of blue light next to his. A sob of relief escapes his throat, and then his hand slaps the ground around him until he finds Vespa's. The buzzing in his head disappears the moment he touches her skin.

"Okay, we found him," the woman with the sheaf says. "Now, how do we get out of here?"

She takes a step away from the wall of boulders and scans the ground with her flashlight, sending Jonah into an immediate panic.

"No, watch out!" he jumps to his feet. "The skulls! Watch out for the skulls! They're going to…"

Two other flashlight beams quickly scan the ground in front of the woman, right where Jonah just saw the skulls, but to his complete shock, they're gone. He snatches Vespa's light out of her hand without asking and sweeps the floor all around him. All he finds are slick, black rocks, and a few tiny specks of fading blue lights. Even the scratches in the floor he saw under the skull's beak are gone.

"They were just…there were two giant skulls right here. Big as dinosaurs. And they…they talked to me," he whispers. "I think."

"Great," the man says. "Kid's seeing shit. They're getting sicker faster than we thought they would."

Jonah continues to sweep the cave floor with the flashlight, and then he lights up the walls and tries to find the ceiling.

"Let's just move," the woman says. She and the man march down the tunnel, leaving Jonah standing stupefied next to Vespa.

"There were two skulls right here. And they were…connected.

Like conjoined twins or something," he whispers as he begins to follow the adults. "I'm not crazy."

Vespa slips her arm under his and grabs his bicep. "Well, they're not here now. And no one is calling you crazy, Jonah."

The cadets walk arm-in-arm in silence before Jonah stops abruptly. "Wait. Where's Paul? Is he still up there? Did those things..."

"We got separated from him, too," she whispers gravely. "Last I saw of him, he was limping into another cave with one of those monkey things in a headlock. Then there was a rockslide, and everyone ran and I couldn't see him anymore. We tried to get to him, but there was no way through. I don't know what to do, Jonah. I'm kind of freaking out."

Jonah touches his bleeding chest with his free hand. "We'll find him. Or, I'm sure he'll find us. But what about the other guy? With the ponytail. Did he make it or—"

"He's dead. Those things tore him apart."

"And Dr. Z?"

"No sign of her."

Vespa's flashlight beam crawls back and forth in front of them, illuminating jagged rocks and wet walls. And then, as she lights up the ceiling, Jonah sees the first symbol. It's six tiny squares inside a triangle, carved deeply into the exact middle of the ceiling.

"Look," he says.

Vespa stops in her tracks and sighs. "Great. That's exactly what I needed to see right now. We're not doing this again. We're not looking for portals or other crazy shit right now. We gotta move."

Jonah takes the flashlight out of her hand and lights up the surrounding rocks. The symbols begin to show themselves, glistening on the wet walls, their sharp outlines shining in the light. To Jonah, the symbols look like an upside down anchor, a curled-up snake with no head, a sideways letter "K," stacked triangles, half of a guitar. There are hundreds of them. Maybe thousands.

"We're not going into any portal, Jonah. Please, let's just get out of here and find Paul and then check on Brooklyn."

"Come on!" the woman yells over her shoulder. "I think I found a way out."

Jonah keeps his beam on the symbols overhead, wondering what each would do if he jumped up there and touched them. He then spins on his heels to light up the ground behind him, checking to see if the skulls have come back, but there's nothing there but a few fading blue spots on the ground.

"Let's go already!" the man shouts before being overwhelmed by a coughing fit.

On the other side of the wall of boulders, the sounds of splashing come echoing down the tunnel. Then comes the collective humming of the mimics. With each new splash, the humming grows louder, and then Jonah can see flickering blue lights in the distance, rising over the wall.

"Shit. They're coming," Vespa says, pulling Jonah farther down the tunnel. She grabs the flashlight out of his hand, and they catch up with the adults who have started to jog. Rocks crash into each other behind them, and they break into a sprint, their beams whipping around the tunnel like strobe lights, and every few seconds Jonah catches a glimpse of a symbol or two. And all he wants to do is stop and examine each one and find the one or two that will stop the voices in his head from visiting him again. There must be a clue in these symbols. There must be a reason he keeps finding them. Maybe if he finds the right one, he thinks, the voices will stop and never come back.

The tunnel winds to the left, and when they make the turn, Jonah smells the humid, sweet air of the Thetis jungle. A pinprick of light appears a hundred yards down. As soon as they see it, all four of them pick up the pace. The humming of the mimics continues to grow behind them, and when Jonah looks over his shoulder, he sees dozens of blue clouds that continually form and dissipate as black shadows burst through them.

"Hurry!" shouts the woman.

The end of the tunnel gets closer and closer, and when they're just a few steps away from exiting, the man turns and fires a series of lasers into the ceiling behind them. Rocks cascade down in sheets, and within seconds, they completely seal the tunnel.

Jonah plants his hands on his head and falls to his knees. "But what about all the…" He stops himself from mentioning the symbols, but Vespa knows what he means. She wraps an arm around his chest and yanks him back to his feet.

"They're everywhere we go, Firstie. I'm sure we'll find more."

He backpedals out of the cave and immediately feels the sun and sticky air on his back. He looks down at his shredded jumpsuit speckled with black mud and his own blood. Anger and frustration suddenly boil over inside him, and he looks up into the sky and opens his mouth to scream when Vespa's voice stops him.

"Paul!" Vespa shouts.

Jonah spins around to see three more cave openings nearby. In the furthest one, Paul leans against its frame with his hand clutching his side. He watches as Vespa runs toward him and whips her arms around his neck, pulling him into an awkward hug. A second later, she has her hand around his waist, guiding him toward the group.

The bald man wheezes as he dips his head under Paul's arm. "I know where the rover is from here. Come on."

Far off on their right, a geyser explodes into the air, and Jonah watches the plume of water rise and fall as he follows the others through the trees. He thinks about the symbols, the skulls, the voices in his head, and he can't help but wonder if he's going crazy. Maybe he needs more medicine. Maybe he needs more sleep. He's going straight to the hospital when he gets back.

The rover comes into view, and they ease Paul into the back. The other four climb into their seats just as Paul lets out a sickly groan, causing everyone to turn and check on him. When the man turns back around to start the engine, he shouts. A dozen or so kids from Module Eight stand in pairs, holding hands just twenty feet away. In the middle of the huddle, sticking out like a scarecrow in a cornfield, is a strange-looking boy nearly as tall as Jonah, maybe even taller, with extremely long black hair. Each of the kids stare at the rover with blank faces and open mouths. And with their free hands, they slowly point to the sky.

From the back, Paul says, "These fucking guys again."

"Just go!" the woman shouts, and the man puts the rover in reverse and speeds them back to the village.

CHAPTER SIX

Paul lies in his hospital bed with his eyes closed, his fingers picking at the edges of the bandage covering his chest. The lines carved into his skin have faded, but they're still visible under the fluorescent lights. Jonah sits on a canvas chair against the wall with his own bandages crisscrossing his chest. He drifts off to sleep every few minutes before being jolted awake by visions of the connected skulls and the mimics and the Module Eight kids pointing to the sky.

A bag of clear liquid hangs from a wobbly hook drilled into the wall above Jonah's head. He watches the medicine drip through the tube and disappear into his forearm, hoping it won't only help keep his eyes healthy, but that it will also help with his mind. He's done with the voices and the hallucinations and the constant paranoia. He's done being used and hunted and pulled against his will.

Guilt pecks at his neck; he should be down the hall checking on Brooklyn. He should also be looking for Kip. He hasn't seen nor heard of the hacker since they arrived on Thetis. After seeing the kids from Module Eight, he worries Kip will fall in with them, if he already hasn't. Jonah should be doing so many things instead of sitting in this uncomfortable chair and trying not to fall asleep, but he's been ordered to stay in this hospital room with Paul. Freeman stands guard outside the door, peeking his head inside every few minutes to ask if the boys need anything.

"Paul?" Jonah whispers.

The cadet opens his eyes and stops picking at his bandage. "What, Firstie?"

"That first night on Achilles, when you went looking for Module Eight after dark, you started acting weird afterwards. What happened to you down there? Did you see something?"

Paul lets out a laugh and then shifts away from Jonah, his muscular back rising and falling with heavy sighs.

"Because I heard you talking to Vespa before we headed west. You said you saw something, and it sounded like it really freaked you out. I want to know what it was. I really need to know."

"You *need* to know? Oh, really? Look, it was just…it was just some stupid residual effects from the wormhole, Firstie. Not a big deal. Hallucinations or some shit."

Jonah takes the bag of medicine off its hook and painfully drags his chair around to the other side of Paul's bed. He sits down directly in front of Paul's face. The cadet's eyes are wide open, his teeth clenched. Sweat beads off his head and soaks the pillow.

"I want to hear about what just happened with Dr. Z and what she was saying about me, but right now, I really need to know about what you saw on Achilles," Jonah says as he sets the medicine bag on his shoulder and gives it a squeeze. "Because I've been…I've been seeing things. And hearing things. Stuff like that."

"Yeah, well that's because you're a fucking weirdo with stuff wrong with you, and plus you're a total wimp."

"Then you're a total wimp, too. Because I know you saw something out there. I saw the way you talked to Vespa about it. I need to know because I think I'm going crazy or something. My head feels crazy all the time now."

Paul rolls over so that he's facing the ceiling. Tears trickle down his cheeks, mixing with the sweat. After a long pause, he says, "Fine. Fine, Firstie. You want to know what I saw out there? Fine. All you kids went to sleep like a bunch of babies after the snouts rolled through, and while that Tunick kid and Sean were out killing the adults and writing shit on them and hanging them from trees, me and a couple other cadets went looking for Module Eight. Took us an hour, but we found it smashed and split open against the bottom of a hill. Do you want to know how many dead kids we saw? How many were splattered all over the ground?"

Jonah takes a deep breath and tries to imagine it all before saying yes, he does want to know.

"Thirty or forty of them. At least. Dead kids just fucking dead everywhere. And some adults, too. Everywhere I turned my flashlight, there was another pile of them, or there was some kid's arm or some dude's leg. I even saw a cadet's head all by itself. But the cadets I was with—Samuel and Mason—they took off pretty fast. Couldn't handle it. Of course, that was the last time I saw those cadets, too. Guess Tunick and Sean got to them, too, I don't know."

Just then the door cracks open and Freeman's head pops through. He sees Jonah sitting next to Paul and smiles. "Need anything?"

"Yeah," Paul says. "I need my life back, man. I need to be done with all this bullshit. I didn't sign up for this stuff; I came here to research and maintain security, not to be hypnotized or whatever by a lunatic doctor and left for, for…for slaughter in a cave."

A weak smile comes across Freeman's face. "How about some water?"

"Whatever, man," Paul says.

Freeman disappears, and Paul looks back at the ceiling. Jonah reaches for Paul's shoulder but pulls back. He wants Paul to keep going. He knows there's more to the story than just seeing so many dead kids.

"So, then what happened? After the other cadets took off and you saw all the dead bodies and everything?"

"I guess it took me about twenty minutes before I found any

survivors down there. It was brutal, man. All those bodies. But I walked around this big hillside and there was this small group of dirty kids all just standing there in a huddle. I practically ran right into the bastards. Their clothes were all burnt up and melted to their skin, and they were just standing there, not saying a word. And yeah, it's the same kids we just saw in the jungle holding hands and acting all crazy. But that night, they were standing there and putting one of their hands on this big black rock that was sticking out of the hill. I ran up to them and yelled at them to come with me, you know, told them I was there and I was rescuing them and to follow me and everything, but they didn't move. They didn't react. At all. Not one of them turned a head."

Jonah gives the medicine bag sitting on his shoulder another squeeze. "That's...creepy."

"Right? Super creepy. So, I start shaking them by the shoulders and kind of tossing a couple of them to the ground, but they got right back up and put their hands right back on that stupid rock. I saw that one of the kids was this really tall demic I've seen before. The really tall one with the long hair, the one that was on the road just now."

Jonah remembers him well. He can see his stony face and long black hair and narrow shoulders hovering over the heads of the other kids.

"So, that guy," Paul continues, "He's like standing there with his hand against the rock, and it's high above all the other kids' hands because he's so tall, and he's saying *something* to the rest of them, but I can't hear what he's saying. So, I get closer and closer until I'm physically pushing my way into their huddle. And I'm yelling in their faces, and I'm yanking them away from the rock and pushing them down on the ground." Paul raises his hands off of his chest in exasperation. "But they just *keep* getting back up. And I mean, I really wailed on this one boy. Used him as a fucking punching bag. Knocked two of his teeth out, I swear to god. Blood all over his white shirt."

Jonah shudders as he imagines Paul taking the opportunity to beat on someone without repercussions. Jonah stands, balancing the bag on his shoulder. "What was the tall kid saying?"

"I couldn't tell at first; it was really fast, over and over, and it sounded like just bullshit gibberish and kind of robotic. I pushed my way out the huddle and got out just as the tall kid is finishing saying whatever he's saying, and then all at the same time they turn their heads—with their hands still on the rock, they never take their hands off the stupid rock—and they look around, staring at nothing, and...I don't know, it looked like they were sleeping with their eyes open and not looking at anything, but at the same time they were definitely looking at *something*. I waved my arms and yelled at them, but they never looked at me. So, I was like 'Fuck it,' you know, and I walked right up to the black rock and put my hand on it, too. And then I started to see..." Paul takes a long, deep breath and then covers his mouth as he tries to hold back a heaving sob. After a few seconds, he steels himself and runs his hands over the blond stubble on his head. "That's when I started to see the ghosts. Or whatever they were. Ghosts? All I know, Firstie, is that when I put my hand on that rock and looked over my shoulder like the rest of them, the entire hillside was covered with these yellow-ish ghost monster things. Hundreds of them marching back and forth and they were see-through and kind of not see-through at the same time. And they were about eight or ten feet high, and they had two bodies that were connected in some way like conjoined twins or whatever. And they had these two scary looking heads like birds or some shit."

Jonah drops back into his chair, and the bag of medicine falls onto the floor with a quiet thud. His mind is back in the tunnel with the blue lights and two connected skulls with beaks he saw in the cave. The ones that just seemingly disappeared by the time Vespa and the others arrived. "That's..."

"Insane? Yeah, it's insane, Firstie. But I saw it. I saw *them*. Most of them were just gliding around, going up and down the hill, just up and down, up and down, but then there was this other small group of them of maybe four or five that circled around me. They'd go sideways up over the black rock and then back on the ground and keep circling. That's when I finally heard what the tall kid was saying because he slowed down."

Jonah clears his throat and reaches down for the medicine at his feet. He can't bring himself to look at Paul's face.

"The kid said...he said, 'We keep the fingers.'"

The door flies open, and Mirker marches in with a tall glass of water spilling over his fist.

"You, get back to where you were sitting," the man says to Jonah. And then he presses the spilling glass of water into Paul's shoulder. "This is for you. Drink it."

Paul stares at Jonah for a long moment before sitting up and taking the glass. He downs half of it in one gulp and then cradles the cup in his lap. Jonah looks from Mirker to Paul with the words "We keep the fingers" on the tip of his tongue, and then he slowly drags his chair back to the wall and hangs the bag on the hook. What does that mean? Whose fingers? These two-headed ghosts want their fingers?

Mirker paces back and forth as Paul takes another sip of water. The man looks as if he hasn't slept in days; dark bags sit under his eyes like rotten fruit, his muscular shoulders slump forward, and the man smells like someone too busy to shower.

Mirker rips the empty glass out of Paul's shaking hand. "You going to tell me what happened out there? Tell me why I lost one of my best men to a bunch of fucking alien apes so we could drag your ass back in here like a little baby?"

Paul connects eyes with Jonah and then looks down at the bandages on his chest. "Honestly, sir, I don't know. I don't remember. I went to sleep in my yurt at 2100 hours, and then when I woke up I was sitting in a cave with Dr. Zarembo standing over me with a sharp stick in her hand and my skin was covered with a bunch of lines. She started saying things, but when I tried to respond, she stabbed me. I woke up again and I see Firstie over here and Vespa and some woman and a hell of a lot of mimics coming at me."

"And what did the doctor *say*, cadet? Before she stabbed you with a *sharp stick*."

"Sir, she was talking about someone. She was talking about... him." Paul nods toward Jonah.

Mirker twists around. "Talking about you? Now, why would the nutso doctor who we had to lock up for attacking you earlier be talking about you?"

"I don't know," Jonah says. "But I also don't know how if you locked her up she was able to get out and take Cadet Sigg outside the perimeter with her."

A huge grin takes over Mirker's face as he squats in front of Jonah, putting his nose inches from the cadet's. "Now, if I remember correctly, I had to save your skinny behind from that crazy little lady just yesterday. You know how much of a pain in the ass she can be. The bitch got the jump on a couple of my officers. Now, if I were to have been there when she pulled that shit..." The man clenches his fist dramatically next to Jonah's face. "She would be on top of the compost heap."

"Where is she now?" Paul asks.

"We're tracking her," Mirker says as he stands up straight. He takes Jonah's bag of medicine off its hook and holds it up to his eyes. "Don't you worry about that. But, Cadet Lincoln, seems to me like trouble follows you wherever you go. Here. On Achilles. I've read your report, kid. I know your background. It's just full of trouble."

Jonah yanks the tube out of his forearm and stands up. He doesn't need to listen to this. Not here. Not right now. "I'm going to go check on Brooklyn."

Mirker snatches Jonah's wrist and yanks him back into his chair. "Like hell you are. What you're going to do is sit here, and you and Cadet Sigg are going to tell me everything that happened on Achilles. From before the crash up until we picked you up with Kip Kurtz. I've been patient, but I'm done waiting. I'm very much done. You're going to tell me. *Now.*"

Jonah looks back at Paul who slowly shakes his head. He doesn't trust Mirker either.

"I was asleep, we crashed, and then we waited around to be rescued," Jonah shrugs. "That's it." Then, in almost a whisper, he adds, "Thank you for rescuing us."

Mirker puts his hand on Jonah's shoulder and gives the cadet a sarcastic wink. "You're very welcome for the rescue. It was our fucking pleasure, believe me. Now, you should know that I've talked to that dopey Griffin kid with the dumbass lion in his hair, and he's told me a bit more of your adventures than you all just sitting around and waiting to be rescued. For example, you kids murdered some of the adults. Hung them from trees. Slit their throats. Stuff like that."

Jonah doesn't know what to say; he doesn't know if he should defend himself and tell him the truth or stay silent. How much did Griffin really tell Mirker?

"That wasn't us," Paul says.

Mirker purses his lips and nods. "So, then what happened, huh?"

Before Paul can answer, Jonah asks, "Does Earth know? Do they know we crashed and most of us died?"

"They know you're here now," Mirker says. "They know poor little street kid Jonah Lincoln made his sad little way to Thetis, and he's being cradled to my bosom, yes."

"Sir, do they know most of us are dead?" Paul asks.

"All they know is that I said we were happy and enjoying life and that we're ready for the *Mayflower 3* to bring us some more people and supplies. Should I get them on the com right now and let them know you boys have been slaughtering scientists and doctors and cooks and hanging them from trees to scare each other like this is all some kind of sick game?"

Paul shrugs and buries his head into his pillow. Jonah sits forward in his seat, ready to leave, to find Freeman or someone else he can possibly trust. Maybe the woman in the farm building taking care of the frosties can help him. He'll run by Brooklyn's room first, put her over his shoulder, and then with Vespa, they'll figure out their next move.

"Here's my big question," Mirker growls. "There was a

second-year cadet on your trip who we didn't rescue. His name was Sean Meebs. What happened to him? Where can we find him?"

Jonah's vision tunnels at the name. It was Sean who took down the ship in the first place. It was Sean who helped his brother Tunick attack the adults and terrorize the kids. *What happened to him*? His arm was practically blown off by Vespa, and then he broke his neck trying to jump over the canyon to chase down Jonah. *The boy is dead.* Jonah swallows the memories and trauma, looks directly at Mirker, and says, "I didn't know him. I didn't know a lot of people. I like to be by myself."

Mirker's shoulders rise and stiffen, and then he pivots swiftly on his heels toward Paul who remains motionless, as if he didn't hear the question. The man grunts, reaches down, grabs ahold of the thin mattress, and he flips it completely over, sending Paul crashing to the floor.

"Motherfucker!" Paul rolls back and forth on the ground, clutching his side. His bandage immediately starts to turn red with fresh blood.

Mirker places a boot on top of Paul's wrist. "Don't you boys lie to me now. I'm the law here. I'm the law and the judge and the jury." He steps down on Paul's wrist, straightening out the boy's trembling fingers. Jonah thinks he can hear bones crunching against each other. "What happened to Sean Meebs?"

Paul grabs Mirker's ankle with his other hand and shouts in pain. The man winds up his left foot and punts away the cadet's hand. "Don't you fucking touch me, boy."

Mirker steps down harder. Paul shouts louder.

"He's dead," Jonah says. "Sean is dead."

Mirker turns his head and exhales through his nose, fire in his eyes. "I thought you didn't know him?"

"I don't. I just figured...if we didn't know him after the crash, then that means he died in the crash, right? Most everybody died in the crash."

"You're a couple of liars. And what about Kip Kurtz? When did he arrive?"

"Kip went into a cave and we lost him," Jonah says. "We didn't see him again until you guys picked us up on the island."

Mirker steps off Paul's wrist and moves quickly toward Jonah, grabbing his jumpsuit and balling it in his fist. He pulls him off the ground and slams him against the wall, shaking the entire room. The door opens, and Freeman's head appears, and when he sees what's happening, the man enters the room with his hands up.

"Sir, they're just boys. Just—"

"Get out of here! Now!" Mirker barks. He raises Jonah even higher up the wall, presses him harder into the wood. The ceiling bows as if it's about to collapse.

Freeman takes another step inside, locking eyes with Jonah. "Put the boy down, sir."

With his free hand, Mirker whips a gun from his pocket and aims it at Freeman's face. "Get out."

Freeman looks from Jonah to Paul writhing on the ground, and then to Mirker's gun. The commander rubs the trigger with his finger and a smile starts to crawl across his lips. Freeman's face goes from concerned to apologetic, as if he's seen Mirker act like this before and knows what he's capable of, and before Jonah can plead for help, Freeman blindly reaches over for the doorknob, opens the door, and sidesteps back out into the hallway.

As soon as the door closes, Mirker tosses Jonah onto the bed frame. The thin metal wires dig into his back and legs. Immediately, the man places a boot on the middle of Jonah's chest and rests his elbow on his knee. "You're going to tell me the fucking truth. Right now. Tell me about Sean Meebs."

"Why do you care so much about one cadet?" Paul asks. He struggles to his feet and shuffles toward the door, blood dripping down his side. His bandage is completely red and peeling away from his skin. "Lots of cadets are gone and missing. Lots of cadets are dead."

Mirker slips the gun back into his pocket and reaches down to touch Jonah's face. Jonah jerks his head away, but the officer places a thumb above the boy's right eye and raises the skin. "Yup, these babies are going to be blue again real soon once we start taking away your medicine. Take a good look at me while you can, street boy. Cadet Griffin told me you were buddies with Sean Meebs, that the two of you went on a little journey on the second day together. You guys were friends, were you not?"

"Who cares about Sean Meebs?" Paul spits.

"I do," Mirker says. "Because that's my son."

The door opens again and in spills Freeman and three other men with rifles in their hands.

"That's enough," Freeman says. "*Sir.*"

Mirker chuckles and takes his foot off of Jonah's chest. The cadet wheezes for a lungful of air, and as the men shout back and forth, all Jonah can think about is if Mirker is Sean's father, then that means he's Tunick's father, too.

CHAPTER SEVEN

Jonah lies sweating and panicking in a hospital bed down the hall from Brooklyn and Paul. He tries to rest, to feel safe with the soldiers patrolling the hallways and Mirker sent away to cool off, but all he can do is stare at the doorknob, waiting for it to turn just an inch. He's decided that the wooden pole next to his bed holding his medicine bag will be his best weapon against whoever, or whatever, will surely attack him in here.

A hundred things sit and swirl in his mind, combining and separating, rising to the top and making room for more and more worries from the past two days: Paul's story about meeting the kids from Module Eight and them saying they want to keep the fingers; the two-headed ghosts that Paul says roamed Achilles and the combined skulls he saw himself in the tunnel on Thetis; Mirker is Sean and Tunick's father and what he'll do when he finds out he and Vespa murdered them; Griffin has been talking to the commander, telling him god-knows-what; Louis in the village says they're all doomed because something on board the ship was destroyed; Brooklyn's not getting better even though she's getting her medicine; Kip has seemingly disappeared with no one knowing where he is and yet Mirker and others talk about him as if they already know him; the voices in his head returning in the tunnel; Dr. Z saying things about him to Paul and how she's on the loose and could be anywhere. Jonah's brain fires with every thought while his toes clench with readiness to jump off the bed in an instant.

There's a quiet knock on the door, and Jonah rips the wooden pole from its stand, sending his bag of medicine sloshing to the ground. He sits up just as the short and skinny Matteo enters the room, his shaggy mop of black hair pulled into a neat bun on the top of his big head. He holds a clipboard in his hand.

"Whoa. Hey there, buddy," he says. "How're you feeling? What's with the big toothpick?"

Jonah aims one end of the pole at his roommate. "What are you doing here?"

"Uh, relax. I'm just checking on you. You haven't been around, and so I asked where you were, and someone told me you were back in the luxurious hospital we have here at the beautiful Athens colony. I heard you had *quite* the adventure outside the gate."

Jonah lies back, balancing the pole across his stomach, his fingers itching to grab and swing it at a moment's notice.

"They caught Dr. Zarembo. I thought you might want to know that."

"Good," Jonah says. The relief that tingles his skin is brief, but strong. He's not ready to fight her again.

Matteo pulls a chair away from the wall and sits down with sigh. "You want me to bring you some tea or something? Read you a bedtime story? I'm just on my break, and we're on lockdown right now, so I can't exactly go exploring."

"Why are we on lockdown if they caught Dr. Z?"

"Oh, there were some animals outside the fence causing trouble, trying to get in or whatever. Happens from time to time. Plus, um, let's not forget about those creepy-ass kids walking around together that you guys brought back from Achilles. They managed to sneak outside the fence and somehow got back inside."

Jonah thinks of Paul's encounter with the Module Eight kids and the black rock and the two-headed aliens. He thinks of the tall boy standing in the huddle on the road in front of the rover, his blank stare, his finger pointing to the sky.

"So," Matteo says, "You feeling better or what?"

Jonah rolls over and picks the bag of medicine off the floor and gives it a slight squeeze, sending a stream of medicine down the tube and into his arm. "I want to know what was onboard the *Mayflower 2* that everyone is so pissed off about."

"So, Mirker still hasn't told you guys? I don't know what he's waiting for, as if it's a huge secret around here. Well, here's the deal: Something that people on Earth don't know about is that the atmosphere here on Thetis ain't exactly what we thought it was. The instruments from the initial probes somehow messed up or something because when we got here we learned pretty quickly that the oxygen level here is a bit too high. By like five percent."

"And that's bad?" Jonah asks.

"Well, if you consider being slowly poisoned over time and everyone dying in a maybe another year or so bad, then yeah, it's pretty bad."

"Are you kidding me?" Jonah rubs his face with his giant hands. The air on Thetis is poisoning them? They can't live here? If they can't live here, then where are they supposed to go? Achilles? Peleus? Back to Earth? It makes Jonah want to curl into a ball and give up. How could they let them come all this way here when they knew it was a death trap?

Matteo stands up and brushes something off the front of his jumpsuit. "So, you see, you guys were bringing us this super important terraforming device that was supposed to be able to alter the atmosphere here and bring the level of oxygen down enough for us to be okay. It was like a satellite that would orbit around the lower atmosphere and release a bunch of super-condensed nitrogen and carbon dioxide and eventually it would change the overall composition of the air over time. I think that's what it was supposed to do, anyway. I only heard rumors about it. I'm not told everything."

"*You* aren't told everything? Jesus Christ, we weren't told any of this shit. Why wouldn't they tell us on Earth about this before letting us take off and come here? And why would we still come here if this place is poison?"

"Well, because I guess they thought they had a good solution with the terraformer and didn't want to panic everybody. There would be egg on faces—a lot of people's faces. A lot of money gone to waste. Top scientists would look like assholes. The terraformer was going to be the big fix. But then…you guys crashed, and shit got broke, and now we're kinda screwed."

Jonah sets the pole back in its stand and stares up at the ceiling. He holds his breath, thinking that perhaps that it will somehow keep him healthy. But then a thought comes to him: "What about gas masks? Couldn't we wear masks until the next ship arrives with a new terraforming thing?"

"Hey, sure, we could all wear masks and have it be Halloween year round, but guess what? They were on your ship, too. So, trick or treat, buddy. Or I guess just trick. You happen to see any of them lying around after the crash?"

Jonah thinks back to all the debris he sifted through and jumped over. The crash site was over a half mile long. He doesn't remember seeing any gas masks or anything like a satellite. But there were so many things on fire and thrown in so many directions. "I didn't see any, no, but I wasn't exactly looking for gas masks or satellites, you know? We were looking for food and water and clothes and guns and this big orange energizer to fix Tunick's ship. Maybe if I were actually looking for them…"

"From what I heard, they did a sweep for the masks and the terraformer when they picked you guys up. They didn't find any of that stuff. I don't know; I think we're screwed, roomie."

Jonah pulls his pillow out from underneath his head and presses it hard against his face. He screams as loud as he can. Once. Twice. He sucks in the cotton and bites on it. And then he screams again

"You done?" asks Matteo.

Jonah pulls the pillow from his face and looks at him in disbelief. "So, what's the plan now?"

"I don't know. There's talk of flying back there to look again, but who knows. I don't think there's enough juice left in the battery for another trip like that."

"So, we're all just going to die."

Matteo shrugs and stands up. "We all die sometime, right? And look at it this way, you'll outlast most of us. You and everyone from the second ship. For the rest of us who have been here, we might have another year. Maybe six months. Everyone feels it differently. But who knows? Maybe our bodies will somehow evolve and adapt, and we'll be fine. I mean, it's just a little extra oxygen. Maybe we'll grow gills or something."

Jonah stares at the ceiling and grits his teeth. "I need to get out of here."

Matteo smiles and claps his hands. "Well, good. Because that's why I'm here, to get you out of here and get you to work." He holds up his clipboard and shakes it over his head. "And I'm your new boss, so don't give me any lip, or I'm going to make you work overtime without time-and-a-half."

Jonah looks down at the tube sticking out of his arm, but before he can say he can't go anywhere until the bag is empty, Matteo leans over and yanks it out.

"Jesus!" Jonah immediately presses his fingers against the bandage on his bicep.

"You know, I don't really think Jesus can hear us in the Silver Foot Galaxy," Matteo says as raps his knuckles against the clipboard. "He's a Milky Way guy. We're on our own up here."

The tube dangles over Jonah's shoulder, dripping onto the floor. "Yeah, so what gods do you all believe in up here?"

Matteo takes a few steps toward the door and then stops and looks over his shoulder. "We're the gods of this galaxy. We're in charge."

Jonah knows who's really in charge here: the two-headed yellow aliens, the voices, the ghosts that Paul saw circling the Module

Eights on Achilles. But he can't bring himself to truly believe that. Maybe Achilles's air is just as poisonous as Thetis's and everyone is simply hallucinating all the time. That's easier to believe than conjoined twin monsters roaming around. With his one hand applying pressure to his bicep, Jonah gets up to follow Matteo. "So, what? I should be praying to you?"

"You should be praying to yourself, man. You're the only one who is going to answer any of your problems up here. But, hey, if you want to pray to me and get down on your knees and worship the ground I walk on, I'm not going to stop you."

• • •

The clipboard has several jobs for Matteo and Jonah to do around the community for the day. It's a welcome distraction for Jonah; his mind is full of so much anger and so many questions that it helps to be put to work. Most jobs were simple and benign: security detail, general maintenance, and kitchen clean up, while other jobs were a bit more mysterious like espionage recon and animal control.

"Animal control?" Jonah asks as they wind their way around the village. "What does that even mean?"

"Our fence keeps out most of the little guys, *and* the big guys, I guess," Matteo says, "But of course there are flying things like the vulture fish and animals that dig underground and pop up and freak everyone out like the pickers. We'll be on animal control around dusk because that's when those little bastards show up."

"The pickers?"

"Yeah, they're like ground hogs or beavers that burrow underground and then pop up inside the fence and literally try to pick up anything they can touch: tent poles, piles of wood, bowls of food, the tires attached to our rovers. Doesn't matter how big something is, these little guys try to pick it up and see if there's anything to eat inside. You'll know them when you see them: They're about as big as dogs and completely white with six legs and sharp teeth, and when we find them, we kill them."

"No catch and release?"

Matteo laughs. "More like catch and squeeze the trigger."

The two boys slowly walk up and down the rows of tents and yurts and sheds looking for maintenance issues. Any time they find a splintered piece of wood on a door or a frayed edge of canvas, Matteo writes it down on his clipboard. Jonah pays more attention to the big picture, counting the buildings, making mental notes of the villagers and seeing who nods at Matteo and who seems to shy away. He wants to grab each person by their collar and tell them that the crash wasn't his fault and it wasn't Vespa or Paul or anyone else's but Sean Meebs, Mirker's own son. He wants to tell them he knows the danger they're all in. But instead, he puts his head down and follows Matteo.

"We use that sucker a lot," Matteo says, pointing to a silver machine that looks like a cannon, except that it's flat and topped with a giant blade.

"And that's a..."

"Wood chopper. Only way we could have put up the fence as fast as we did or build the farm building and other stuff. Anyway, this way."

In the southeast corner of the village, Jonah finds himself in the shadow of the Woesner Telescope. The giant black tube extends out of the building's roof at a forty-five-degree angle, and when Jonah follows the angle up into the sky, he sees it's pointed right at Achilles. The moon looks beautiful from where he stands; it's blue and red and purple and dotted with clouds. It looks so close that Jonah feels like he can almost touch it. He squints to look for any signs of smoke or fire on the moon but sees none. It's an incredible feeling knowing what type of mess is up there when it looks so peaceful from this spot.

"They definitely use that guy a lot," Matteo says as he begins to circle a neighboring tent. "Day and night, someone's in there looking into the sky."

Jonah stands in the telescope's shadow until a wave of goose bumps sweeps over his body. "I pretty much pinned all my hopes and dreams on this thing when we crashed. Lots of us were depending on it for you all to see us up there from down here and then come and get us."

Matteo reappears on the other side of the tent, his clipboard under his arm. "So, hey, can you tell me what actually happened up there? I'm *unbelievably* curious about you guys. Like, how did you even survive? I think I would have freaked out and like died on the first day. Did you have to eat any of the animals to survive? And how come only one adult was rescued with all you kids?"

"All the adults..." Jonah starts. He doesn't even know how to say what happened to them, how they were tortured, killed, carved into, and written on like warning signs. "They pretty much all died in the crash."

"All but one? But that doctor?"

Jonah stops staring at the telescope and looks at his boots caked with dried black mud from the caves. He still can't believe Dr. Zarembo turned on him like that. She must have seen what Paul and the kids from Module Eight saw. Maybe she knows what those ghosts want. Maybe she's hearing the same voices in her head that he hears, what Tunick heard. After he tracks down Griffin to find out exactly what he told Mirker, she's next on his list to talk to.

"Yeah," he says. "Dr. Z was it. The only adult to survive the crash."

The cadet walks around the telescope's building with Matteo quietly on his heels. When Jonah finds the door, he takes a deep breath and pulls on the handle. It's locked. Or stuck. He pulls again, harder.

"Whoa, you can't go in—"

The door suddenly opens, sending Jonah backpedaling into Matteo's chest. Standing in the doorway is the short Indian woman from the rescue mission to find Paul. When she sees Jonah, she immediately grabs the door and pulls it closed, leaving just her face visible.

"You can't be here," she says to Jonah before eyeing Matteo behind him. "You know better than to let him inside here. What were you thinking?"

Matteo puts a hand on Jonah's arm and tries to pull him away. "Come on, we have work to do."

"But I want to see the telescope," Jonah says. He thinks about Hopper and Malix and the Splitters leaving on Tunick's ship. They could be on the other side of Achilles, which should be visible from the telescope right now, or they could be on Peleus, or they could be orbiting Thetis right now looking for a good place to land. "I want to talk to someone about looking at Peleus with it. When can I do that?"

The woman looks from Jonah to Matteo, and without saying another word, she closes the door and locks it.

"Wait! Why can't I see it?" Jonah yells into the door.

Matteo gives his arm another tug, spinning the cadet around. Before Jonah can ask why the telescope is off limits, he sees that standing behind Matteo in a tight huddle are the kids from Module Eight. There are a dozen or more of them, kids of different ages and heights, and each of them holds another's hand, save for the tall boy who stands directly in the middle of the huddle. For the first time, he sees his long black hair is burnt and uneven, angling up his back like a steep hillside.

All their faces are blank, their shoulders relaxed. A girl no older than twelve breaks off and steps toward Jonah, leaving her partner with his hand up and out, awaiting her return.

Her blonde hair is covered in dirt, and when she raises her face up at Jonah, a thin blanket of dust falls from her head onto her shoulders. Jonah thinks of Paul's story and doesn't know if he should fear this girl or try to save her. He wonders if they all still see the giant two-headed ghosts. Perhaps several are circling them right now. Jonah looks left and right. If Paul could see the ghosts, then maybe he can, too?

"Follow us," she says in a flat tone.

Matteo puts his hand up. "Just get out of here, freak. We have work to do."

The girl extends a finger, pointing right at Jonah's face. "Follow us."

Jonah looks from the girl to the huddle of kids behind her. Their faces remain blank, but it's then Jonah notices their milky eyes constantly shifting. They *do* still see the ghosts, Jonah realizes. And those ghosts are all around them right now. Jonah spins around with his breath caught in his throat, squinting and focusing, trying to see what they see. He feels something. The air suddenly feels electric. He whips one arm out from his side and waves it back and forth in front of himself. Maybe he's doing nothing but creating a little bit of breeze, or maybe he's pushing his arm right through some entity's ghostly body.

Matteo sighs and pushes the girl's finger out of Jonah's face and then turns her around. "Seriously, get the hell out of here. Shouldn't you all be locked up or something? Or at least on some kind of medication? Nobody is following you weirdos anywhere. Why don't you follow me to the med tent?"

The girl's shoulders rise and stiffen, and a second later she's in the air, leaping at Matteo with both hands out like claws. Jonah reacts immediately, and with one arm, he intercepts the girl in midair. The cadet sets the girl on the ground, turns her around, and pushes her back toward the huddle, shouting, "Leave me alone!"

The girl spins around and again leaps at Matteo. Jonah has no choice but to put his foot out, and he kicks the girl right in the chest. She stumbles backward, falling into the legs of the rest of the Module Eight kids.

The tall boy with the burnt hair lowers his forehead and flares his nostrils. His eyes stop shifting and focus only on Jonah. Without breaking eye contact, he bends down and whispers into the fallen girl's ear. When he straightens back up, the girl slowly gets to her feet and points at Jonah and screams, "Follow us! Enter the exit! Exit the entrance! Follow us! We keep your fingers! They choose you! HE CHOOSES YOU!"

She then slowly lowers her hand back to her partner's and takes it. The Module Eight kids begin shifting their eyes again, and then a moment later, they turn to the left in unison and walk up to the telescope's building. They each place a hand on the wall, bow their heads, but then a few seconds later, they walk away.

"What the hell was that?" Matteo asks. "She chooses you? For what?"

"I have no idea." Jonah's hands are shaking. He watches the huddle disappear amongst the tents, and when he's sure they're gone, he falls to his knees. *They choose you.* That girl just repeated what the voices in his head have been saying. *We keep your fingers.* Paul was telling the truth.

Matteo takes a quick glance at his clipboard and then drops it to his side. "Were they like that on Achilles? Or did they get like that because of the wormhole, or what?"

Jonah pushes himself back up to his feet. "Where do we keep the prisoners?"

"Prisoners?"

"Where do people get locked up?"

Matteo scratches his neck. "At the guard's station. In the northwest corner next to the gate. But you won't be able to—"

Jonah turns and runs. Matteo yells something, but he's already too far away to hear it. Jonah flattens his hands and breaks into an all-out sprint, his head swiveling back and forth the whole time trying to locate the huddle of Module Eight kids or Griffin or Vespa or Mirker. He passes other villagers who stop whatever they're doing to stare at him as he flies by.

He pounds on the door under the red light bulb for a solid minute before the man wearing the red ball cap stumbles out. Again, he reeks of alcohol.

He squints at Jonah as if he doesn't remember him from that morning. "Yeah?"

Jonah wipes a layer of sweat from his face. "I need to talk to Dr. Zarembo, if she's inside. Just for a second."

With his hands on his hips, the man chuckles and starts to close the door with the toe of his boot.

"Wait!" Jonah yells. "I was on Achilles with her. I think I might know what's wrong with her. Maybe I can help her not be crazy anymore."

The man stops closing the door, but he doesn't open it back up, either. "Yeah, and how are you going to do that?"

"By talking to her. She's a good person. Or, at least she was. And if I could help her get well, then there would be another doctor around here to help out. Isn't that why she was on the trip here in the first place? So we could have another doctor here? Maybe she can help find a cure for the atmosphere problem here? Maybe she's the key to saving us all."

A few seconds pass as the man mulls over Jonah's words, and then he looks over his shoulder and into the room as if he wants to make sure no one is listening. Leaning forward, he says in a slur, "Look, I know she's a good person. I knew Laura, I mean Dr. Zarembo, back on Earth when we were stationed in Baltimore together. But I..." He pauses to look back over his shoulder again. "But I think the wormhole really did a number on her."

"It wasn't the wormhole that turned her like that."

"Yeah? Then what happened to her, smart guy?"

Jonah takes a step toward the door. "That's what I'm going to ask her."

The man hesitates but gets out of Jonah's way. The concrete room is small and cold and drab with nothing on the walls. A desk made of fuzzy black wood sits in the corner, covered with hand-drawn maps and field notes, plus there's an empty plate of food and a sheaf standing up, curled into a half circle showing different video feeds. On its screen, Jonah sees the huddle of Module Eight kids standing against the fence near the hospital, and then the screen changes to a view of a drone sweeping over a steaming body of water.

"She's in here. All the way down," the man says as he fumbles with a key ring. He unlocks a door next to the desk and bows sarcastically. "Your date awaits, my lord."

Jonah walks into a narrow dark hallway that smells like sweat and rotten food; he covers his mouth and nose as he makes his way to the end. There, on the left, stands a thick door with a small barred window that Jonah has to lean down to see into.

"And hurry up," the man slurs from down the hall. "Because if Mirker knows you're in here, I'm a dead man, man. But then again, we're all dead men. So, fuck it, I guess."

It takes a moment for Jonah to see Dr. Zarembo inside the dimly lit cell. He finds her by her voice; she's standing flush with the wall, her nose practically touching the concrete. Her one hand is flat against the wall while her other hand jumps wildly above her head, opening and closing, pointing at the ceiling. Instantly, Jonah is reminded of Tunick's erratic behavior when they found him on the island. She mumbles something Jonah can't understand, so he holds his breath and listens closely. After a few seconds, he understands what she says: "Eat the seeds. He has to eat the seeds. Eat the seeds. He has to eat the seeds." Over and over and over.

Jonah takes a deep breath and then puts his mouth in between the bars of the window. Quietly, he says, "Dr. Z? Hey, Dr. Z? It's me, Jonah Lincoln from the ship. I'm here to check on you just like you checked on me after we crashed. I wanted to see if you're okay."

The woman's body stiffens at the sound of his voice and both of her hands fall to the side. Slowly, she sets her head against the concrete wall and then turns it toward Jonah. Her forehead is covered with bruises and scrapes and dried blood. An evil grin grows across her dried lips when she sees Jonah's face.

"I need to know what happened to you on Achilles," Jonah whispers. "What did you see? Who is telling you we need to eat the seeds?"

"Eat the seeds. He has to eat the seeds," she says. "Eat the—"

Jonah snaps; he wraps his hands around the bars and shouts, "Shut up about the stupid seeds! Did you see the ghosts, Dr. Z? Who are you talking to? Damn it, who is telling you about the seeds?"

Dr. Z starts to laugh. It's quiet at first, and then it grows into something menacing. She places her forehead against the concrete wall and starts knocking against it. Fresh blood quickly dots the wall. "Enter through the exit," she says. "Exit through the entrance."

"Please stop," Jonah pleads. "I'll listen to you, to whatever you have to say."

Dr. Z pauses, her head inches from the concrete. She brings her hands up to her red hair and pulls them through to its burnt ends. For a few seconds, the woman mouths something and makes herself shake with laughter, and then she pounces at the door to wrap her hands around Jonah's on the bars. Her grip is strong, but she doesn't seem to be trying to hurt him.

"You okay down there?" the man asks at the end of the hall. "Just a couple more minutes, okay? So, fix her already. Make her stop saying all that shit all the time, it's driving me bonkers."

"You're long enough," she whispers into Jonah's face with rancid breath. "You're long enough and smart enough and long enough and smart enough and long enough and—"

"For what?" Jonah asks. "I'm long and smart enough for what?"

"To be their God."

A shiver runs down Jonah's spine. "What are you talking about? To be whose God? Who is telling you all this? Who are they?"

Dr. Z's hands get tighter around Jonah's, and she brings her face through the bars. She takes a deep breath before screaming at the top of her lungs: "Kill the red one!"

The man rushes down the hall with a flashlight and shoulders Jonah out of the way, breaking Dr. Z's grip on the boy. Jonah crashes into the concrete wall and falls to the ground. Dr. Z points a finger at the bearded man. "You will die."

"What happened to you, Laura?" He whispers to Dr. Z. "We were friends back on Earth. We…we went on three dates before I left. How do you not remember me? We crashed that moped, remember? We almost fell into that lake?"

"You will die," she laughs.

Jonah scrambles to his feet just as the man crushes Dr. Z's hands with the head of a flashlight. She stumbles back into the cell with a hiss, and when the man points his light inside, Jonah sees the walls are covered in symbols drawn in blood. He recognizes many of them from the caves on Achilles. There's a sudden pull on his mind, a tunneling feeling that draws him forward, and without thinking, he reaches both arms through the bars. He wants to touch the symbols. He must touch the symbols.

The man yanks on Jonah's shoulder. "What the hell are you doing, man? Get back!"

The need to touch the symbols is too strong, so he holds his ground. He reaches farther into the room and then slaps his hands on the inside of the door, feeling for symbols, carvings, answers. He knows he should listen to the man. He knows he should back off once he sees Dr. Z walk toward him with a sadistic grin on her face. Instead, he finds himself reaching toward her.

"Dr. Z," Jonah pleads. "Help me understand."

"I said…" the man wraps his arms around Jonah's chest and pulls. "Get…the…fuck…back."

Dr. Z approaches Jonah's outstretched hand. Slowly, she opens her mouth and places his index finger between her teeth. As she bites down, the trance or the pull or whatever keeps Jonah from wanting to run away, breaks. The pain is immediate, and he screams for her to stop. He tries to yank his hand away, but she grabs his wrist with both of her hands and then leans back as if trying to pull him through the tiny window. She puts two more of Jonah's fingers in her mouth, and he can feel her freezing cold tongue on his skin and what feels like loose teeth slipping between his knuckles.

The first gunshot zips through Dr. Z's hair, blowing a wide hole clear through it, but the second shot from the man's gun grazes her right shoulder, sending her twirling into the back wall. Jonah falls onto the hallway floor, his bleeding hand balled into a fist. He jumps back to his feet and looks inside the room to see Dr. Z standing motionless against the back wall with her head down. Blood drips from the top of her shoulder and makes its way down her arm, creating a small puddle on the floor.

"I need a medic in the jail block," the man says into a walkie-talkie. "Now. Right now."

The symbols of the room begin to call to Jonah again, but this time he resists and backpedals down the hallway with his fist up to his chest. He can still feel her loose teeth and cold tongue on his fingers as Dr. Z begins to laugh in her cell. Her voice echoes down the hall and follows Jonah into the room where he slams the door shut with his foot and falls to his knees in exhaustion.

Two people run past him and rip open the door. Dr. Z's echoing laughter appears for a second until the door closes again. Jonah sits back on his heels and takes a deep breath. Then he opens his bloody fist to find three white seeds in his palm.

CHAPTER EIGHT

THE HAMMOCK GROANS UNDER JONAH'S WEIGHT. THE CADET listens to it with his eyes closed, his arms crossed over his chest. Bandages cover the tips of the fingers of his right hand. He reminds himself to breathe. He reminds himself that, despite everything, he's okay. For now. He reminds himself that he's lucky, to not only be alive after everything that has happened in the past several days, but to be off Earth with its wars and loneliness and uncertainness. But he can't convince himself; he doesn't feel lucky. Not everything is okay. He can't just breathe. After all, the air here will poison him soon enough.

The encounter with Dr. Z rolls back and forth in Jonah's mind. She said he was chosen to be their God. Whose God? To the people here on Thetis? Or to these two-headed ghosts that everyone is seeing? Jonah raises his hand from his chest and stares at the verve seeds. They're no bigger than his thumbnail, pebbled and rough on one side, and on the other they're smooth and chiseled from Dr. Z's teeth.

He brings one of the seeds close to his lips and holds it there, inches away. He knows what will happen if he eats it; he remembers the mania and the visions, the rays of lights appearing out of his chest, the sudden burst of strength and self-confidence, the inability to feel pain or follow a rational thought. Jonah rolls the seed down the bridge of his nose and over his cheeks as he thinks back to Tunick's cave where Hopper and Michael became best friends, where Portis forgot he was shot and bleeding to death in the jungle, where Aussie and Christina begged to be punched because it sounded fun.

There's only one bulb hanging in the yurt, but its light reaches every corner, and Jonah crawls his eyes slowly over the floor. Are the alien ghosts in there right now, circling him? Are they walking right through the walls, aimless like clouds? Are they walking right through *him*? Jonah waves his other hand wildly at his side to ward off any spirits that might be nearby, and he wonders what he would have done if he were Paul that night he found Module Eight and the kids touching the black rock.

A list in Jonah's mind keeps getting longer: find Griffin, check on Brooklyn, get into the telescope building and try to get a peek at Achilles and Peleus, avoid the Module Eight kids until he knows how to connect with them, talk to Freeman about Mirker, stay away from Mirker, tell Vespa everything he's heard, find Kip to help him uncover some of the mysteries of the symbols in the cave he fell into, and so on and so on.

Jonah brings both hands back to his chest just as the door opens and Matteo marches in with his clipboard. He sees Jonah lying there and tosses the clipboard onto his own hammock and drops down into the chair. The boys stare at each other for a few moments before Matteo says, "So, uh, you do know you're supposed to help out around here, right? That's kind of the deal for being chosen to live here?"

"I know," Jonah says. "I'm just...trying to figure things out. Been a busy day."

"Yeah, well, look, you better start contributing soon before Mirker and some of the others hear that you're just hanging out in here doing shit. They run a pretty tight ship. Or, at least they try to."

Jonah tries to shove his hands into his pockets, but it's difficult to do because of the way the hammock practically wraps around him, and the three verve seeds he tries to hide fall to the floor. Matteo leans forward to get a look at what it is, and before Jonah can jump to the floor to grab them, Matteo has them in the palm of his hand.

"Shit. Not good, Jonah," Matteo says as he backpedals toward the door. "This is…not good. This is bad."

"Someone gave them to me just now. I haven't even—"

And then Matteo is out the door.

Jonah untwists himself from the hammock too quickly and crashes to the floor. "No! Wait! I wasn't going to eat them!"

The cadet bursts out the door and then pauses, looking both directions for Matteo. He needs to get to him before he finds Mirker. Jonah can't be locked up like Dr. Z. Or worse, with her. To his left, several villagers slowly walk toward the middle of the village, their heads down and their shoulders slumped. A small drone hovers over them as if herding them toward a pen. On his right, Jonah sees a group of teenagers heading toward the garden. No sign of Matteo. He runs to his right and toward the hospital, looking up and down the alleys for his roommate. Jonah turns right and makes a looping circle back to the center of the village.

"Matteo?" he yells. "Has anyone seen Matteo?"

He receives a few shrugs and blank stares from those around.

"Shit," he seethes.

He takes off running again, and when he rounds a line of tents, Jonah sees the Indian woman leaving the telescope building. She has her head down, talking into her sheaf. Jonah watches the door to the building slowly close and then crack back open; it didn't lock behind her. Then, far off on his left, he spots Matteo running toward a group of men with his clenched hand held over his head. Jonah takes a few steps toward Matteo and then stops. He knows he won't get there in time to defend himself properly, and so he turns and runs in the opposite direction. By the time he reaches the door to the telescope, the woman is out of sight. Jonah pushes the door open with the heel of his shoe and backs inside. He pulls the door shut and locks it.

Jonah slaps the doorframe for a light switch until his hand finds a flat, cold square on the left. The moment his fingers touch it, a dim light overhead hums to life. He spins to find a rolling chair sitting directly below the lens of the giant black telescope. All around the room, monitors on dusty tabletops stare blankly at Jonah, their screens dark or showing a blinking cursor asking for a password. He knows he doesn't have a lot of time, thinking that the moment he touched that square near the door, security was on its way. The cadet jumps into the rolling chair and sails into the nearest table, crashing against its leg. A few monitors blip to life showing photos of galaxies and stars and a sphere that Jonah immediately recognizes as Achilles. These are just desktop background images, though, with blinking cursors appearing in the middle. Jonah stares at Achilles and its huge ocean and jigsaw continents and hazy purple atmosphere, and instead of trying to figure out where the *Mayflower 2* crashed or locate the tiny island where Tunick hid his ship, Jonah pushes himself away from the table and rolls back directly under the lens of the scope.

The lens is warm against his eye socket. Nothing. Completely dark. Either the telescope is aimed at a giant black hole, or it's turned off. As his eyelashes brush the glass, Jonah reaches up and wraps his hands around the metal tube, looking for knobs or buttons or anything to turn it on. A group of people run by the building, the crackles of walkie-talkies following behind. Jonah leaps out of the chair, sending it spinning across the room, and he hides in the farthest corner under a table. He pulls a wastebasket in front of him just as hears a key ring jingle, and then the knob on the door begins to turn. A large shadow appears in the doorframe. It just stands there silently, as if waiting for Jonah to give himself up. The cadet cradles the wastebasket, making himself as small as possible. Finally, the shadow backs out of the building and closes the door with a click.

Jonah waits several minutes before moving, and as he sits there crouched under the table, he looks into the wastebasket. It's full of crumpled papers scribbled with crossed-out calculations, lists of numbers and measurements, hand-drawn pictures of planets and landscapes. He pulls a few papers out and quietly flattens them against the floor, and as his eyes crawl over the numbers and pictures, he quickly realizes how little it all means to him. He sits back in frustration and his foot accidentally tips the wastebasket over. Dozens of torn pieces of paper spill out from the bottom. Jonah immediately starts to line them up.

It's an easy puzzle; within a minute, Jonah has the pieces of paper in order, and even in the dim light, he recognizes the hand-drawn circle of Achilles. There's an "X" scratched onto the right-hand side of the moon, and next to it are coordinates and the words, "*Mayflower 2.*" And next to the larger "X" is a smaller "X" with a dash mark pointing to the letter "T."

Jonah stares at the drawing and the markings, and it isn't long until he realizes the "T" has to be for Tunick. The Athens community knew where Tunick and the Splitters were located? And where the *Mayflower 2* went down? But how? The crash site is on the other side of the moon, and there's no way the telescope could see it. Is there a satellite orbiting Achilles that he doesn't know about? Jonah crawls out from under the table and gets to his knees to look at the images stuck on some of the screens. There's nothing there to help him connect the dots. He digs back into the wastebasket and pulls out more pieces of paper, putting them together in an instant. As he slides the last piece into place, he finds the word "Zion." He stares at it in disbelief. *Zion?* That's who Tunick said was killing everyone on Achilles, the name the Splitters said Tunick used for himself. And then, just before the ship arrived from Thetis, the voices in his head shouted, "We are Zion."

Jonah stares at the name for a solid minute before feeling his hands and feet and heart again. He gathers up the pieces of paper and stuffs them back in the basket.

He needs to go. He needs to find Vespa and Paul. Quietly, Jonah rolls the chair back under the lens and tries looking through it one last time. Still nothing but blackness. Before opening the door, he makes sure everything is where he found it. He knows once he steps back into the village, he's going to be accosted and interrogated, possibly thrown into a cell where Mirker will try to beat information out of him, but if they found out he was snooping around in the telescope building and saw something he wasn't supposed to, then they may just kill him. He cracks the door open and sees no one is around, but just as he's about to make a run for it, he realizes he has nowhere to run to. His own yurt is off limits now, as is every other inch of the village, and he doesn't even know where Vespa's tent is. There are drones constantly hovering overhead. He's sure there's been an announcement to report him upon sight. Still, he can't stay in here. There's only one place to go now: outside the gate.

Jonah slips out of the door and keeps his back flat against the wall of the building, slowly circling until he's facing the direction of the guarded and locked gate. It's at least two hundred yards away. When the coast is clear, he sprints, not stopping until he makes it to the garden where he dives into the rows of corn and quietly crawls to the edge of the plot.

"Hey," a whisper comes from his left. The cadet slowly turns his head to see a tall girl with long blonde hair wearing a black jumpsuit. Behind her stands a small group of kids, each of them looking pale and scared and desperate.

Jonah shakes his head and puts his finger to his lips. He doesn't need this right now. He doesn't need whatever problem they're about to make for him. He sticks his head outside the stalks of corn, but the girl and the others advance in a tight group. Two men suddenly jog by with rifles in their arms, causing Jonah to duck back inside the stalks. The group of kids gets closer, and Jonah turns and waves them off, but they still come.

"Please. Get away from me. Go," Jonah whispers as he watches faraway villagers mill back and forth between the tents. A small drone zips over the farm building. How is he going to get to the gate without being seen? And even if he does, how is he going to get through the gate?

"Where are you going?" the blonde girl whispers.

"Don't worry about it," Jonah seethes. "Please, just leave me alone."

"Take us with you," a boy of about twelve says. His hair is half shaved, long in front and buzzed in the back. His face and neck are marked with bruises, some new and some old and fading.

Jonah sits on his heels, bouncing with anticipation. "Look, I'm in trouble, and if they find me I'm pretty much done for. I can't take anyone with me. But I don't even know where I'm going. I need to get outside the gate, but I don't know how."

The blonde girl nods to the other kids and quickly they stand around Jonah and start to examine the corn on the stalks, blocking him from view.

"We know how you can get out of here," the girl says. "It's close by. But if we show you, we get to come with you."

"If you know a way out of here and want to leave, why don't you just leave? Just go yourselves."

A tiny girl with short black hair quickly ducks down next to Jonah. The rest of the group squeezes together, hiding the both of them. The girl digs her knees into the ground and places her small hands on her thighs. "I talked to your friend Brooklyn."

Brooklyn. He needs to take Brooklyn with him. And Vespa. And, he can't believe he's thinking this: Paul, too.

"She told me about what you did on Achilles," the girl says.

"She did? How is she? She's awake? Can she see? Is she still blind?"

"She's still blind, yeah."

Jonah falls onto his butt and sets his head on his knees. Poor Brooklyn, still blind and waiting in that hospital, her eyes probably just as blue as the day they arrived. He knows he has to bring her with him. Or, at the very least, come back for her.

"What did she tell you?" Jonah asks the girl.

"She told me how brave and strong you are, and if there was anyone who was going to figure out what's going on around here, it was you. And we need someone to figure out what's going on around here."

"They found something," the boy with the half-shaved head says. "Something big."

"What do you mean?"

The blonde rips an ear of corn off of a stalk. She takes a long, wheezing breath before saying, "We'll explain more when we get outside."

Jonah grabs a handful of soil and squeezes it through his fingers, the black dirt falling back to the ground like worms. In fact, when he looks closer at the thick coils of dirt smooshing out of his hands, he sees tiny red worms escaping its clumps. As soon as a worm hits the ground, it unfolds in two different directions, like miniscule "Xs" that slowly crawl back into the shadows. Jonah looks up and through the kids' feet to see dozens of boots running this way and that way. He hears the drones overhead. He has no choice.

"You get me out of here, and you can come with me," he says. "But I can't promise you I'll be able to figure anything out around here. You probably know more than I do."

"What about our trackers?" one of the girls says. "They'll find us."

"Trackers?" Jonah asks.

"We all have tracking chips in us. You do, too," the blonde girl says. "In our hands."

Jonah looks at the back of his hands but doesn't know where to start; his hands are covered with scratches and bumps and bruises. "Where?"

"We'll show you on the outside," the boy says before jumping to his feet and disappearing. A moment later, he's back with a large wooden wheelbarrow. A couple of the other kids stand and begin to shovel a nearby mound of the black dirt inside. Jonah can hear each of their lungs straining with the work. They do it as slowly as possible, seemingly waiting for the right moment…

"Now," the blonde girl whispers. "Get inside."

Jonah doesn't hesitate, he army crawls over to the wheelbarrow, and in less than a second, he's inside and curled into a ball. Large clumps of the black soil immediately fall on top of his legs, the shovels working so fast they blur over him. Soon, his entire body is covered, and a few small hands reach in and carve out his nose and eyes so they're the only parts of him exposed. He can feel the tiny worms crawling all over him, up his sleeves and pant legs. Dozens slowly make their way under his collar and onto his chest. He wants to jump out and rip his clothes off. He wants to scream. But instead, he continues to lie there.

He watches the purple and white sky move as he's wheeled down a nearby alley. They turn left, right, another left. The worms move up his neck and start investigating his ears and lips. Just as he can't take another second, the top of the wall comes into view.

"Okay," the blonde girl says. "Get out. Hurry. Now."

Jonah pushes himself out so quickly that the wheelbarrow tips over, and he rolls onto the ground where he slaps his hands all over trying to rid himself of the worms. He rolls a few more times and finds himself on top of a square piece of wood.

The blonde girl bends down to pull on the wood and it opens on hinges, revealing a deep hole. "Maintenance crawl space. Don't touch the pipes down there, they'll burn you or cover you in…" She looks over her shoulder at Jonah, and then past him. "Shit."

Jonah turns his head to see the kids from Module Eight huddled together just fifty feet away. They stare at Jonah and the others for a moment before walking straight toward them, the tall boy with the uneven hair pointing directly at Jonah.

"Get in," the girl says, pushing Jonah toward the hole. "Now."

• • •

Jonah punches the door above his head twice before it swings open into the blinding brightness with a vibrating clang. He pulls himself out of the hole and immediately crawls to the outside of the fence and flattens his back against it. To his right, the wall disappears after just a dozen yards, angling around the corner, but to his left the wall looks to go on forever. It takes a moment for the sounds of the forest to reach his ears: creatures howling, chittering, and singing, geysers exploding and splashing water all over the trees, branches shaking, rocks rolling over each other. While he waits for the blonde girl and the others to pop out of the hole to take him who-knows-where, Jonah reaches into the chest of his jumpsuit to pull out several more of the red worms, whipping them to the ground where he stomps his boots on them and grinds his toe back and forth. Then he flips his hands over, again looking for an incision where a tracker might be embedded, but nothing stands out among all the scratches on his skin.

"Come on," Jonah whispers at the open door. "Let's go, let's go."

Finally, he hears someone climbing the wooden ladder. They are moving too slow, though, and Jonah knows it's only a matter of minutes before a drone floats over the fence and spots him on the outside, or a patrol unit comes running around the corner on his right. He needs cover. He needs to move. He pushes off the wall and runs and slides over to the hole on his knees. He reaches his long arms down into the darkness.

"Hurry, come on," he barks into the hole.

A small hand fumbles for his, and when its fingers wrap themselves around his palm, Jonah feels a jolt of electricity shoot up his arm. He screams as lightning pops in his throat and hits his brain with a repeating, pulsing wave of static. Suddenly, his head feels too big, too full, as if it's about to rise off his shoulders like a balloon. Pink and purple blobs float in his vision, bouncing into each other, eating each other. And then the blobs blow away like sand in a storm, disintegrating in every direction before several yellow, double-headed figures appear and circle around him. They glow like light bulbs with fuzzy outlines, or with no outlines at all somehow, and they constantly change shapes, moving from a dozen feet taller than he to no taller than his waist.

The fingers grip his hand so hard it feels as if his skin is going to be pulled right off. The lightning inside Jonah's body intensifies, and his back goes rigid, his vertebrae lining up as if fused together, and he falls backwards like a felled tree, pulling a small boy onto the dirt who, in turn, pulls up a teenage girl. Jonah's brain stops popping for a second, just long enough for him to recognize the kids as Module Eights.

The two kids slowly get to their feet with their hands still held together, and the boy refuses to let go of Jonah's hand. A new wave of electricity runs up Jonah's arm and he begins to writhe on the ground. The circling yellow figures slow their pace around him, and then one breaks off and floats right through Jonah's body, bringing an icy chill to his throat.

The boy dips his blank face down to Jonah's until their noses touch. Jonah can't break away. He can't even turn his head. The boy pushes his nose harder into Jonah's, and his eyes vibrate as he says, "Door four."

A moment later, the girl has her face smashed against Jonah's cheek. Her lips are ice cold as they open and close on his skin, repeating: "Door four, door four, door four."

Another yellow ghost breaks from the ongoing circle and passes through him. His body goes numb. His mind sharpens, and then a tunneling stream of colors overtake his vision. His eyes are open, staring right back into the boy's, but all he sees are flashes of reds and blues and yellows. It's almost as if he's back in Tunick's cave with a verve seed clinking against his teeth. Then the flashes begin to swirl and flatten out and create sharp lines. He sees…a giant pyramid. He sees several giant pyramids in the middle of a vast, empty landscape.

The voices of the boy and girl cut through the visions, repeating, "Door four, door four, door four."

In his mind, the pyramids rise from the ground and rotate, and then they rush toward Jonah at an alarming speed. More noises cut through the vision: heavy breathing, the ground scraping near his head. Then, right before he hears a bone break, there's a familiar voice: "Let. Him. Go."

The pyramids vanish, and the lightning suddenly stops running through his body, and the circling figures disappear just as quickly as they arrived. Jonah sits up gasping for air, and after shielding his face from the sun, he sees Vespa standing over him, her boot planted directly on the Module Eight boy's wrist.

"You okay, Firstie?" Vespa asks.

Jonah can't find his voice as he pushes himself up to his knees where he immediately falls back on his butt. What just happened? Did he just see what Paul saw back on Achilles? He must have. There were ghosts. All around him.

Vespa puts even more weight on the boy's wrist, and Jonah watches in horror as a white shard rises out of the boy's wrist with a pool of blood. The boy doesn't make a sound or a face, as if he doesn't feel a thing. Vespa then wheels back her other foot to boot the girl in the chest, disconnecting her hand from the boy's, sending her rolling away in cloud of black dust.

The blonde girl from the garden pops her head out of the hole and reaches up to grab the side of the wooden door. Her eyes are as wide as Peleus and Achilles overhead. "You need to go. Now. More are coming. There's something they built down there that you should see. Just go half a mile that way down in the trees. Follow the path." She points over their shoulders and into the forest. "Come back for us. Please. And get rid of your trackers."

Before Jonah can say a word, the girl pulls the door shut.

Vespa reaches down and yanks Jonah to his feet. "Let's move."

"But we can't. We'll be tracked by some kind of implants in our hands somewhere. They'll know exactly where—"

The cadet pulls a knife out of her pocket and quickly examines her hands. Her thumb moves something in the back of her right hand and she immediately places the blade to it. Without hesitating, she slices open her skin and digs out a small green microchip with the knife tip. She holds it in front of Jonah's face and it glistens with her blood. Vespa is about to fling it to the ground when Jonah says, "Wait. They'll figure out you removed it, or they'll think you're dead."

"That's not a bad thing," she responds.

But Jonah carefully grabs the chip off the tip of her knife and then bends down to the boy on the ground. With a held breath, Jonah forces the chip into the open wound on the boy's wrist, squeezing it under the broken bones sticking out of his skin, doing everything he can not to vomit.

"What about you?" Vespa asks.

Jonah shows her his scarred hands. "I don't even know where to start."

Vespa snatches his hands and squeezes his skin until she feels something that makes her nod. She places the blade to his skin and asks, "You ready?"

A drone sounds somewhere nearby.

"Just hurry."

Vespa makes a tiny, careful incision and digs out the green chip. She holds it between her fingers and asks, "Where do we put it?"

The small Module Eight girl gets to her knees and stares at the cadets, but before Vespa can make a move toward her, something tickles Jonah's arm and then a cluster of red worms falls out of his shirtsleeve.

"Give it to me," he says

Vespa keeps staring at the girl. "But…"

He takes it from her hand and slowly smashes the small green chip into the cluster of worms. It sticks to one and it squirms away.

"Now, let's go," he says.

Vespa charges forward, stopping only to boot the girl in the side, sending her rolling away, and then the two cadets run into the forest.

CHAPTER NINE

Pushing through the forest with Vespa is much easier than cutting through the jungle on Achilles with a group of kids in tow, Jonah thinks, but he sure could use one of the electric cycles or LZR-rifles they had on the moon. They move quickly, though, darting between black trees whose trunks shed off in massive sheets the moment they're touched, sending columns of dust into the air; climbing over boulders as soft as sponges that suck on the bottoms of their boots; and dodging hundreds of low-flying creatures that look like pink jellyfish with snail shells. Water constantly bubbles out of unseen pockets in the ground, soaking their boots and pant legs, and twice they step on active geysers, barely escaping being shot into the tops of the trees.

Jonah wants to fill Vespa in on everything he's learned, but she's too fast and too angry, always several feet ahead of Jonah, making it impossible to have a conversation. At the same time, he doesn't know how much he should tell her. She'll think the Zion stuff is crazy, that the ghosts he's seen and voices he's heard mean he should go back for more medicine. Maybe she'll turn on him, leaving him behind.

They continue in the direction the blonde girl pointed them, and eventually Jonah and Vespa come to a huge waterfall feeding a glassy pool hundreds of feet below. That pool spills into another waterfall that sends water into another pool and another waterfall, and it goes on like this for what looks like forever.

"On the left," Vespa says, her hands on her knees. They're both completely out of breath. "Look. There's a path right there. Some of the Athens people must have carved it out."

With his hands on top of his head and his chest heaving for air, Jonah scans his eyes along the cliffs of black trees and exploding geysers until he sees a narrow road cutting through the vegetation, a path that could only have been made by a human. Overturned trees and rocks edge the road that winds its way toward the valley below, and as Jonah follows its path, near the bottom he sees a large gray structure sticking out of the trees. The roof looks curved like a dome, and it must be fifty feet tall.

"You think that's what that girl was pointing to?" Jonah asks.

"Probably. But I'm getting some major déjà vu standing up here. I mean, didn't we just do something like this about a week ago?"

"You mean standing on the top of a cliff with me and we're about to head west without knowing what the hell is out there?"

"We're heading south, I think, but yes," she says as she takes her first careful step down the cliff. "That."

Jonah continues to stand there, watching Vespa's black hair shine in the bright white sun as she finds a way along the side of the cliff toward the road. He remembers standing on top of that cliff on Achilles with Vespa and all the other kids, how Paul looked terrified and begged Vespa not to go because of something he saw—the circling yellow ghosts that Jonah himself just saw—and how he and Brooklyn watched the marine layer of clouds crawl toward the beach that seemed so far away. *Brooklyn.* She should be there right now with them, muttering her smart remarks, kicking ass, showing him what real bravery is like.

He takes a shaky first step after Vespa and asks, "Have you seen Brooklyn lately? How is she?"

Vespa stops moving and puts her hand on a large pink boulder that appears to suck on her fingertips. She immediately pulls her hand away and wipes it on her jumpsuit. "Not well. Not like you."

"Damn it. What do her eyes look like?"

"The same, Jonah. Blue. Blind. They're the same. And she doesn't seem to feel any better, either. But she woke up, which is something. I honestly don't know if..."

Jonah catches up and sets his foot on the boulder, allowing it to suck on the bottom of his boot. Within a couple of seconds, his treads are cleaned of any dirt or loose rocks. "You don't know if what?"

She picks a long, spindly black branch up off the ground in front of her and launches it into the valley below like a javelin. The two of them stand silently as they watch it twirl end over end in the swirling wind until it disappears into the tops of the distant trees.

"You don't know if what?" Jonah repeats.

"*Christ*, Jonah. If she's going to live. If she will survive. What did you think I was going to say?"

"I was hoping something different," he mumbles.

They walk in silence along the crumbling cliff, stopping briefly to watch an insect that looks like a slimy green piece of paper inch its way down a tree trunk. When it folds to pull itself along farther, Jonah sees three smaller ones fold and inch their own way along the back of their mother or father or big brother. Or, perhaps, Jonah thinks, they're stuck to the back of their enemy. Is that what he's doing on Thetis? Stuck to a planet that wants to kill him as he inches along with Vespa and Brooklyn and a few others?

After a half hour, they make it to the narrow road and immediately pick up the pace. Jonah knows a drone could rise overhead and spot them at any moment, or maybe there are remote cameras stuck to the nearby trees, or maybe there is a laser perimeter set up to trigger a cage to pick up more animals for their experiments. Jonah thinks about the red worms he shoved his tracking chip onto, hoping they're still alive so Mirker and the others believe he's still near the village.

The road zigzags around boulders too big to move, and as they get lower and lower into the canyon, the gray structure they saw up on the cliff is completely invisible. And when they reach the end of the road, they find themselves out of breath, facing a thick wall of the black trees.

"Which way is that thing?" Vespa asks as she rotates on her heels.

Jonah jumps off the road and pushes a few yards into the trees on the right. Ducking this way and that way, he sees slivers of the domed structure. It looks as if it's made of cement, making it one of only three cement buildings on Thetis. Why would they use such precious construction material on something so far away from the village?

"This way," he calls, and within minutes, Jonah and Vespa stumble out of the small patch of forest and find themselves in the shadow of the sphere. Immediately, the hairs on Jonah's arms rise. He takes a step backward and lowers his eyes to the ground in fear; he knows exactly what it is they're building out here: a portal, just like the one on the island where Kip disappeared. Just like the broken dome of Tunick's cave.

"It kind of looks like..." Vespa mumbles as she circles the cement base. "Is it an observatory, like for another telescope?"

"Observatories usually go on top of mountains, not down in valleys," Jonah says as he follows close behind. As they get near the opposite side, he sees a large doorframe cut into the wall. "Honestly, I think this is another portal, like the ones on Achilles. That means... Vespa, that means they know what's going on with all the symbols and portals and..."

Jonah freezes in the open doorway and all of his thoughts disappear. The same carved symbols he saw on Achilles cover the inside of the dome, but these have obviously been made with human hands and tools, their lines far too shallow and uneven. At the bottom of the sphere, sitting in a ball with his head up and staring at them, is a thin boy of Asian descent. He looks familiar to Jonah, but he can't place him immediately.

"Holy shit!" Vespa yells. "What are…who are you?"

The boy closes his eyes and sighs in what looks to be relief to see the two cadets. His knees carelessly drop from his face, and he leans his head back against the wall with an echoing thud. Black dirt covers the boy's neck and face, and his bare chest heaves with slow, painful breaths.

Another second passes. And then Jonah recognizes him. They met on Achilles.

"His name is Everett," Jonah says as he takes a cautious step inside the sphere. He doesn't get the same overwhelming feelings he got on Achilles when he entered a portal. "I met him right before I found you and Brooklyn with Lark and Krev and the others. He and Hess followed me after I escaped from Tunick, and they forced me to open up a portal on Achilles. And when I got it working, I pushed him onto it. He disappeared and didn't come back."

"Until now," Vespa whispers.

"How long have you been here?" Jonah asks the boy.

Everett raises his trembling hand to show them five fingers, and that's when Jonah sees a thick plastic cord cuffs his wrists together. Another cord tethers him to a hook drilled into the base of the wall. A couple feet away from the boy sits an old tray of food scraps and an overturned cup.

Vespa jumps to the boy's side. "You're being held in here? Someone is keeping you here? Who?"

The boy opens his mouth, but no words come out. He then points to his throat and shakes his head.

"You can't talk? You lost your voice?" Vespa asks as she pulls a small blade out of her jumpsuit pocket. She puts the blade to the plastic cord around his wrists, but just as she's about to cut it, Jonah sets his hand on hers.

"Wait. Just wait."

Vespa stands up straight. "We have to free him, Jonah. He could die out here."

"Just let me think for a second," Jonah says as he paces back and forth. "He and Hess threatened to kill me. They blackmailed me.

They tried to sacrifice me and use me as an experiment, to see what would happen when I went through the portal. They were prepared to kill me, Vespa. They didn't give a shit about me."

Everett's eyes widen, and he shakes his head furiously in his defense, but Vespa puts her knife back in her pocket and sits down against the opposite wall. "So, what, we're going to just leave him here to starve and get eaten by something? I mean, someone has him in here as a prisoner, Jonah."

"You know, I bet those guys coming back the morning Paul went missing with Dr. Z, they were down here messing with him. Remember they said they were delivering breakfast? Maybe Everett has some answers they need. Maybe he has some answers we all need."

"Maybe he does," a man's voice says from right outside the door. Before Vespa can get to her feet, Mirker walks inside with his fists on his hips, his broad shoulders pulled back like wings, his long gray beard blowing in the wind. He looks both pissed and pleased to see Jonah and Vespa inside.

Paul stumbles through the doorway with his wrists held by a plastic cord. He falls to his knees right in front of Everett and collapses onto his chest. Dried blood and fresh wounds cover his head.

"Paul!" Vespa jumps to his side and cradles him in her arms. A quick bolt of jealousy shoots through Jonah, but he shakes it off.

Mirker pulls a blue handgun out of a side holster and scratches his beard with it. "Little Everett Hwang here stole my best ship a year back, didn't you, boy?"

Everett draws his knees up to his chest and looks down.

"So, you two think you can cut out your tracking chips and we wouldn't find you, huh? Think you're pretty smart?"

"There's two of them inside us," Paul coughs. "They put two chips in us."

"Now, Cadet Sigg, where did you hear a silly rumor like that?" Mirker asks as three men appear in the doorway holding rifles.

"You know, I can't exactly remember. Someone in the village told me, I think—someone who really hates your guts and thinks you're a shitty leader—but that's not really narrowing it down at all, is it?"

Mirker barks incoherently and kicks Paul so hard in the stomach that he rises off the ground and rolls on top of Vespa, pinning her onto her back. Mirker steps toward the cadets; his rage suffocates the room, causing Everett to curl up into a ball and cover his head. He has seen this before.

Jonah jumps in front of Vespa and Paul, casting a tall shadow on the wall. He doesn't know what he's going to say or do, but he knows he can't just stand there and watch Mirker hurt anyone else.

Mirker laughs and immediately reaches out to shove Jonah aside, but the boy catches the man's wrist with both hands and flings him into the wall. Mirker bounces off the concrete and falls to his knees. Slowly, the man puts his hands on his waist and lowers his head. Everyone is surprised, including Jonah. The cadet then drops down into a fighting stance, ready for round two. Mirker stays on his knees facing the opposite direction for a moment, though, and then his shoulders start to bounce with laughter.

One of the men rushes over to pull Mirker up to his feet, but the commander shoves him away and keeps laughing.

"Come on, get up," Jonah begs as he pulls on Paul's arm. "We got to go."

Just as Paul staggers to his feet, releasing Vespa to do the same, Mirker jumps up and turns around. A thin line of blood runs down his chin. He points his handgun at Jonah's chest. In what feels like slow motion, the man sneers before pulling the trigger. Vespa leaps, pushing Jonah out of the line of fire, and the blue laser misses Jonah's shoulder by an inch. It hits the curved wall of the sphere behind him and ricochets into the floor, and from there the laser bounces around the room until hitting the thigh of one of the men standing in the doorway. The man screams as he backpedals out of sight.

"Now!" Jonah yells. He lowers his shoulder and rams through the two other men with Vespa and Paul right on his heels.

"Shoot them!" Mirker's voice echoes inside the sphere.

Jonah looks over his shoulder to see which way to zig and which way to zag from the incoming fire, but to his surprise, no one raises their rifles. One of the men runs over to the man just shot to see if he's okay, and the other one, a stout man with a black beard, points to Jonah's right and mouths: "That way."

Mirker shouts, "I said, shoot them!"

On his right, Jonah spots a narrow crack in a rock wall, and without saying a word to the cadets huffing behind him, he takes a sharp turn and squeezes into the crack. He hears Vespa do the same, and then Paul's heavy breathing enters the small space. The path keeps narrowing, and the only way Jonah can get farther inside is to turn his shoulders and shuffle sideways.

"Where are we going?" Vespa asks.

"Just go faster, Firstie!" Paul begs. "I'm a sitting duck back here!"

A gunshot rings out and the three cadets cover their heads. They don't see a laser, but black rocks and dust begin to rain down on them.

Paul shouts, "Go!"

The space veers to the left and gets even tighter, the mossy rock walls practically touching each other. Jonah tries to squeeze through, but it's impossible; he can't go any farther. Vespa rams into him and whispers, "Come on, come on. What are you doing?"

"It's a dead end," Jonah wheezes. "We're trapped."

Paul shoves his head over Vespa's shoulder with fire in his eyes. He rubs the plastic cord tied around his wrists frantically against the rock wall, sawing right through it. "Crawl, you idiot!"

Jonah looks down to see that there's space at their feet. Maybe just enough space to squeeze through. He struggles to his knees, the rock wall hugging him tightly as he tries to lower himself to the ground. Paul and Vespa do the same thing, but Vespa loses her balance and falls into Jonah, sending him onto his back. He's stuck like that, on his back like an overturned turtle.

Another gunshot rings out and more black rock and dust blow through the narrow space like a wave of water barreling into a cave at high tide.

"Fucking go!" Paul yells.

Jonah reels his heels into his body and then pushes off. He blindly scrapes his way a few feet down the space and tries to push off again when Vespa suddenly crawls over him, her head moving up his body until their eyes meet. She gives him a quick wink and says, "I'm taking over, kid," before clenching her jaw and pulling herself completely past him. He feels her heels push off his shoulders just as Paul begins to scramble up his legs. When his eyes meet Jonah's, he shakes his head and growls, "Faster, Firstie. You're going to get us killed."

"I'm *trying*," Jonah snaps back, and as soon as Paul passes over him, Jonah rolls back and forth until he finally turns onto his stomach. He army crawls as fast as can, and within a few seconds he catches up to Paul's boots. He considers grabbing the cadet's ankles and pulling himself past, but then the space begins to widen and widen until the three of them spill out into a clearing circled by trees.

Jonah gets to his feet first and reaches down for Paul's hand. The Fourth Year refuses it; instead, he presses one hand to his chest wound and pushes himself up with the other. As Jonah pulls Vespa up by her armpit, Mirker's voice speeds down the narrow crack and assails their ears, loud and as clear as if he's standing in the clearing with them.

"You can hide all you want, but I can find you!"

Paul puts his head into the space and shouts, "Come and get it, old man! The next time you see me, I'm going to kill your ass!"

Mirker's laughter echoes back. "Kid, you have *no* idea what I can do to you and your friends. Jonah, if you don't come back soon for your medicine, you're fucked, boy! You are going to go right back to being blind! Think about that!"

Vespa and Paul turn to Jonah who can only respond with clenched fists. He hadn't thought of that. He forgot how tied he is to the village. He finds himself taking a small step toward the crack, toward the village, but he stops and takes a deep breath. What is he going to do?

"Don't worry about that," Vespa whispers. "We'll get your medicine somehow. Screw that guy."

"We're not going back," Paul says.

"We have to," Vespa answers coldly.

Mirker's voice comes through again: "And let's not forget about your little friend, Brooklyn! Here's a little secret for you: She's only still sick because I *want* her to be sick. I'm not giving her the right medicine! You hear me? I'm keeping her sick! And I'm going to let her die unless you come back here right now and tell me what I want to know!"

Vespa slips her arm under Jonah's and gives a little tug, but he barely registers she's next to him. All he can hear are the electronic beeps in Brooklyn's hospital room.

"That's right!" Mirker shouts. "I'm going to let her die! And you're as good as dead, too, Jonah! Without your medicine, YOU ARE DEAD!"

Jonah places his forehead against the stone wall and tries to work through his anger. Now what? Mirker has him by the throat, Brooklyn by hers.

Vespa comes up behind him and sets a hand on his shoulder. "Paul? Where's the other chip in our bodies? Where did they put the second one?"

"I don't know," he says. "I have no idea. But we're not going back for any of that medicine, I'll tell you guys right now. They'll kill us as soon as we get there."

"Maybe *you're* not going back," Vespa says. "But we are."

"Why? Because of your lover boy, Jonah here, or for that stupid little girl, Brooklyn?"

Vespa doesn't take the bait and continues, "I'm going back for both of them. They both helped me get off Achilles and stay alive, and I'm going to help them stay alive. Now, if they put one chip in our hands, then the other one must be..." Vespa rolls up her sleeves and starts looking for marks on her arms. When she finds nothing there, she yanks her pant legs up just past her knees and examines her skin. "Come on, come on..."

Jonah follows suit, checking his arms and legs for bumps or recent cuts, but to his chagrin there are dozens and dozens of scratches and half-healed wounds from the past week.

"They wouldn't put it where you could see it or get to it," Paul says. "It's probably on your back or something."

"Jonah, take off your shirt," Vespa orders. "Let me check your back. Hurry up."

At her request, he unzips his jumpsuit and starts to shrug off its shoulders when he remembers what the skin on his back looks like, scarred from the Pacsun twins who tortured him with scalding hot rocks when he was just eleven, leaving a huge cluster of bubbling scars like a school of fish. There are also several long, thin marks crisscrossing his lower back from Mr. Wexler's dressiest belt, the one with the silver tip shaped like an arrowhead. Without saying anything, he starts to zip his suit back up. But then Paul gets his hand on the back of his collar and rips it down, leaving Jonah naked from the waist up. The cadet feels his entire body flush with shame.

"*Jesus*," Paul whispers as he backpedals. "I don't know where to fucking start."

Vespa is silent for a few seconds before circling around to face Jonah with her one hand covering her lips. Her eyes brim with tears. "Did Mirker do that to you? Is that from Tunick? What... happened?"

Jonah shoves his arms back into their sleeves and pulls the suit back over his shoulders, zipping it all the way up to his throat. He takes a hard swallow and whispers, "Foster family stuff."

"What the hell does that mean, Firstie?" Paul asks.

"*Paul*," Vespa begs. A tear finally runs down her cheek, and she doesn't bother wiping it away.

Jonah hates it. He hates his scarred, ruined back. He hates Vespa's tear running down her face. He hates Paul's question. He hates this clearing. These trees and this alien sunshine. The air that's poisoning him. He hates Mirker for making Jonah expose his past. He hates, hates, hates.

"What?" Paul laughs. "The kid shows us his jigsaw puzzle back that's all messed up and I'm not supposed to ask what happened? *Fine.* Here. Look on me."

Paul strips to his waist, exposing a mountain range of muscles on his shoulders, chest, and back. Dr. Z's designs still rise from his skin, a riddle to solve at another time. Below the fresh bandage on his chest, his stomach is a bruised washboard. The huge gash on his side he suffered from the Achilles crash has been healing nicely, leaving a crescent moon–shaped scar that runs from his stomach to the top of his left shoulder blade. His white skin shines in the sun as he raises his huge arms and slowly twirls around. "Tell me if you see anything you like."

Vespa walks up to him and slaps a hand on his shoulder to keep him from twirling. "Hold still, asshole." Jonah watches her scan Paul's back with envy; she doesn't recoil or cry like she did when she saw his skin, even if there is a faint map scratched into it. She doesn't circle around to Paul's face to look at him with wonder or sympathy. She doesn't see him as damaged goods.

"Well," Paul says, "Hurry up. Anything back there?"

"Besides Dr. Z's handiwork? Not yet…" But then Vespa pauses her eyes on the middle of his upper back. She leans in, practically pressing her nose and lips on his skin. "I think I found something. Jonah? Look."

He swallows his shame and then takes a close look, and there in the direct middle of Paul's back, the place where no one can reach themselves and touch, sits an incision no longer than an inch. It looks clean and new.

"What'd you find? A pimple?" Paul asks.

Vespa turns to Jonah and clenches her jaw. He knows what she's going to say before she even says it. "I'm sorry to ask, Jonah, but I need to see your back again. To compare."

Jonah takes a deep breath and unzips his suit again.

"Or, you know you could always take off your top, V," Paul says over his shoulder.

This makes Jonah move faster, and soon the top of his suit

hangs from his waist. He turns his mangled back toward Vespa and waits.

"Yup, you have it, too."

Paul marches over. "Let me see."

Jonah feels Vespa's finger press into his skin. "Right here. See it?"

"Oh, yeah," Paul says. "It's right in the middle of all the other gross shit on his back, but I definitely see it." The cadet must notice Jonah's back stiffen and his shoulders narrow because he follows up with, "No offense, Firstie."

"I guess the only way to be for certain…" Vespa's finger drops from Jonah's back and he hears the sound of a zipper.

"Now we're talking," Paul whispers.

"Don't be a dick," Vespa responds.

Jonah pulls his suit back up over his shoulders and turns to see Vespa's exposed back crisscrossed by black bra straps. He can't help but clear his throat as he looks over the smooth skin covering her tight muscles. Tiny, almost invisible white hairs stand up in the cool air, shining in the sunlight. Both boys stand dumbfounded, not knowing what to do next.

"Do I have it, too, or what?" she asks. "Hurry up."

Both boys step closer, their shoulders pushing against each other for the best view. Jonah sees the same mark between her shoulder blades.

"You have it, too," Jonah says.

"Yup," Paul says. "Hold still for a second." He places two fingers on either end of the incision and pushes on her skin. After a little prodding, Paul pulls back a little and the outline of a small pill or pebble shows up between his fingers. "Got ya."

Before Jonah can memorize another inch of the beautiful, smooth skin in front of him, Vespa reaches over her shoulder and hands Paul her knife.

"Get it. Take it out."

The Fourth Year carefully puts the tip of the blade over the mark and cuts. Vespa gasps and her shoulders flex, but in a few seconds, it's over. Paul holds up a small, blood-covered silver object.

"Here she is," Paul says, placing it in Vespa's palm as she pulls her jumpsuit back over her shoulders. She silently looks at it for a moment before placing the tracker against the stone wall and smashing it with a rock.

"Fuck you," she whispers to it.

"Okay, now me," Paul says. "Then the ugly Firstie."

Once Vespa spins away from the wall, her face drops and her jaw stiffens. Jonah looks over his shoulder, and there, standing in a long line along the perimeter of the trees, is a herd of red-feathered mimics.

A humming noise slowly fills the air.

"God damn it," Paul growls.

• • •

Jonah counts twenty-three of the apes standing shoulder to shoulder under the black trees, their red feathers blowing back and forth in the wind. The air is suddenly full of red fluff that dances and twirls over their heads. The animals stand motionless, seemingly waiting for one of the cadets to make a move.

Paul's exposed torso begins to heave with adrenaline; Jonah can tell the boy is ready for the fight of his life. Again. The cadet tosses Vespa her knife back and then flexes his neck and stretches his fingers, cracking his knuckles, and the apes mimic his movements. When Paul takes a step forward, all twenty-three do the same.

"No, Paul," Jonah says. "Try stepping backward a couple times."

The Fourth Year grumbles but does what Jonah says; he takes three steps back until he's right next to Jonah. The red apes follow Paul's lead and soon they're a few feet inside the forest, half hidden by aqua plants and black tree trunks. Jonah puts his hand on Paul's wrist and pulls him back another few steps. Within a few seconds, the mimics are practically invisible, save for a few patches of bright red peeking through the foliage.

Vespa pulls out a second knife and whispers: "Good job, but they're still right there. What do we do?"

"We fight, or we go back whence we came," Paul says.

"What about Mirker and the others?" Jonah whispers through stiff lips.

A large mimic with blue-tipped feathers drops out of the closest tree. It stands stoically between its herd and the cadets, its triangular pink face unmoving as its shoulder and chest feathers wave in front of its eyes.

"I think I like my chances with Mirker better than these things." Paul takes another few steps backward with Jonah until they are right in front of the crawl space.

Vespa sidesteps along the wall with the knives in her hands. "What if they follow us in there? There's no way we'd make it all the way through."

"We crawl backwards," Paul chuckles. "The stupid things will do the same thing until they're so far away they'll—"

All twenty-three feathered apes march back into the clearing until they flank the leader. They advance together until they're just a dozen feet away from the cadets, forming a half circle around them, closing in slowly.

"Now what?" Vespa whispers.

Terrified, Jonah rubs the back of his neck. The mimics stop advancing long enough to rub their own necks. Jonah drops his hand and they follow suit. A few seconds later, though, they start to inch closer again. The leader begins a hum, triggering a chorus. Out of the corner of his eye, he sees Vespa slowly spin the knives in her hands. There's no way they'll be able to take on so many of the beasts; they may be able to take down a half dozen, maybe ten, but there's simply too many to fight. They need reinforcements, at least ten more cadets fighting on their side. Suddenly, Jonah has an idea.

"Just trust me here," Jonah says as he grabs Paul's bare shoulders with both hands and squares his body with his.

"I'm not fucking dancing with you right now," Paul seethes.

The mimics do the same, pairing off, setting their hands on each other's feathered shoulders.

Without warning, Jonah sends an uppercut into Paul's sternum. The Fourth Year howls and doubles over, the wind knocked out of him, and he falls to his knees.

"Firstie, you stupid mother..."

Sure enough, one of the mimics in each pairing strikes the other in the chest. The animals howl and spit in pain.

"Now, hit me," Jonah orders. "But just maybe not so hard?"

A sadistic grin comes over Paul's face, and in an instant, he tackles Jonah to the ground. He quickly crawls up Jonah's body and punches him hard in the cheek. Jonah and Paul look over to watch the apes mimic everything they're doing, tackling each other, striking each other in the faces. The blue-tipped leader takes a pounding. Paul reels his fist high over his head again, but before he can swing down at Jonah again, Vespa dives in and tackles Paul and punches him hard in the throat.

Paul gasps for air as Jonah painfully sits up to wipe his bloody lips, and all around them, the red apes are in an all-out brawl. They no longer pay attention to the movements of the cadets; they're blinded by rage and pain. Feathers drift in the air, slowly falling onto Jonah's heaving chest.

"Now," Jonah whispers, and he quickly turns over onto his stomach and crawls backward toward the opening in the wall. Paul and Vespa slowly get on their knees and begin to follow him, and it looks as if Jonah's plan is going to work, but then one mimic—a short, squat creature with one red eye and one yellow—is sent flailing out of a fight and toward the cadets, falling right on top of Jonah's back, flattening him on the ground. Within seconds, another mimic jumps on top of the first, and its mouth lands right next to Jonah's face, where it roars in his ear.

Paul grabs the top ape off of the pile by its neck and whips the beast into the stone wall behind them. The mimic bounces off and hits the ground in a lifeless heap. A few of the other animals see this, and they begin sprinting toward the wall to ram themselves against it, falling to the ground either completely knocked out, or pretending to be.

Jonah reels his arms into his body and rolls violently to his left, knocking the remaining mimic off his back. The creature reaches out and grabs ahold of his bicep, though, and yanks Jonah toward it with a demonic growl. It gets on top of him and opens its giant mouth full of sharp, brown teeth, and then drops its head onto Jonah's chest, but before it can take a bite, Vespa plunges one of her knives into the back of the ape's skull with a sickening squish. She then kicks the beast off Jonah and pulls the cadet to his feet.

Half of the animals continue to fight each other, seemingly unaware the cadets are still there, while the other half of the apes slowly advance toward them in silence, including the leader. The humming in the air ebbs and flows, like waves lapping at the beach.

"Someone take my other knife," Vespa whispers out of the side of her mouth.

Still stripped to his torso, Paul steps in front of Vespa and Jonah, blocking them from the advancing animals. Over his shoulder, he says, "Give it to Firstie." He flexes his enormous back and rolls his neck from side to side. "I can handle these things myself."

Vespa slips Jonah a knife and then steps forward and stands next to Paul. Jonah quickly stands on the other side of Paul, squeezing the handle of the knife as hard as he squeezed his sheaf when the *Mayflower 2* went down. The three cadets take a collective breath, and then without warning, Paul shouts into the air and rushes forward to tackle the two closest mimics. Vespa follows his lead and rushes into the mix, swinging her blade into the side of one as it tries to jump on Paul's back. The beast flails in pain and strikes Vespa across the face with the back of its paw. Vespa crumples to the ground where three more apes dive on top of her and claw viciously at her jumpsuit.

A switch flips in Jonah; a wave of adrenaline rushes through him and he boots one of the apes off of Vespa, sinks his knife into the back of another. The third animal continues to claw at Vespa's side, shredding the waist of her jumpsuit, until she's able to sit up and slash her knife across its neck, killing it.

"Thanks," she wheezes, and then she's scrambling over to help Paul who has a mimic's throat in each hand while he kicks a charging third in the stomach. Jonah runs to join in, but the animal he stabbed in the back grabs his ankle and trips him. He reaches back with his knife and slices the ape's wrist, sending a fountain of watery yellow blood into the air. As he tries to get back to his feet, he sees a small handful of white seeds and recognizes it at once. Verve. They must have fallen out of Vespa's shredded pockets. She must have gotten them from the hospital floor after Dr. Z attacked him. Jonah quickly scoops them up and shoves them into his pocket, and then he's at Paul's side, slicing his knife back and forth, doing anything he can to survive and help his fellow cadets.

The dead and wounded mimics now outnumber those still fighting each other and those squaring off with the cadets. Paul's chest and back are covered in the yellow blood of the beasts, and he seems to heave with excitement of possibly adding to it.

But just as they feel like they have the upper hand, a new herd of purple mimics appear through the trees. There must be thirty or forty of them, and they just stand and watch patiently, waiting for their turn at the cadets. Jonah watches in awe as a blue-tipped, red-feathered leader howls for its herd to stand down. It then slaps its paws on the ground and howls at the purple group to stay back.

"That's just too many," Vespa says, taking a few steps backward. Jonah agrees and steps with her, not stopping as he grabs Paul's thick forearm and gives it a tug.

"Until next time," Paul says.

They step in unison toward the stone wall and its narrow passage, and within seconds, the red leader marches forward with its arms out wide, no longer mimicking their moves.

Once they get in front of the crack, Jonah slowly gets down on his stomach.

"You first, Firstie," Paul says.

Jonah shuffles backward into the crack, keeping his eyes on the leader until it disappears behind Paul's legs. Vespa follows him, and then Jonah hears Paul mumble and grunt inside the opening. There's a sound of rocks shifting and crunching into each other, and then Paul yells, "I blocked the entrance! Now go!"

They move quickly. Jonah's elbows and knees are raw by the time they reach the other side, but all he can think about is Brooklyn lying on her bed, her eyes blue and blind—and Mirker standing over her with a devilish grin. The man is just like his sons, Tunick and Sean, sadists with no regard for reason or empathy. Jonah stands and peeks his head out, scanning the road for soldiers. On his left, sitting quietly at the end of the road, the concrete sphere appears empty, save for Everett curled into a ball, and to Jonah's right, the path is empty, winding its way up the cliff. No soldiers. No red or purple mimics. No two-headed yellow alien ghosts walking in circles.

"Before you go out there..." Vespa whispers.

He turns to see her wiping a knife blade back and forth on the front of her destroyed jump suit, cleaning off the yellow blood. An apologetic, yet stern, look appears on her face.

"Right," Jonah says. He exposes his upper back in a flash and grits his teeth. When the tip of the blade pierces his skin, Jonah shoots his arms above his head and grips the edges of the rock. Within seconds, Vespa places the tiny silver tracker in the palm of his huge hand. He sets it on the ground and stomps on it.

Vespa then removes Paul's tracker and smashes it with the butt of her knife, and a minute later, they're crouched behind the sphere and whispering for Everett to answer them.

"You still alive in there or what?" Paul asks.

"Make some kind of noise if Mirker is still here somewhere," Jonah says.

When Everett doesn't answer, Vespa beings to creep around the curve of the sphere. Jonah and Paul keep their eyes on the road and the forest, ready to protect Vespa at a moment's notice.

"Guys, get in here. *Now*," Vespa says, her voice echoing.

The boys enter the sphere to find Everett on his side, gasping his last breaths with wide-open eyes. A small pool of blood shines under his neck, slowly expanding across the concrete. Vespa cuts the plastic bindings from Everett's bruised wrists and the boy rolls limply onto his back. A smile slowly crosses his cracked lips. He tries to say something, but no words escape his moving mouth.

"Everett, it's me, Jonah, from Achilles. Can you hear me?"

To their surprise, the boy nods.

"Okay!" Jonah says. "Everett, why are you down here? When you went through that portal on Achilles, is this where you showed up?"

He nods again.

"Fuck that, there's no way," Paul whispers. "You can't just get zapped from a moon to a planet. Kid's lying, or he's gone crazy."

Vespa peeks out the door to be sure the coast is clear, and then she kneels beside Everett and hovers her face over his. The boy's smile immediately widens, blood bubbling through his teeth.

"Everett, did Mirker tell you why he chained you up in here? Is there something he wants from you?"

Another nod.

"Speak, god damn it," Paul says. "Just tell us."

Everett's mouth moves quickly, as if he's telling a grand story, but again not a word comes out. Not even a whisper.

Vespa gently sets her hands on the boy's cheeks. "We can't hear what you're saying. What does he want, Everett? What does Mirker want?"

Everett slowly raises his right arm and then points to the ceiling of the dome: the dozens of symbols carved into the concrete, an attempt to copy what the people of Thetis have found elsewhere. This strikes Jonah hard, knowing that they've discovered what could be the writing of an ancient alien civilization, and that it hasn't been reported back to Earth. They are keeping secrets. Huge secrets. But why?

"What are we even looking at?" Paul asks. "I just see a bunch of shapes up there. Does it say something?"

Jonah lies down right next to Everett and follows the boy's vision up his trembling arm. There's no doubt in Jonah's mind; Everett points to a stick figure with exaggerated legs and arms. It's relatively small compared to all the other symbols, and it's positioned right below several triangles. Jonah jumps to his feet to get a closer look, and very faintly, he reads his own name scratched alongside the figure.

"Shit," Jonah whispers.

"What?" Vespa and Paul both ask.

"It's me," Jonah says, "It's a picture of a person and there's my name. Right below those triangles."

Vespa gasps when she finally sees it.

"That's not good," Paul says. "Or, maybe it is good. Hey kid, you carve Firstie in there yourself or what?"

When the cadets look down, Everett's arm is draped across his chest and his eyes are closed. Vespa puts her ear to his chest and then shakes her head. "He's gone."

Jonah takes another look at the stick figure. At his name, clear as day. He feels wobbly and confused. His hands shake so much that Vespa grabs them and holds them up against her cheeks.

"Hey, look at me. We have no idea what that means, so don't dig too deep, okay?" she says.

Jonah stares at her green eyes and nods for a second before looking back at the carving overhead. Maybe Mirker did it. Maybe Everett himself scraped that up there. Maybe Captain Tejas put this all together. Maybe, maybe, maybe...

Paul rotates, his eyes scanning the cement. "Am I somewhere, too? Look for a big strong guy who can bench press 340."

Vespa says, "Jonah, we'll figure this out later, okay. Right now, we have to go."

"Go where?" Paul asks.

"To get Brooklyn." Jonah continues, "We go save Brooklyn and then figure out what the hell is going on around here. And I think we have to get inside the telescope building to get some answers."

Paul pushes past Jonah and steps outside. He picks up a yellow stone and throws it against the outside of the sphere, shattering it. "It's a trap, you know that, right? That asshole is just waiting for us to show up. He's probably got ten men just sitting in Brooklyn's room, waiting for you. Hell, one of the guys probably has his hand over her mouth right now, suffocating her while he whispers messed up shit in her ears."

"Okay," Jonah says. He shakes off what he just saw. For now.

"Then we don't go to the hospital and try to break her out. Instead, maybe we get her to come to us."

"And how are we going to do that, Firstie?" Vespa asks.

"I don't know yet."

Jonah takes a moment to drape Everett's other arm across his chest. He wipes blood away from his cheeks, sweat away from his forehead. Looking down at the boy, Jonah's anger rises and falls until a wave of sadness washes over him. Yes, the kid pointed a gun at Jonah's face and forced him inside that Achilles cave. And then he tried to force Jonah onto the white portal after it started up. But then Jonah shoved him onto it, apparently sending him back here. And then Mirker got to him. So, it was Jonah who had this boy tortured and killed. This is his fault.

"Sorry," he whispers, and then Jonah steps out of the sphere and squints up into the greenish sky. He looks for Peleus and sees its faint outline over the trees. It doesn't matter if he's on Thetis or on one of its moons, death will follow his every step.

The cadets edge the path up the mountain, staying hidden just inside the tree line. Jonah keeps an eye out for drones while Paul stays on watch for more mimics or other creatures. Vespa moves silently with her shoulders raised on high alert. They get to the top of the cliff in under an hour and then hide behind a pile of boulders covered in smelly purple moss. They can see the top of the fence surrounding Athens. Far beyond the village, Jonah sees the giant white modules sitting empty at the bottom of mountain.

Paul turns to Jonah and Vespa. "So, who has a plan? How are we going to get Brooklyn out of there? And how are we going to get Jonah's meds? You need me to put on a show or something?"

"How are your dance moves?" Vespa says.

"Pretty damn good, actually."

Jonah runs his hand over the purple moss, petting it gently as he thinks. He goes over the interior of the village in his mind, picturing the different buildings, the layout of the garden, the trapdoor he escaped through. He sees his yurt and Matteo sitting on the one chair inside. His mind circles the telescope building and the farm building. And then he pictures Brooklyn groaning on her bed with Mirker standing over her with his arms crossed, ordering one of his men to remove the tubes from her arms. Faces from the village flood his mind: Matteo, Freeman, the Indian woman, the man with the red cap, the kids from Module Eight. Is there anyone who can help him? While other faces run through his mind, Jonah loses his balance and falls on his butt and feels the verve seeds in his pocket. Now it hits him. He knows how he can create enough chaos inside to get Brooklyn out. It's going to come with a major cost, though. He's going to have to promise something he doesn't want to do, but he thinks it's the only way.

"I'm going to go inside and get someone to help us," Jonah says. "I'll get Brooklyn out here. I'll get her to come to us."

"Yeah, and who is going to help us?" Paul asks.

"If I tell you, you're just going to say I'm crazy and try to talk me out of it. But I think it will work. I just need to get inside without them seeing me. Any suggestions?"

"You're looking for a diversion?" Vespa asks. Her eyes begin to scan the landscape.

Jonah reaches up and pets the moving purple moss one last time. "Yeah, a diversion would be nice. But still, I need to get back inside somehow. And I don't think going through that trap door I came out of is going to work. It has to be monitored or locked."

"Or boobytrapped," Vespa says.

"Can you climb the fence?" Paul asks. "I mean, it's only fifty feet high with spikes on top and people with rifles watching at all times."

Vespa's eyes continue to scan. "But they won't be watching the fence if they're watching something else."

"You want to start a fire, don't you?" Paul says, chuckling. "You *love* your fires, V. That should have been flagged at some point in the academy."

"I may have an idea." Jonah backs away from the boulders and hides behind a nearby tree. The two cadets quickly follow him. "All we have are Vespa's knives, right?"

Vespa holds both blades up and twirls them in her hands.

"Firstie, if you're going to suggest we go back and skin a couple of those apes and then wear their hides as disguises," Paul says, "I would say I've heard worse ideas, but not many. Also, I'm totally in."

Jonah cringes at the thought. "No, I was thinking you guys could do some kind of damage with the modules from the ship. Somehow push them over or cut something off of them or—"

Vespa raises her eyebrows. "Set them on fire?"

"Sure, yeah," Jonah says. "We don't have much time. The longer we're out here, the more pissed off Mirker is going to be. The question is, can you get over there and make something happen in the next thirty minutes?"

The cadets study the giant modules in the distance. They must be a mile away, or more. Two of them are stripped to their metal shells, their material used to make tents in the village. But another three stand out there like giant marshmallows waiting to be skewered for a campfire.

"Even if we light them up, I still don't know how you're going to scale the fence," Vespa says.

"That's what your knives are for," Jonah says. "I stick them in the wood and keep pulling myself up."

Paul shrugs but then nods at the idea and Vespa quickly slaps the knife handles into Jonah's hands. A second later, the two cadets sprint inside the tree line, curving their way toward the modules. Jonah watches until they're out of sight and then slowly moves toward the village wall. Two drones zip along the top of the perimeter, buzzing back and forth, while another two hover near the gate. He slides down an embankment and gets himself in position. From this vantage point, he can no longer see the modules; they're hidden behind the spiked wall looming over him. There, he waits.

Jonah hates that he's sent Vespa and Paul off together. He hates the thought of them working together, planning, laughing, reconnecting; it's ridiculous to think about his feelings for Vespa at this moment, when he's curled up in a ball in an embankment waiting to scale a fifty-foot wall with nothing but a couple of knives, but his desire to be with Vespa is simply undeniable. Everything about her makes his heart jump. Even when she dismisses him.

He also thinks about Lark and Krev and Tunick and Hess and all the other kids who left Thetis because it was no longer safe for them here. He now fully understands that Thetis is, in fact, a very bad place to be. It's killing every human here. *Still*, Jonah thinks, *maybe they can find a way to breathe the air without getting sick, and the community can still be turned into the alien utopia promised to them.*

He keeps his eyes on the wall and the drones zipping back and forth overhead. Forty-five minutes pass. But then smoke appears in the distance; a huge black and twisting plume spreads out like wings over the mountaintops. A few seconds later, the two drones monitoring the fence nearest Jonah suddenly take off toward the smoke. He hears shouting. He thinks he may even hear the gate open on the other side.

Jonah moves quickly, sprinting the last fifty yards to the wooden fence. He flattens his back against it, looks left and right and up, and then twists around and jumps straight up. He plunges the right knife hard into the wood and it sticks, leaving him hanging by one arm until he swings the left knife over his head and sticks it higher than the right. The toes of his shoes scramble over the boards until getting a slight grip, and then Jonah pulls himself up. He yanks out the right blade and plunges it higher. Then the left. In a matter of thirty seconds, his eyes peer over the spikes at the top. In the distance, the cloud of black smoke has gotten bigger, and he can see the tips of the flames dancing along the tops of two of the white modules. *Good work, guys*, he thinks. He counts five drones moving toward the fire. Below, Jonah watches villagers sprint back and forth among the tents and buildings. Mirker stands in the middle of it all with his hands on his hips. Two men face him and point fingers in different directions, arguing with him. Another man drives a cycle over to Mirker and jumps off and offers him the handlebars. Mirker swings a leg over the seat and speeds toward the gate, popping a brief wheelie along the way. He's met by two idling rovers, and as soon as Mirker arrives, the gate opens halfway, barely allowing the three vehicles to squeeze through before closing with an echoing thud.

The moment the gate closes, Jonah pulls himself between two of the spikes and descends the inside wall just like he scaled the outer; he plunges the knives over and over into the wood until he can safely jump to the ground. As soon as his feet hit the black dirt, Jonah sprints behind the nearest tent. Voices come from inside, an argument between two women about never being able to leave the village, and Jonah runs to the next tent. He's able to avoid the few remaining men in military outfits, sprinting and hiding, sprinting and hiding, and soon he's close enough to the gate to see the red button high up on the wall.

Jonah shoves his hand into his pocket and rubs the verve seeds between his fingertips. He can't believe he's about to execute his plan. It's a huge gamble; if it doesn't work, he's done for. Trapped. Maybe even tortured and killed. And then Vespa and Paul are done for, too.

He watches the gate for another thirty seconds, and when it's clear, Jonah jumps into action. He sprints right for the huge doors, but then makes a sharp right turn toward the cement building next to it. He rams his shoulder into the door. The wood splinters and crashes inward. Jonah stumbles inside and sees the sheaf standing on the desk, a red ball cap next to it. He rips open the door to the hallway in the back.

It's almost completely dark inside the hall as he sprints to the end. He gets to the last door on the left and squints through the bars in the window. There, rocking back and forth in the corner under a naked light bulb, sits Dr. Z.

"Dr. Z," Jonah whispers.

The woman's head jerks upright to stare at the wall in front of her.

"It's me, Jonah."

The doctor flips over onto all fours and crawls toward him. When she gets close to the door, she disappears from Jonah's sight, but then her face suddenly pops up and appears in the small window with a sadistic grin. Her teeth are yellow and broken, and one of her eyes is black and blue, swollen shut with crusted blood. Jonah gasps and stumbles backward into the darkness. *This is a mistake*, he thinks. *There has to be another way.*

"You're too late, too late," she says in a grave voice. "They're going to choose someone new soon." She drums her dirty hands on the top of her head. "The tall boy with the hair. They want him. He wants to choose him now."

Jonah clears his throat and takes a small step forward. He tries to reconcile this broken woman before him with the doctor who saved his life after the crash on Achilles. She couldn't have been kinder back then, more concerned with everyone's safety. He remembers how at the makeshift hospital, after another child died and was covered with a blanket, she spun around and launched a rock into the night sky with so much anger and defeat. She cared so much for everyone. She cared so much for him.

"Am I still chosen? Do they still want me?"

Dr. Z smashes her face into the bars of the window and when she laughs, spit covers her chin and drips onto the ledge. "Yes. They still want you. He does, he does. But you don't listen. If you don't listen, you don't get to go."

"Go where?" he asks.

"You don't get to be their God. You don't get to save the old boy."

"Save who?"

The woman backs up a few paces and then slowly points all over the room, her trembling index finger following nothingness around her empty cell. "Them and him. Them and him. Them and him."

She sees them right now, Jonah thinks. The two-headed ghosts. He whips his head back and forth in the dark hallway, wondering if he's surrounded by them at that very moment.

As he watches Dr. Z continue to point and say "them and him" over and over, he knows time is running out. He's not going to get the answers he needs from her. At least, not clear ones. Not right now. So, he says what he came to say: "Dr. Z, if you do something for me, if you help save my friend from the hospital here and bring her to me outside the fence..." He hesitates to say the next part, but then moves forward with his plan: "I will eat the seeds. I will listen to them or him or her or whoever you want. All of them. I will let them choose me."

Dr. Z stops pointing and then charges at the window. Her one good eye shifts back and forth to stare into Jonah's face to see if he's telling the truth. "Free me and eat the seeds. Eat the seeds and listen to them. Listen to them and save us all. Eat the seeds, kill the red one."

"I will only eat the seeds once you bring my friend, Brooklyn, to me outside the gate. Alive. Not until then."

She laughs and then paces back and forth in the small cell, huffing and growling like a lion. Her lips move constantly, her head tilted toward the sky. She grumbles and argues with the air around her, and then she stops in the middle of the room and lowers her face to the ground where she stands silently for almost a minute. Jonah watches terrified; he knows he made a mistake. This isn't going to work. She's too far gone. All of this is too far gone.

"I will bring her to you," she says with her face still aimed at the ground. "And then you will eat the seeds."

"You bring me Brooklyn...and you bring me her medication *and* my medication, and then I'll do whatever you need me to do."

Jonah reaches into his pocket and retrieves the verve seeds that fell from Vespa's pocket. He then holds them up to the window for her to see.

"Let me out," she whispers. "Let us all out."

Jonah closes his eyes and takes a deep breath. Is he really going to do this? Is Brooklyn's life really more important than his own? What if the seeds kill him? What if he never stops seeing the alien ghosts and they haunt him forever like Dr. Z and the Module Eight kids? He feels the air around him, knowing that these beings are there watching his every move. He opens his eyes again to see Dr. Z smiling at him with her broken teeth.

He pauses for one last second and then runs back down the hall and into the front room. Keys. He needs to find the keys. As he slaps his hands all over the desk and rummages through the pockets of the two jumpsuits hanging from a hook on the wall, Jonah catches glimpses of the sheaf's screen rotating through different feeds. He sees the village from several angles: people darting back and forth into tents, the Module Eight kids huddling next to a section of the fence, swaying in unison. He sees outside the village, and the giant smoke plume widening, a shot from one of the drones moving in. No sign of Vespa and Paul. He hopes they're okay, running in this direction as soon as they set the modules on fire. Maybe he should have brought Vespa with him. Or Paul. No, he thinks, they would never let him eat the verve seeds and sacrifice himself.

His fingers touch metal in a jumpsuit pocket, and he brings out a small ring of rudimentary keys. The way they shine in his hands instantly reminds him of the metal disc that hung around Lark's neck on Achilles. He had never seen that kind of metal before, until again just now. Jonah runs back down the hall and stops in front of the cell door. Inside, Dr. Z stands in the back of the room with her face to the wall. As soon as he puts the key in the lock, she spins around and marches toward him. He pushes the door open and the doctor walks right past him, turning into the hallway, never breaking her stride until she gets halfway down the hall. There, she looks up to the ceiling and holds her hands to her temples. She shakes her head, whispering, "Yes, yes, I will. I understand. If he doesn't eat them, he dies. Yes, yes."

Hearing this, Jonah's whole body shakes, and it takes everything in him to say, "I need Brooklyn alive, and her medicine and my medicine. The medicine is in clear bags. Meet me in the trees right outside the gate."

Dr. Z twists around and nods twice. Then she holds out a dirty palm and wavers back and forth. "One seed for me. One seed for me. To give me the powers."

The cadet quickly digs into his pockets and finds the keys and then Vespa's knives. He could end this right now, killing this woman and never worrying about her again. He could go rescue Brooklyn himself. The thought of him stabbing Dr. Z is too much, though. He finds and brings out the white seeds. He walks toward her and drops the largest one into her hand. A sick growl comes from the woman's throat before she shoves the verve into her mouth and takes an echoing *crunch.* She raises her arms over her head and clenches her fists. The muscles in her neck are suddenly visible and pulsing. And then she turns and sprints down the rest of the hallway, disappearing through the doorway.

CHAPTER TEN

JONAH PLUNGES THE KNIVES INTO THE WALL RIGHT NEXT TO the gate and starts climbing toward the red emergency button, but blue laser fire sends him crashing back to the dirt. He ignores the shouts for him to freeze, and he picks himself up and sprints along the fence toward the dark tunnel that got him outside in the first place. He just hopes the Module Eight kids aren't there waiting for him.

He darts down an alley, and a man shouts for him to stop, and then another man joins in the call, but Jonah just puts his head down and takes a sharp turn between a cluster of yurts. He turns again and again, zigzagging between different tents and buildings, sprinting through the shadows of the farm building, catching sight of the three frosties stacked on top of each other. He runs right past a small group of villagers with their heads up and their hands flat above their eyes, watching the dark cloud of smoke rising in the distance.

The two men get closer, their heavy, laboring breaths just a dozen yards behind him, and so Jonah speeds around a yurt, circling around and around its circumference until he hears their confusion on the opposite side. He's not only trying to lose the men but also trying to buy Dr. Z some time. Maybe even get a few of the guards from the hospital to leave and give chase. He pictures Dr. Z kicking down doors and roaring like a madwoman, fighting Mirker's soldiers with everything she has. He pictures her draping Brooklyn over her shoulder, grabbing an armful of medicine bags, and then charging back out into the village with the verve blasting through her veins. *How is she going to get outside the gate?* he wonders. He should have thought about that. But if she got out once before with Paul, he thinks she can figure it out again. Especially with Jonah's promise to eat the seeds hanging in the balance.

Jonah sees the telescope in the distance and tears straight for it. He flattens his back against the building's cement wall and gathers his breath. His heart beats in his throat as he whips his head around, trying to get his bearings. Which way is the tunnel from here again?

Voices come from his left and Jonah quietly rounds the building until he's in front of the door. He tries the handle, but it's locked. He reaches for the knives in his pockets to pry the door open, but instead his fingers find the keys. With trembling hands, he tries three different keys until the fourth one clicks when he turns it. A second later he's inside, locking the door behind him. Jonah crouches against the door, putting as much weight on it as possible. Whoever follows him is now just on the other side. He sees the shadow of a face peering through the window, and then he hears the handle being turned. But when they realize the door is locked, they leave to look elsewhere.

Jonah puts his head in his hands, wondering how he's going to get out of there. When he looks up, he sees the telescope rests at a different angle than before; in fact, it's facing the complete opposite direction, and near the top of the huge tube five long panels stick out of it like flower petals open at midday. Time is running out. If he's not in the trees waiting for Dr. Z when she shows up with Brooklyn, there's no telling what she'll do. To Brooklyn. Or to him. But he can't help himself and jumps in the rolling chair under the lens and presses his face against it. Then he lets his fingers crawl over the sides of the lens until he finds the right switch.

Like a sheaf coming to life, the lens expands and curls around his head, and then a red and gray ball appears in front of his eyes. It's small, the size of a fist, but still, Jonah can tell this isn't Peleus. And he knows it isn't Achilles. He finds the zoom function, and soon the object grows closer and closer until he sees red mountains and green rivers and then moving waves on a rust-colored coastline. His fingers try to zoom even closer, but they hit a different button, and the telescope begins to move by itself, shifting a couple inches down and then to the left. When it stops, Jonah presses his forehead against the lens as several triangular shadows form in his view. The image gets sharper and sharper until it's unmistakable. Pyramids. He's looking at pyramids in a desert. He's instantly reminded of the pyramids in his visions when the Module Eight girl grabbed his hand outside of the tunnel. And of the triangles carved above the stick figure in Everett's sphere. Who built these? And where is this?

And then, moving in and out of the giant shadows of these pyramids, Jonah sees thousands of tiny figures. They go in every direction, some in groups and some off on their own. Jonah tries to zoom in for an even closer look, but it won't go farther. But then the telescope shifts again under its own control—just slightly—and Jonah watches the red landscape crawl to the right and up a mountainside, and when the telescope stops and focuses, Jonah gasps and falls to the floor, knocking the chair over in a resounding clang. With held breath, he gets up on his knees and presses his face against the lens.

"What the hell?" he whispers to himself.

Carved into the mountainside is a giant crescent moon with the three circles sitting inside it. The same symbol that has been haunting him for a week, following him from Achilles to Thetis to wherever he's looking at now. Using the digital specs on the periphery of the lens, the symbol appears to be over five hundred yards long. It must have taken someone years to make. But why? And by who?

The light in the telescope building changes; a man's face

appears in the window, his hands cupped to his temples. When the man sees Jonah inside, he shouts the word "keys" over his shoulder and then tries to ram the door in. Jonah gets to his feet and runs a circle around the room, looking for another way out, but finds none, and so he hides next to the door with his fingers reaching for Vespa's knives. His shoulder hits a switch, triggering a motor somewhere that shakes the whole building. The ceiling separates and a second later Jonah stands in a ray of sunshine.

The man rams the door again, this time splintering the wood, and Jonah pushes off the wall and jumps right at the telescope. He wraps his arms around the tube and quickly begins to shimmy his way up. Vespa's knives push out of his pockets and fall before he can reach for them. They hit the cement floor with an echoing chime. "Damn it," Jonah whispers. He's twenty feet off the ground when the door breaks away and a half-dozen men charge into the room. They dive for the papers and monitors on the desk, checking for what's been taken.

"Where the hell did he go?" asks a pudgy man with a tuft of white hair on the top of his head. He stands directly over the knives. "Check the cabinets! Come on out, Jonah. Mirker's asking for you. We're not going to hurt you. He needs your help, son."

Without making a noise, Jonah pulls himself higher and higher along the telescope until he leaps out of the crack in the ceiling like a rabbit darting from its borough. He lands on the roof just as one of the men looks up, missing him by a second.

"*What the fuck*?" the pudgy man yells. "He can't just disappear! And shut this thing off already. Pick up those papers. Call Mirker."

"He's not answering," another man says.

"Then someone go get him!"

A click echoes from the room and a motor begins humming below Jonah. The roof begins to shake and pinch together. He leaps out of the way and then drops to his stomach and crawls to the edge of the roof. A tall man bursts out of the broken door and charges toward the hospital, barreling through a couple of small children playing in the grass.

From the roof, Jonah can see everything, and no one can see him, save for drones, but there don't appear to be any around. They must all still be at the fire, which continues to add more and more smoke into the black cloud spreading across the sky. The peaks of the mountains in the distance remind Jonah of the pyramids he saw through the telescope lens. And that reminds him of the giant symbol carved into the mountainside. The image haunts him. He needs to know what it means. Before he eats a seed, *if* he ever gets outside, he's going to demand Dr. Z tell him everything about the symbol, once and for all.

The pudgy man with a tuft of white hair leaves the building flanked by three other men. They stop a few feet from the doorway and huddle together, and Jonah scoots back a few inches to remain hidden.

"What do you think?" one of the men asks before spitting on the ground.

The pudgy man bites his lip before answering, "I think he looked through the telescope and saw what he saw, and he saw the papers and knows about Zion out there and maybe the Kurtz guy. I don't know if the kid slipped out the door when we weren't looking, or what, but we have to find him before he tells anyone."

"Yeah, and then what?" a blond man asks. He holds Vespa's knives in his hands, examining them. "What if he comes at us? We can't just kill him. We need him for the thing."

"We hold onto him. But let's just find him first."

Jonah scoots back even more on the roof. Sweat beads down his face and neck, soaking his collar. Need him for *what* thing? And what about the Kurtz guy? Kip? He hears them run off, and when he sees no one around, Jonah dangles his legs over the side and jumps. He rolls to a stop and looks around. He can't go through the gate, and he can't go back over the fence without the knives, so he has to get outside some other way. And quickly. He's already wasted way too much time.

Sprinting from tent to tent, Jonah moves toward the maintenance tunnel. He catches glimpses of a few stragglers, but mostly the village feels like a ghost town. When he gets near the farm building, Jonah hides behind a small tent and sees a few creatures pacing in their pens. A bright yellow capstone runs back and forth, its long arms dragging behind as it searches for a new rock to put on its head. He wants to stop and ask Francesca for help, to somehow sneak him outside in a cage or something, but that's when he sees the silver, cannon-sized contraption on the side of the building: the wood chopper. Matteo showed it to him on his tour, saying they could never have built the fence as fast as they did without it. He makes a break for it.

He's halfway past the farm building when Griffin steps out of the shadows with his arms crossed.

"What do you think you're doing, Firstie?"

"Getting out of here," Jonah says, running around him, never breaking his pace.

Griffin is on his heels, "Then, I'm coming with you. Some shit is happening. Dr. Z escaped and everyone's freaking out. I think they're going to start shooting people."

Jonah doesn't know if he can trust him, but he doesn't have time to argue. He reaches the wood chopper and begins to shove it toward the fence. Griffin gets next to him and pushes with all he's got.

"Where the hell we going with this?" Griffin asks.

"Outside," Jonah says.

They reach the fence and Jonah immediately begins looking for the controls. Griffin shoves him aside and presses a small black screen on its underside, and a second later, four metal legs descend from the chopper's belly and plant themselves in the soil. The blade pulls back, ready.

"We're just going to bust a hole in this fence, or what?" Griffin asks as he runs his hand through the lion in his hair.

"Just do it."

The cadet presses a button and the blade shoots forward, slicing right through the fifty-foot log standing in front of it, sending bits of wood and dust all over them. Jonah gets ready to move the chopper to the right so they can make the hole even bigger, but to his surprise, the log separates from its base and slowly tips away from them, falling toward the jungle. With a resounding boom, it hits the ground and leaves a small gap in the fence.

"Go, go, go," Griffin says, pushing Jonah.

Jonah jumps over the three-foot stump left behind and then ushers Griffin through. When Griffin squeezes past, Jonah sees the Module Eight kids huddled together inside the village, just a couple dozen yards away. They begin to walk toward the cadets.

"Run!" Jonah yells.

They sprint into the trees as the black smoke from the modules moves over the jungle, blocking the sun.

"Now what?" Griffin asks.

"Now, we look for Vespa and Paul and watch out for drones and Mirker and his people and the kids from Module Eight."

"*Jesus.* That all?"

Jonah takes a sharp left toward the rendezvous point. He needs to get to the cadets before Dr. Z finds and attacks them—or before Paul and Vespa attack her.

Through the trees, Jonah keeps an eye on the fence, which is fifty yards on his left. Four men pace back and forth in front of the gate. The short pudgy man from the telescope building is there, talking into a walkie-talkie while pointing at one of the other men who holds his palms up and shakes his head. The gate opens slightly and several more villagers spill out, some just kids. *Where's Mirker?* Jonah thinks.

As they get closer to the section of forest where they are supposed to meet the cadets and Dr. Z, Jonah and Griffin slow down and begin to move as quietly as they can, using tactics learned in the academy. After a few minutes, Jonah catches sight of Vespa's green jumpsuit through the trees. He darts to a cluster of spiky bushes to get a closer look, seeing Vespa hiding behind a thick gray tree trunk with Paul next to her. Paul has his arm around Vespa's waist and she leans her head against his chest. Jonah holds his breath as he watches Paul push hair out of Vespa's face and kiss her cheek.

Instantly, Jonah wishes he would have sent Paul into the village to free Brooklyn instead.

"Sigg!" Griffin half-shouts as he runs past Jonah. "Hey, Paul!"

Paul and Vespa quickly separate; Vespa sprints to another tree and ducks out of sight while Paul twists around to face Griffin.

"Get out of here, cadet. Right now," Paul growls. "You don't want to be involved with this."

Before Jonah can step out from behind the bushes, Vespa leaps out from behind the tree and tackles Griffin, blindsiding him. Griffin lets out a shout as the two roll right into Paul's legs where the Fourth Year places his boot right on Griffin's throat.

Paul spits over his shoulder and says, "I'm telling you. Get out of here."

"Wait," Jonah says as he comes out from behind the bushes. "He came with me. It's okay, it's okay. Griffin helped me escape."

Still on top of Griffin, Vespa turns her face toward Jonah with a smile. "Jonah. You made it, thank the gods."

He can't help but smile from the way she says his name. But the rush of adrenaline Jonah had been running on suddenly leaves his body, and he's left shaking and exhausted. He plants his hands on his knees and whispers, "Barely."

Paul removes his foot from Griffin's neck and nods over his shoulder. "You boys like our little fire? Seems to have done the trick, right? Tons of people are over there. Drones. Rovers. Quite the diversion we put together, if I do say so myself."

"Yeah," Jonah says. "Looks like the entire—"

"Wait. Jonah? Where's Brooklyn?" Vespa stands and spins around. "Where is she? You were supposed to… Is she okay? Oh god, don't tell me."

Jonah takes a deep breath. "She's coming. She'll be here. I hope."

"What does that mean?" Paul grunts as he yanks Griffin off the ground by his collar.

"I have zero clue what's happening right now, but I like it," Griffin says.

Exasperated, Vespa opens her arms. "Jonah? Seriously, what *does* that mean? That mean that she's healthy enough to get here on her own? She can see now? She can walk?"

Men's voices suddenly enter the forest, sending the cadets hiding behind different trees. A rifle fires, and Jonah sees a flash of blue light zip far off on his right.

"Motherfucker," Paul seethes. "You guys led them right to us."

"My knives. Give them to me," Vespa whispers.

"I kind of lost them," Jonah responds.

"*Damn it, Firstie*," she grits.

Branches crunch a few dozen yards away; they're coming right toward them. Jonah crouches down and grabs a rock. The noises get closer and closer, coming in from the right, and Jonah is the first line of defense. When it sounds like the men are right on top of him, he jumps out from behind his tree, raising the rock over his head. But before he can swing it down, he sees it's Dr. Z. And draped across her shoulders is a lifeless Brooklyn in a hospital gown, medical tubes sticking out of her arms.

As soon as Jonah and Dr. Z lock eyes, he lowers the rock and the woman shrugs the sick demic to the forest floor with a huge smile on her wicked face. Her yellow teeth chomp together three times before she tosses a small bag at Jonah. It hits his chest and falls quietly at his feet, several bags of the clear medicine spilling out.

"What the fuck, Firstie?" Paul says, pointing at Dr. Z. "What the actual *fuck*?"

CHAPTER ELEVEN

Vespa rushes to Brooklyn's side and places an ear to her chest. "She's still breathing. She's alive."

Dr. Z steps over the girls and walks slowly up to Jonah like a lion approaching its prey. Her one good eye is just a giant pupil, dark and glassy, and her burnt red hair blows around her cheeks and chin. The stench from her breath sends Jonah back a few steps as she says, "Now your turn. Your turn now." She comes closer, pinning Jonah against a tree. "Eat them. Eat the seeds."

"Firstie? What the hell is going on?" Paul asks.

Vespa scrambles over to the bag Dr. Z tossed to Jonah and looks inside. Her face suddenly falls. "Jesus, there's like only six bags of medicine in here. That's not enough. That's not enough for Brooklyn, let alone for the both of you."

Jonah looks over Dr. Z's heaving shoulder. "That should get us through a couple days maybe. And then we can try to—"

Dr. Z's right hand shoots to Jonah's neck and squeezes, cutting him off. She shoves her dirty left hand inside his mouth and pulls his jaws apart. "You eat now!"

Just as Paul slams his hand onto Dr. Z's back and rips her away from Jonah by her collar, more noises appear in the forest. Feet stomping on fallen branches. Muffled voices. Jonah massages his throat and locks eyes with Dr. Z. "I will eat, I promise. But not here. We have to find somewhere safe first."

Dr. Z smiles and nods rapidly, and then she spins around and ducks down to wrap her arms around Brooklyn's waist. She sits the small girl up and a low groan escapes her cracked lips. Dirt and fresh scratches cover the demic's face; Jonah can see she must have had a brutal ride through the jungle on Dr. Z's shoulders. He whispers into her ear, "It's me, Jonah. It's really good to see you, Brooklyn. And you're going to see me soon, too." Before he can say another word, Dr. Z hoists Brooklyn onto her shoulders and jogs farther into the trees.

Vespa scoops up the bag of medicine, and they all rush to catch up, Paul growling at Jonah the whole time, berating him for bringing the madwoman along for their ride. Dr. Z flies through the trees as if she isn't carrying one hundred pounds on her shoulders, bounding up and down hills, bursting through walls of sharp leaves, jumping over gaps in the ground without breaking stride.

"Where are we even going?" Vespa asks.

"I have no clue," Jonah huffs. Watching Dr. Z carrying Brooklyn like this reminds him of running along the reef on Achilles, the demic bouncing on his shoulders like a backpack as he tried not to fall in the water and get to Tunick's ship before it left the moon. He left Brooklyn on the edge of the canyon. To live. To die. He doesn't even know anymore. But he knows that right now, he's never going to leave her behind again. He picks up his pace and runs right alongside Dr. Z.

"Follow me, follow me," Dr. Z says as she leads them between two huge orange boulders at the base of a mountain. Jonah has to shuffle sideways through the path, and at the end of it, they come to an enormous field of geysers shooting thick columns of water high into the air.

"You really taking us through that shit?" Paul asks. "I say we hide and fight. Take Mirker down right now, get the jump on him. What are we waiting for?"

"I agree!" Vespa yells.

"We can't," Jonah says. "Look, I have to do something first with Dr. Z, and *then* we'll go after Mirker. Trust me. I think I can get us some answers if I just do something first."

Griffin pushes his way to the front of the group and shakes his head. "Uh, no way we're going through all that. Look at that shit. We'll fucking burn to death!"

Without saying a word, Dr. Z walks between the closest two geysers with Brooklyn balanced across her shoulders. She opens her arms out wide and both holes erupt at the same time, launching scalding columns of water right into the doctor's palms. She's knocked off balance and falls to her knees. Brooklyn slumps to the ground, lying flat on her back. Jonah runs to his friend as the woman slowly twists around to stare at him. She points a steaming, bright red finger at Jonah and motions to come to her.

"What is she even doing here, Firstie?" Vespa asks. "Get away from her! Why would she be helping us?"

"Because I promised her if she brought Brooklyn to me and grabbed our medicine, I would do something for her!" Jonah calls.

Vespa puts her fists on her hips. "And what did you have to promise her?"

"I told her…I promised her that I would eat some verve and hear her out."

Vespa and Paul look at each other as the field of geysers blasts in front of them. Jonah doesn't know what else to say.

"What's verve?" Griffin asks.

Vespa says, "It's the shit that made those kids Tunick and Sean go crazy and kill everyone, and it's what made the other kids from Thetis leave this place and go to Achilles. It's a drug. A really powerful drug *that Jonah should definitely not take.* What the hell is wrong with you?"

"I'll take some," Griffin says with a laugh. "Been bored out of my skull since we came here. In fact, this is somehow as far as I've gotten outside the fence."

Jonah pulls Brooklyn's head onto his lap, her eyelids flittering and showing slits of her bright blue eyeballs underneath. He hugs her to his chest, blocking her from the hot mist blowing over them.

"You're not really going to take it, are you, Jonah? Because the last time...you said it was too much," Vespa says as she steps onto the geyser field. "You said the other kids went crazy on it. They were homicidal."

Dr. Z gets to her feet and stands over Jonah and Brooklyn, her sleeves dripping water onto Jonah's neck. "It's time to eat, so you can speak to them now. We're almost there. Follow, follow."

"He's not eating anything!" Vespa shouts. "Get the fuck out of here! Leave us alone. You're free now, so run away."

Vespa's words transport Jonah back to Achilles with the warnings written on the cook and legless man hanging from the tree. He could just grab Brooklyn and try to lose Dr. Z amongst the geysers. But he's tired of running. And he's tired of all the mystery and being in the dark. It's time he learns what the voices want, what that symbol means, what the two-headed ghosts need from him. If he listens, then maybe everyone will finally leave him alone. And just maybe it will help him figure out a way to help everyone live a long happy life on Thetis.

"Seriously, lady," Vespa continues. "Get the hell out of here. Leave Brooklyn and just go."

Dr. Z turns toward Vespa with her hands shaking and her eyes on fire. But before she can even think about attacking the cadet, Jonah holds a palm up to her and says, "I'll eat the seeds, okay? I will. I promised you, and I will. But not here; I need a safe space, someplace where we can't be attacked."

A grin spreads across Dr. Z's blue lips. She then whips her head skyward and clicks her teeth together, and a chill runs down Jonah's spine as he knows she's listening to the alien ghosts. "I see it, yes. I'll bring him, I'll bring him." The woman lowers her eyes to Jonah and says, "I have a place. They showed me a place where you can eat. The old boy is there."

She leans down and rips Brooklyn from Jonah's lap and hoists her back onto her shoulders. Ahead of her, hundreds of columns of water blast rhythmically, blanketing the air high over their heads with thick layers of steam. Dr. Z walks between the first two geysers, disappearing in the water, and Jonah begins to follow her.

"I told you guys," Griffin says, "There's no way I'm running through all those geysers and burning my face off!"

Paul grabs Jonah's bicep and pulls him back. "You're not going in there, cadet. That's an order. You're not following that piece of shit lunatic. I'm not going to let you. I'll...I'll just go kick her in the back and send her into one of the geysers and grab Brooklyn and then we'll make a plan. But a *good* plan this time."

"I promised her. It's the only way we'll ever know what's going on around here," Jonah says, yanking his arm away from the Fourth Year. The two boys look at each other for a second and Jonah sees the fear in Paul's eyes. Jonah gives a sarcastic salute and turns to jog into the field. And within seconds, Vespa is right by his side, mumbling how stupid everything is.

"You guys are gonna die!" Griffin yells.

"You, too, V?" Paul calls. "Oh, come on!"

Vespa shouts over her shoulder, "She has Brooklyn! You guys do whatever you want!"

As the two cadets jog through the first two geysers, the one on their left explodes upwards with the force of a freight train, knocking Jonah to his knees. Hot water rains over his back and shoulders, but Vespa immediately rips him back up to his feet and together they stumble forward, swaying back and forth as if they're on a boat lost in a storm. Dr. Z is barely visible as she marches through the field.

Jonah and Vespa hold onto each other's sleeves as they pull themselves this way and that way, dodging a dozen more geysers, shielding each other from the burning columns of water that come from every direction. Jonah spins away from a giant hole just as it erupts, covering the top of his head with his hands, and he can barely see Paul and Griffin standing on the edge of the field. They're arguing. But not with each other. As several water jets between the two groups collapse and fall back into their holes, Jonah sees the cadets are yelling at the huddle of Module Eight kids marching toward them. Jonah tries to take a few steps in their direction, but Vespa yanks him back.

"Come on! We're losing her!" she yells over the roar of the field.

Jonah watches Paul point at the Module Eights and then look for Jonah and Vespa in the field. Jonah hesitates before jogging after Vespa, who still has eyes on Dr. Z. They lock hands and begin to run, taking turns pulling each other out of danger.

After a hundred yards, Vespa and Jonah find themselves in the middle of the field, soaked and staring at the doctor who stands near the lip of an enormous crater. It's easily the largest geyser they've come across, thirty yards in diameter, with waves of steam dancing over its darkness like ghosts. With Brooklyn still across her shoulders, Dr. Z turns and curls her finger inward, beckoning them closer. "Now, you follow."

And then Dr. Z turns back around and leaps into the hole, disappearing.

"Brooklyn!" Vespa shouts.

The cadets dash to the edge of the hole and see Dr. Z a dozen feet down, standing in the entrance of a cave cut into the side of the geyser wall. Brooklyn lies at her feet, motionless. Dr. Z looks up at the surface and beckons again, then she grabs the demic by one wrist and pulls her farther into the cave, vanishing.

Vespa nods at Jonah and together they back up several feet to get a running start. They charge ahead, palms flat, heads down, but just as they are about to leap, the giant geyser roars and explodes upward, sending a building-sized pillar of scalding water into the air. Jonah and Vespa scream and separate, both looking for any kind of shelter as the water rains in sheets. Jonah falls onto his stomach and rolls onto the lip of another geyser, only to crawl out of the way just as it activates. He gets up and jogs along the perimeter of the hole that Dr. Z jumped into, waiting for the column to collapse. He spots Vespa doing the same thing on the opposite side. Finally, the geyser ends; without hesitating, Jonah and Vespa run right at it. As

Jonah leaps down into the darkness, he hears Paul shout somewhere in the distance.

The top of his foot hits the ledge of the cave and Jonah falls onto his stomach. He opens his eyes just as Vespa's feet land inches from his face, spraying his cheeks with hot mud.

"Get up," she says, "Hurry. Before this thing blows again."

Jonah stands and looks upward just as Paul comes flying into view. Griffin is less than a second behind, both cadets waving their arms at their sides like helicopter propellers. They land on their feet, right next to Vespa.

"Holy shit," Griffin says. "You assholes see that? I was like Superman or something."

Paul grabs Jonah and Vespa by the arms and yanks them farther into the cave that leads to a tunnel. "Come on, before they get any—"

The cavern begins to rumble violently and a column of steam flies past them and up and out of the hole. A shadow appears in the steam, leaping right for them, and Jonah sees it's a Module Eight boy no older than ten. The geyser erupts and sends a wall of water skyward, shooting the boy straight up and out of sight. If he isn't killed by the scalding water, Jonah knows the fall will surely do it.

"Come on!" Paul shouts.

The four cadets sprint into the cave while water pools at their feet and rushes past them as they descend farther into the tunnel. It's almost completely dark, save for brief patches of sunlight that must come from other geyser holes above them. The ground levels out, and they pick up speed, but soon they come to a circular room with several tunnel openings. It's damp and hot and dark; no one knows where to go next. To make matters worse, dozens of feet echo behind him. The Module Eight kids are close behind.

"Dr. Z!" Jonah shouts. "Where are you?"

The cadets see a light flicker inside a tunnel on their right, and they run down it. The flickering light gets brighter and brighter, but when they round a corner, the light disappears, leaving them in complete darkness.

"Shit. Now what?" Vespa whispers.

"No one has a light?" Paul asks. "Nothing? A flashlight?"

"Wait, I have this. I have a sheaf that has a little bit of juice left," Griffin says. A second later, a rectangle of dim light glows in Griffin's hands, illuminating several feet in every direction. Jonah stands in front of the Third Year, staring through the back of the transparent sheaf, trying to read what's on its screen, but it's backwards.

"This way," Paul says, pointing them to the left.

Griffin leads the way, running down the tunnel while Jonah continues to try to read the screen of the sheaf. Just as daylight appears at the end of the tunnel, Jonah stops in his tracks. He finally reads what it says: "Welcome, Jonah."

"Wait. Where did you get that? Where is that sheaf from?" Jonah asks.

"Don't stop, Firstie! Let's go!" Vespa yells.

"Griffin?" Jonah asks. "Did you find that on Achilles?"

"Found it the last day we were there, yeah."

Jonah runs after them. "Look at the name on it; that's mine. That's my sheaf. I was looking everywhere for that. It's—"

Paul twists around, jogging backward. "Who cares, Jonah? It's our flashlight right now."

The thought of seeing the photo of his parents again instantly gives him another wind, so Jonah sprints ahead until he's right next to Griffin. He can't take his eyes off his sheaf; the last time he saw it, the *Mayflower 2* was grinding against the surface of Achilles, and his module was breaking apart, sending kids and adults and debris everywhere. He's not going to lose it again.

The end of the tunnel gets closer and closer, the pinprick of light becoming an eight-foot high exit, but just as they are about to run outside, Dr. Z's head pokes out of a small hole carved into the bottom of the wall.

"Follow, follow," she whispers before pulling her head back inside the hole.

"Forget that," Griffin says as he blows right past the hole. He reaches the end of the tunnel and bounces on his feet, waiting for the others to join him. "Let's just go. Let's just keep running. Come on."

Jonah looks from Griffin and his sheaf to the hole where Dr. Z waits inside. He knows he has to follow Dr. Z and fulfill his promise and save Brooklyn, but he doesn't want to lose his sheaf. Not again. "I don't care where you go, just give me my sheaf back."

Griffin whips his head back and forth, checking the jungle behind him. "You want it back, then you guys come with me. Let's go somewhere. Let's hide. Those zombie kids will be here any second."

Brooklyn's low moans come from the hole at Jonah's feet. He even thinks he hears her say his name. He turns to Griffin, "Just don't lose it. I need it back."

And with that, Jonah lowers himself to his knees and ducks inside the dark hole. It's musty and warm and the rocky floor beneath him sweats a slimy liquid that sticks to his skin. He hears Vespa and Paul whisper behind him; it sounds as if they decide to leave him and take off with Griffin, but then a second later Vespa pushes on the soles of Jonah's boots and tells him to move faster.

As soon as Jonah enters the space, there's an odd electricity to the air and an overwhelming feeling envelops him like a blanket, telling him he's safe inside. He stands in complete darkness, but he's not afraid. He hears Dr. Z giggling somewhere in the corner of the room, but he doesn't hesitate to seek her. When he gets to what feels like the middle of the space, he holds his arms out at his side—the slime slowly drips off of his clothes and hands—and he allows the electricity that swirls around to consume him. Nothing can hurt him in here, he thinks. Nothing and no one.

Vespa and Paul crawl into the room, their breaths heavy and full of fear.

"Firstie?" Paul asks. "Where'd you go?"

With a hiss, a light comes to life in the corner of the space, and there sits Dr. Z with her legs crossed, holding a long match in her dirty hand. Brooklyn lies flat on her back next to her with eyes flittering. And next to her sits a pink-haired Kip hugging his knees to his chest. He doesn't look older or taller like Vespa said on the ship; in fact, he actually appears younger than he did on Achilles, maybe nine years old. Is he the "old boy" Dr. Z keeps talking about? He's not old, though. He's young. Maybe she means the tall Module Eight boy with the burnt hair.

Dr. Z slowly pulls a small opaque disc out of her pocket and presses it between her fingers, lighting the object up just as the match goes out. Her face is frozen in a sadistic smile, her yellow teeth wet and glistening. She tosses the disc of light into the middle of the room, right at Jonah's feet, and that's when he sees the symbols covering the walls.

"Jesus, not again," Vespa whispers. "Please no one touch the walls. Jonah? I'm talking to you. Just don't. That's not why we're here."

"But that is why I'm here." Jonah rotates on his heels, his eyes crawling over several familiar symbols and new ones he's never seen before: a six-pointed star with a square in its middle, a curved line hovering over it like an umbrella; two ovals stacked on top of each other with three lines intersecting them; a rectangle without its bottom line; an "S" with sharp angles instead of curves; a pair of feathers standing on their quills. There are hundreds of them, maybe thousands, repeating and also appearing at random. And once he spots one of the Cs with the three circles inside, he begins to spot dozens more.

"There you are," Jonah whispers. Before Dr. Z can even ask, Jonah reaches into his pocket and empties it, the keys clanging on the floor. He opens his hand to reveal three white verve seeds to the room. Dr. Z gasps loudly at the sight, and then she begins to rock back and forth in delight, smacking her knees with her palms. "Yes, yes, yes. Talk to them. Talk to *him*."

Jonah holds one of the seeds up to his eye, studying its pebbled surface. He remembers what happened in Tunick's backyard: the visions, the nausea, the undeniable strength and aggression. It took everything in him last time to fight against the onslaught of chemicals attacking his brain. This time, though, he's going to let it all take over. This time, he's not going to fight until he finds some answers.

He puts the seed into his mouth, moving it to his back gums with his tongue. "Someone take Brooklyn away from her before I do this."

Paul springs into action and scoops the demic up into his arms and then sets her up against the wall behind him. Her head rolls from one shoulder to the next, her eyelids throbbing. "And give her the medicine."

Vespa rips open the small sack and pulls out a bag of clear liquid with a long plastic tube wrapped around it. She finds the end of the IV needle still stuck in Brooklyn's arm and attaches the tube. Vespa then stands and holds the medicine above Brooklyn's head.

Jonah sits and takes a deep breath, letting his eyes wander from the symbols on the walls to Paul to Vespa to Brooklyn and then to Dr. Z and Kip. The seed clinks along his back teeth until he gets a small grip on it and shaves off a sliver between his molars. A bitter taste fills his mouth.

"Jonah?"

He whips his head over to look at Brooklyn whose lips slowly smack together. Her eyelids separate to show the two deep blue eyeballs behind them.

"Brooklyn?" he asks.

The demic's chin lowers and a strand of drool falls onto her leg. She coughs twice before snapping her head back up in alarm. Her one arm rises slowly from the floor and she points a shaking finger in Dr. Z's direction. "Don't trust her. She's going to kill us. She's going to kill all of us. She told me."

Jonah tries to respond, to ask why she would say that, but his head and shoulders are suddenly too heavy. He lies on his side and opens his mouth to speak to his friend, but his tongue simply falls out and touches the slimy ground. He watches in horror as his tongue appears to grow and slither its way toward Brooklyn's ankle, turning black along the way. *The hallucinations are starting*, he tells himself. *That's not real.* Jonah closes his eyes and concentrates, and when he opens them back up his tongue is still in his mouth, rolling the seed back and forth along his teeth.

"You okay, Firstie?" Paul asks, kneeling beside him. Jonah feels his energy before he sees it; a yellow glow suddenly surrounds the cadet like rays coming off of a sun. He's the hero, Jonah thinks. He's the one. Paul puts his hand on Jonah's wrist. "I think you should spit that shit out. We have Brooklyn. Let's just get out of here. Screw all this."

Vomit shoots up Jonah's throat and explodes out of his mouth, an orange liquid that fills the room with a horrible stench. Vespa shrieks over Dr. Z's growing laughter while Paul jumps to his feet and flattens his back against the wall. Jonah watches the seed escape his lips with the next wave of vomit, floating in his sickness, and he quickly reaches out and shoves it back into his mouth.

Dr. Z crawls up to his face, indifferent to his vomit. "Don't be afraid. You have been chosen. You will save us all."

"But what if it's Paul? What if he's the hero?" he whispers as thick saliva fills his mouth. His brain begins to crackle as if someone has shoved a hundred crystal orange wrappers into his ears with an electric fork, and the noise is enough for him to sit straight up and bang the palms of his hands against his temples. His sight comes and goes. One second he sees a terrified Vespa standing over Brooklyn, administering the medicine, and the next second he's alone in the room with nothing but the symbols on the wall, which glow green and crawl over each other like ants swarming a meal.

The crinkling gets louder and louder. It's as if he's underwater. As if he's gone too deep. Jonah springs to his feet to swim to the surface in his mind and then Dr. Z's voice is suddenly in his ear and he turns his head to get away from her and his eyes begin to follow random symbols along the walls, which speed up and overlap, blurring into a mess of lines and curves. He hears Paul say something, and an invisible hand falls onto his shoulder, but Jonah bats it away. He takes a deep breath and bites off another slice of the seed and sucks on it as hard as he can until his mind goes blank and the crinkling noises stop. Jonah opens his hands out in front of him and they glow a brilliant, blinding white, as if he's holding two of the brightest stars in the Silver Foot Galaxy. The stars begin to melt; the light drips from his hands like water and splash onto the ground, covering every inch of the floor before creeping up the walls. Within seconds, Jonah stands alone in a bright white room. The only colors are the blurred green symbols that change speeds along the walls.

"Vespa?" he asks in a voice that seems to come from behind him. "I'm alone. I'm all alone."

He hears Vespa answer him but can't make out her words. Just the thought of her being nearby gives him enough strength to stay on this journey. Jonah sucks on the seed and clenches his fists, waiting for what's next.

A burst of purple shoots out of his chest and explodes against the wall, turning into a thick cloud of smoke. A man's angry face appears. It's the same face from Tunick's cave when Jonah made his escape. Back then, this face looked wise and familiar. Now, the face appears to be furious, ordering Jonah to help him. Jonah has done something wrong, he thinks. He's in trouble. He shakes his head violently and pounds his fists against his chest and closes his eyes, and when he reopens them, he's back in the dark cave with the others. There's Vespa and Brooklyn. There's Paul pacing back and forth, pointing his finger at Dr. Z who claps and bounces in place. Paul notices Jonah looking at him and yells his name. Jonah blinks, and instantly the room changes and he's looking at the purple smoke face in the white room again. A different man than before steps out of the cloud and offers his smoky palm to Jonah. It's his father. His father is here. Jonah reaches for his father's hand, but before he can touch him, the man changes shape, widening at the shoulders, stretching like clay. His father's head splits down the middle until it's two different heads with giant beaks that move away from each other along growing shoulders. Soon, Jonah stands before two separate beings connected at the hip. Purples change to yellows until Jonah stands before one of the conjoined twin aliens he saw after escaping the village.

Both of its faces remain blank. They have no eyes. No ears, no noses. Just the large, beak-like mouths sticking out of the bottom of their yellow heads. The left alien points a long, thin appendage at the ceiling. When Jonah looks up, he sees a dozen of the glowing green symbols crash together and then spread out like constellations, dimming and brightening in a white sky. The symbols flip forward and backward and then spin so fast that they're completely indecipherable. Letters then begin to float off of the blurry symbols, and Jonah reads: *We are Zion.*

Jonah's eyes begin to water; he can feel tears streaming down his face.

A few of the symbols spin in the other direction until the word "We" turns into "You."

You are Zion.

Jonah takes a deep breath and concentrates just enough to keep his rising panic from taking over. He asks, "What am I supposed to do? What is Zion supposed to do?"

The words above him pulse and then fade away. The whiteness of the room takes over and grows until it's so bright Jonah has to shield his face. He takes another bite of the seed and tastes the bitterness slide down his throat. When he opens his eyes again, he's floating in a blue sky. Wind whips at his clothes and blows into his ears. He looks left and right and sees nothing, but when he looks down, he sees a red and green blob over a gray backdrop. He's flying, he thinks. He can fly. But the blob below gets bigger and bigger, turning into the size of a rover, then into the size of a house; Jonah, he suddenly realizes, is falling. And he's falling fast.

His screams are silent, lost in the sky as he plummets toward a continent that grows and spreads out below him with every second. Jonah starts to make out green rivers and lakes, red mountains and beaches, thousands of acres of trees and grasses. He can see individual waves break toward a line of red cliffs. He's descending so fast that in another ten seconds, he realizes he's going to hit the ground, and so he waves his arms frantically at his sides. Instantly, he shoots forward like an arrow, the wind pulling at his cheeks and flooding his eyes with tears until he hovers over a section of land that looks oddly familiar, but he knows this isn't Earth. The colors are all off. The air even tastes different. *Is this Peleus?* he wonders. *Or is the other side of Achilles?*

Eight huge shadows grow below him at the base of a mountain range; as he floats in a wide circle, he sees that the shadows are sharp and triangular, changing positions as he glides overhead. He's over the pyramids he saw in the telescope. And that means he's near the symbol carved in the mountainside.

• • •

Jonah circles the pyramids for another few seconds before descending again; this time far more slowly and with less panic. His feet point downward, and his arms shoot out at his sides, and as he lowers himself closer and closer to the ground, electricity seems to zip through his body. He feels invincible, like he's part machine, a spacecraft with thrusters and brakes.

When he's just fifty feet above the reddish-orange ground, the beings below shout and gather, pointing with sticks and tools. Jonah can start to make out their upturned faces, which are humanoid with four horizontal eyes, and each has two horns stretching from scalp to chin, encircling a bright gray face that glows in the sunlight. When Jonah's feet finally touch the ground, he lowers his arms to his sides and rotates amongst thousands of them. He's more than three feet taller than the largest being, towering over them like a lone tree in a field of wild grasses.

"Hello," Jonah offers in a voice that sounds static and almost demonic, much like the alien voices that have infiltrated his mind telling him to eat the seeds.

In perfect unison, the thousands of beings shout "Hello!" back to him in perfect English, but Jonah sees that their gray lips keep moving as if they are still talking, and their horns pulse with different colors. They're not speaking in English, they're not greeting him back, but it's what he hears in his mind.

"I am Zion," Jonah finds himself saying as he takes a step forward with his palms up, showing he means no harm. He then slowly walks through the herd of beings, allowing them to safely shuffle out of his way as he moves through. A sense of calm envelops Jonah, and every step is taken with confidence, as if he knows exactly what he's doing here and knows exactly where he's going. The pyramids loom like giants in front of him, far taller than those he's read about on Earth. And as he walks between them, he sees the enormous symbol dug into the mountain beyond: the "C" with three circles inside.

Jonah turns his head to look at a pyramid on his left, and he can see thousands of symbols carved into its rocky sides, many of which are the same ones from Achilles and Thetis, while others are new and difficult to make out. He walks toward the pyramid and right through a door cut into its base. Shouts of "Hello!" follow him as he ducks inside. But when he walks through the doorway, he's somehow transported onto the mountainside, right into the middle of the symbol of the "C" with the three circles inside. He looks up into the sky and loses his breath: A constellation of stars forms the exact same "C" shape overhead. And inside this massive, packed constellation are three objects that Jonah instantly knows as the planet Thetis, and its moons Achilles and Peleus.

There's a flash of light behind Jonah's eyes, and he falls to his knees. It feels like his brain physically expands against his skull. The alien voices return to his ears: *Destroy them!*

Through the pain, Jonah squints up at the constellation and then down in the valley where the gray beings calmly wander back and forth as if Jonah hadn't just descended from the sky.

The voices in his head continues: *Destroy them, so you will not be destroyed. Destroy them, so we will not be destroyed. Together, we are Zion. You are Zion.*

Jonah tastes the verve seed in his mouth, feels it scraping along his teeth. Without thinking, he bites off another piece and his chest swells with newfound energy. His mind begins to focus despite the symbols crashing inside it, and when he blinks, he's transported into a room with three slanted walls and one small window that's waist-high. He gets down on his knees and looks out the window, realizing he's inside the tip of one of the pyramids.

Frightened, he crawls away from the window and stands up. Carvings line the walls, showing a series of scenes lined up like the panels of a comic book. A tall human-like figure walks through a jungle in one box, and in the next the figure stands on a raft floating in the sea while creatures attack from below. The next panel shows the figure sliding down a slanted wall. In the next, the figure stands in a circle. Jonah recognizes these scenes; they are pictures of what he went through on Achilles. Panel after panel, Jonah sees himself running on a reef, wrestling with another figure, jumping over the fire in Tunick's cave. He battles the snouts and pushes Everett into the portal and stands at the bottom of the canyon, watching the spacecraft lift off.

Jonah twists around to look at the wall behind him, his breath echoing in the room, and he sees images of himself on Thetis: lying in a bed, finding Paul in a cave while surrounded by the mimics, running in the village, standing over Everett in the broken sphere, looking up into the telescope, running through the geyser field.

The third wall stands dark and blank, smooth like silk. But a second later, a thin band of white light breaks through the stone, shooting bits of rock into Jonah's chest. The light moves left and right, carving a new picture with Jonah in it: He descends from the sky in a spacecraft. Another image appears with Jonah standing over the gray beings as they raise their hands to him in worship. More and more images explode out of the wall, showing Jonah in a cage, sliding down a tunnel, running over the surface of a sea. And then Jonah sees a picture of a large circle—it almost looks like Earth, is it Earth?—cut in half and exploding. As soon as the circle explodes, Jonah feels a sick feeling in his gut and falls to his knees. It *is* Earth. Or, it was.

But then the exploding image of the Earth moves in reverse, the pieces of the planet coming back together until it's whole again and slowly rotating. The image quickly disappears, replaced by an image of Jonah standing in a slender room with his long arms stretched out wide at his sides, touching small symbols on opposite walls at the same time. Thick arrows point to his stretched arms, glowing brighter than anything else on the wall, forcing him to close his eyes. And when he reopens them, he stands before one of the yellow alien ghosts. The creature charges at Jonah, sandwiching him between its left and right bodies, squeezing him until his ears pop and his bones crunch. The two heads begin to speak rapidly in his ears, but he can't make out what they say, and he focuses so hard on trying to hear them, that he begins to cry and begs them to speak up. To slow down. To let him go and just say what they want to say.

Jonah's cheeks squeeze together, and he hears Vespa saying his name, her voice mixing with the aliens'. He blinks and suddenly finds her holding his face in her hands, her lips opening and closing silently, panic in her eyes. He shifts his gaze to Brooklyn sitting against the wall with her head resting on her knees and Kip staring at him with cold eyes. And then there's Paul pointing his finger over Jonah's shoulder, barking orders at someone he can't see. In a daze, Jonah pulls his head away from Vespa and twists around to see the Module Eight kids standing silently in front of the hole with their heads down. Dr. Z buzzes around them, laughing.

Jonah continues to hear the whispers of the aliens in his ears, coming from somewhere directly overhead. He looks up and raises his hands and says, "Just tell me. Just tell me what you want."

The whispers get louder and he can almost understand what they say, but then Vespa grabs one of his wrists and twists him back around, breaking him from his concentration. In anger, he wrests his arm away. And before he can stop himself, he shoves Vespa with all his strength. She flies backward into the wall and then crumples to the floor. Jonah doesn't feel any guilt as he watches Paul kneel down next to her; all he cares about is finishing his vision and hearing what the alien ghosts want from him. He moves the seed between his molars and crunches down, sending a bolt of lightning through his body as the seed completely disintegrates.

Jonah opens his arms and feels his muscles pulse with the newfound strength. His skin tightens. His neck thickens. He feels taller, wider, more focused. He feels like he could punch a hole right through the stone walls surrounding him. Paul shouts and then shoves Jonah in the shoulders, but he doesn't even move. Next, he punches him in the gut. Jonah feels nothing but a tap. When Paul hits him in the face, Jonah simply laughs at him. He spits a huge gob of liquid over his shoulder and then punches back, hitting the Fourth Year square in the jaw. Paul falls flat on his back and writhes in pain.

The doctor appears in his face, her yellow smile widening as she stares into his eyes. "You become their God and you destroy them," she whispers. She reaches her hand into his pocket and takes the remaining two verve seeds. She takes a huge bite, the crunch echoing even in his skull. And then, in a monotone voice that sends a shiver down his spine, she says, "Follow us *or we keep your fingers*."

"Yes, yes. Of course, of course," Jonah hears himself say. He looks up at the ceiling and mumbles, "Tell me, tell me, tell me."

Jonah swivels on his heels, and in unison, the Module Eight kids raise their heads and smile, the tallest boy with the burnt long hair smiling the biggest. The youngest girl steps forward and says, "We will show you now. We will show you how to get there."

One by one, the Module Eight kids duck back through the hole in the bottom of the wall. Someone yanks on his shoulders, but he simply shrugs them off. He follows the last of the kids through the hole just as a new surge of verve blasts through his veins. He's never felt so much energy; he sprints to the nearest wall and runs up its side until flipping himself over, landing in a crouch.

One by one, the Module Eight kids try the same move, running up the stone wall and flipping over. Some land on their faces while others complete the acrobatic move with ease. The last kid to try it, the tall boy, runs past Jonah in a blur, holding his left arm out straight and hitting Jonah in the back of the head before running farther up the wall than anyone, flipping down to the ground with grace and ease.

"Good, good," Jonah says. His skin buzzes with excitement while his brain continues to battle itself and the verve. He stretches his neck from side to side and walks out of the tunnel, the sun hitting his face, giving him even more energy. The Module Eights surround Jonah on all sides, absorbing him in their tight huddle, and when Jonah takes his first steps, they walk in perfect unison. Dr. Z emerges and marches past them, walking into the forest spread out before them.

"Jonah!"

He turns to see Vespa dragging a semi-conscious Brooklyn behind her by her collar. Paul then appears, holding his red cheek with his hand.

The Module Eights huddle around Jonah even tighter, not allowing him to move toward his friends. A young boy with dry blood on his shirt takes a few steps away from the huddle and points at Vespa.

"Leave us, or we will kill you. He is ours now."

"If you motherfuckers don't get away from him right now," Paul says, "I'm going to rip your arms off and shove them up your asses. And don't think I don't remember you, kid. I beat the shit out of you at the black rock. That blood on your shirt is from me."

The boy says nothing and rejoins the huddle. Jonah has a moment of clarity and wants to reach an arm out for his friends; he needs them to come along, to take care of him once the verve wears off. In fact, he needs them to help him now, *before* it wears off in case he is about to do anything terrible. But the children around him are too close and too strong; he can't even lift his arms.

As Vespa heaves Brooklyn onto her shoulders, Paul charges ahead and asks, "Firstie? What did you see in there? What did you learn? Can we stop all this now?"

Jonah opens his mouth to tell Paul about the planet he just visited and its gray people and the "C" symbol both carved into the side of the mountain and showing up majestically in the stars above the planet, how he was sent there to either help or destroy them—he's still not sure—but a strong wave of verve sweeps over his body, closing his throat and clogging his ears. Shards of purple and blue lights appear on his chest, and they lift off into the air and swirl above him like leaves caught in the wind. He shakes his head and they're gone, but a second later, his mind loses focus again and the lights reappear, twisting off into the sky until fading into nothing. White rays of light emerge from his chest, shooting forward and around a tree, disappearing into the forest. He remembers this from Achilles; he knows he's supposed to follow the light.

"Jonah?" Vespa tries. "Listen to me. We have Brooklyn now, so let's just go. You don't need to be with these people. Let's figure out a way to get all the medicine for you and her and then we'll—"

A blue laser blasts over Jonah's head, crashing into a twisted gray trunk of a nearby tree, sending a swarm of white bugs in every direction. Jonah and the Module Eights turn their heads in unison, and there, on the peak of a nearby hill, stands Mirker with a smoking LZR-rifle in his arm. The man takes aim at Jonah and fires again, hitting the boy with the bloodstain instead, blowing a hole right through his chest. When the boy falls to the ground, the other kids simply close up the gap, further protecting Jonah in the middle. They start to slowly move toward the trees.

"What are you doing? Run!" Vespa shouts.

Mirker fires again, missing the group by inches, sending a cloud of debris into the air. Jonah's head buzzes, and the white light reappears on his chest, speeding off into the forest.

Mirker shoots another kid in the huddle and the boy spins away in a bloody mess. There are only nine of them left; they're getting picked off too easily, incapable of putting up a fight. They have just one mission, Jonah thinks, and that's to protect him. But they're not doing a good enough job. With fewer kids around him, Jonah is able to raise his arms and push through the huddle and then he's running. He follows the white arrow rising out of his chest, looking over his shoulder only to see the Module Eights jog after him like a flock of sheep. And there, up on the hill, behind Mirker and raising a large rock over her head, is Dr. Z. She slams it down on his shoulders, sending the man to his knees and his rifle bouncing along the rocks. Preventing him from waiting to see if Dr. Z will finish what she's started, another arrow of light shoots out from Jonah's chest, directing him left and then right and down a hill. Vespa's voice fades into the background, overtaken by a nearby geyser.

Jonah keeps following the arrows, the Module Eights right on his heels, until he gets to a cliff. Waterfalls appear on both sides of him, descending the mountainside to land in small pools that quickly cascade into more waterfalls that fall to another level, and it goes on like this for a thousand feet, one waterfall crashing into another waterfall until joining a large, raging river running across the valley far below with alien birds circling above it. Halfway down the mountain, Jonah sees the pig-faced creatures from the day before jumping in the pools and going over the side.

The cadet turns to face the fast-approaching huddle of Module Eights, waiting for the verve to send another arrow of light, but none come. He clears his mind and closes his eyes, willing the light to appear, but when he opens his eyes, he only finds that the kids have come closer.

"Where do we go now?" Jonah asks through the fog overtaking his brain. He doesn't know if he's directing the question to the sky or to the kids before him, or if he's asking a race of alien ghosts who might be circling around him.

The small girl with a space between her teeth breaks from the group and walks right past him. She enters the pool of water on his left without pausing, walking in up to her shoulders. The current sweeps her forward, to the lip of the falls where she rotates once before going over the edge.

Jonah watches the girl fall headfirst to the next level, splashing into a lima bean–shaped pool that churns with greasy suds. She floats to the surface on her stomach and Jonah thinks she's dead, but she flips over onto her back just before going over the edge of the next waterfall. After that, she's out of sight.

"Is that what you want?" Jonah turns to asks the others. They're just ten feet away, dead eyes fixed on him. The tall boy pushes forward and bumps Jonah with his chest, shoving him toward the water.

"Don't do that," Jonah warns him.

The boy bumps him again, causing Jonah to take another step back. Another few inches and he'll be in the water. As Jonah begins to panic, neon green lights rise from his shoulders and arms, blurring into the humid air. He clenches his fists and rolls his neck, encouraging the verve to take over every muscle. In a few seconds, his arms feel like steel beams, his legs like tree trunks. The tall boy goes for the final push to send the cadet into the water, but Jonah reaches up and snatches the boy's thick wrist. He yanks down and the boy doubles over, then Jonah sends his knee rocketing into his chest.

The sound of the boy's sternum breaking is sickening; the bone plate cracks so loudly that Jonah can hear it over the dozens of waterfalls crashing below. Normally, Jonah would back away after delivering a blow like this, allowing the person to recover or retreat, second guessing his role in yet another fight. But the verve surges through him; anger blends with adrenaline, and before Jonah has a moment to think, he finds his fist landing squarely on the boy's jaw. The boy stumbles forward with blood spurting from his mouth, then he tips forward, plunging into the water like a rock.

Jonah realizes he can't control the verve like he did on Achilles; instead of his compassion breaking through and saving the boy, he flexes his arms at his sides and lets out a wild roar. He wheels around to pick his next victim from the huddle of kids but standing next to them is Dr. Z. Blood stains her arms and hands, her shoulders heave. She licks her lips in anticipation.

"Enter the exit," she says, pointing to the water behind Jonah. "And then you will exit the entrance. We will be waiting for you. Door four, Zion. Door four."

Jonah steps forward instead of backward. He did what she asked; he ate the verve. He saw the visions. He heard the voices. He just needs the time to decipher them. Now, though, he does what *he* wants. And what he wants now, what he feels in his gut and possessed mind, is to destroy this woman.

Dr. Z bites down on a seed and spits a long strand of white saliva down the front of her jumpsuit, and then she lowers her head and charges. The Module Eights take her lead and run right after her.

Jonah lowers himself to one knee and clenches his fists. He wants this fight. He's been waiting for this fight. Dr. Z reaches him and swings, but he explodes from his knee and tackles her around the waist. They crash through the trailing huddle of kids like a bowling ball, rolling over a small boy who gets his arm smashed against a rock. Jonah hears his arm break, but his focus is entirely on Dr. Z, who quickly gets to her feet.

A girl jumps on Jonah's back and scrambles up to his shoulders where she bites the top of his head. Jonah reaches up and he immediately reaches over his shoulders and yanks her off by her neck. He holds the girl up to his face and roars, covering her freckled face with his spit. He wants to punish her. He wants to end her. He plants his feet to launch her over the cliff, but his mind pops and clears for a split second. *She's just a kid. She doesn't know what she's doing. She's just a kid, just a kid, just a kid.* Before the verve can regain control, Jonah places the girl back on the ground and shoves her in the opposite direction.

Two more of the Module Eights jump on him, but Jonah spins around and around until they lose their grip and bounce away. That's when Dr. Z pounces; she gets his neck in her grip and slams her heel down onto Jonah's foot, buckling him to his knees. The woman squeezes with all her might, the verve making her ten times stronger than a normal person. Jonah yanks on her wrists, gasping for air, but she has leverage and pushes him flat on the ground. Dr. Z then scrambles onto his chest and sits there, choking Jonah with a smile on her face while several Module Eight kids stand expressionless around him. They're allowing her to do this. He thought he had a mission to carry out for them, but maybe the entrance through the exit—what they've been asking for—is Jonah's death.

CHAPTER TWELVE

Jonah tries to roll onto his side, but Dr. Z only squeezes harder, laughs louder. Her eyes roll into the back of her head as white drool drips from her lips and into his left eye and ear, rolling down into his collar. The huddle of Module Eights above him gets tighter, their temples touching each other's as they wait for Jonah to either die or finally give in and join them. Red and black dots begin to clog his vision, and Jonah knows it's not the verve, but the last thing he's going to see.

Dr. Z's body suddenly shifts on top of him, and her fingernails scrape along Jonah's throat, clawing to stay there. Jonah takes a huge gasp of air. His vision returns just in time to see Griffin's foot connect with Dr. Z's stomach, loosening her grip. The cadet takes a giant step back, and with a Module Eight girl's arms wrapped around his waist trying to yank him away, he kicks with all his might, knocking Dr. Z off Jonah.

Jonah flips onto his stomach and crawls away to catch his breath. A small fist quickly tangles itself in Jonah's hair and yanks back violently, but he's able to swat it away and get to his feet.

"Jonah," Griffin wheezes.

Jonah looks back to see Griffin struggling in Dr. Z's arms near the edge of the cliff. She turns to stare Jonah in the eye as she bites down on a seed. She then drives her fist into Griffin's side, doubling the boy over, knocking something shiny from Griffin's pocket. Jonah couldn't mistake it: his sheaf.

Dr. Z tosses Griffin over her hip, sending the Third Year rolling toward the cliff. The boy goes over the edge, only to save himself by sticking his hand into a crack. "Jonah! Help!"

Jonah sprints toward the cadet, but three Module Eight kids jump on top of him, slowing his sprint to a staggered walk. Dr. Z watches with a snarling smile as she backs up a few steps and places her foot on Griffin's hand.

"Dr. Z!" Jonah pleads. "Please stop. You're a doctor. You're supposed to be helping us. This isn't you! You aren't this! Get the voices out of your head and get back to being Dr. Zarembo from Earth. You are not the verve! You're our friend!"

Something sparks behind Dr. Z's eyes at his plea. She shakes her head and stands up straight, confused for a moment, as if she doesn't know where she is. Griffin struggles to hold onto the cliff below her feet, and when she looks down to see him, she gasps as if surprised. *It's working*, Jonah thinks, *he's getting through to her*.

Dr. Z watches Jonah stagger toward her with the Module Eights hanging on for dear life, and then she looks back at Griffin who is beginning to climb back to the ledge. He reaches a bloody hand up for the doctor to take, whispering, "Please."

She reaches down and takes the cadet's hand, and as she leans over, a long strand of white drool drops from her lips. Instinctively, Dr. Z sucks it back up into her mouth and cocks her head back. Her shoulders shudder, and she falls to her knees with closed eyes, still holding Griffin's hand.

"Hold on!" Jonah shouts.

He's just a few feet away from Griffin when Dr. Z opens her eyes. She looks over at Jonah, and her cracked blue lips form a devilish smile, sending shivers down Jonah's spine.

"No!" Jonah yells. "Don't!"

Dr. Z lets go. Griffin falls, his eyes as wide as the moons orbiting above. Jonah shrugs off the kids from his back and dives to the edge and reaches out, but his hand merely grazes the lion shaved into the side of the boy's head. The cadet plummets without a word or movement, a bird killed in flight. Jonah watches Griffin fall, fall, fall, until the boy is out of sight. There are no waterfalls directly below him. No pools to catch him. Only rocks.

Jonah sits back on his heels in shock. His hand touches the rolled up sheaf on the ground, and he shoves it into his pocket without thinking. He stands on wobbly feet and stares at Dr. Z, amazed that she is this far gone, this far out of her mind.

A pair of kids grab each of Jonah's arms, pulling them behind his back. Dr. Z looks down at her hands as they clench into fists then reaches into her pocket and pulls out two long knives. Jonah recognizes them immediately as Vespa's, dropped below the telescope. She must have fought for them. And won.

Jonah backpedals toward the water, dragging the four kids with him. He tries to wrench his arms free, but their grips are too strong. Dr. Z follows closely with a knife pointed right at his chest. "We keep the fingers."

Jonah thinks about how Sean had him cornered in the canyon on Achilles, how the barrel of his rifle lit up just inches away from his chest. And then just before Sean pulled the trigger, a laser blasted through his arm. Vespa's laser. Jonah scans the forest for Vespa and Paul, hoping they'll burst through the trees with Mirker's gun and find an open shot. But they're not there. They're not coming. This time, he has to save himself. He bends his knees and leans forward, bringing himself just inches from Dr. Z's blade, but then he swings his arms forward at the same time he leans back, slamming the four kids holding onto his wrists together in front of him. The knife pierces one of the boy's sides and goes all the way in. Blood instantly spills out of his mouth as he falls to his knees. The boy looks up at Dr. Z to say something, but Jonah doesn't stick around to hear it. He whips his arms like ropes and escapes the other's grips, and then he turns around and jumps into the water.

"No!" Dr. Z shouts. "We keep the fingers!"

The warm water rises to Jonah's chest as he swiftly pushes his feet along the slimy pool floor in long strides. Dr. Z jumps in right after him, her one knife swinging back and forth over her head as she gives chase. The Module Eight kids jump in, too. The water rises over their heads, but they move quickly, slogging along the floor toward Jonah and the doctor.

Jonah dives underwater, swimming as fast as he can. Almost immediately, though, a strong current shoves him several feet off his path. He rises to the surface to catch his breath, but as soon as he does, another current hits him, pushing him over the edge and into the waterfall.

He goes over headfirst, screaming, waving his arms, and it feels like an eternity before he crashes into the next pool. The falls above shove him deep underwater until he's pinned to the floor. Jonah pulls himself along by his hands until he's able to breach the surface. But as soon as he does, he's swept up by another current and thrown over the edge.

Every ten seconds, Jonah falls into a new pool only to be swept up and thrown over again. He loses his bearings, concentrating solely on getting a breath of air when it's possible. A few times underwater, some last dregs of the verve in his blood surges through his body, giving him just enough energy to survive the next crashing falls and the next pool of currents that scrape him along the rocks. He bounces into a few warm, furry objects, opening his eyes to find the pig-faced creatures bobbing all around him.

After several more falls, Jonah finds himself hugging two of the small creatures to his chest, using them to stay above water. He's completely drained of energy, floating aimlessly in a bubbling, hot pool. Jonah lets go of one of the animals and watches it rotate lifelessly in the water, its small face smashed and oozing green blood. With his trembling free arm, Jonah swims to the side of the pool and hoists himself onto a rock and coughs and coughs and coughs.

He lets go of the other animal, and it quickly jumps back in the water and splashes around. Jonah flips onto his back and squints upward. All he can see are hundreds of waterfalls spilling down the side of the cliff. No Dr. Z. No Module Eight kids. No Vespa or Paul or Brooklyn. A wave of panic suddenly hits him as he thinks about Griffin falling to his death. The boy saved Jonah's life up there on the ledge. And for that, Jonah will be forever grateful.

Jonah pulls himself out of the water and hugs his legs to his heaving chest. He looks for a path back up the cliff, or a cave entrance behind the falls, but to his dismay, the only place to go is down; two more falls crash below him and empty into the river running through the valley. Birds circle the mouth of the river before, one by one, they dive into the water and never resurface. A slanted slab of rock borders the river's left side, and on the right side, tall yellow grasses wave in the wind for a half mile.

I can hide in the field, Jonah thinks, *and come up with a plan there.* Jonah takes a deep breath and then slowly reenters the hot pool. He raises his legs and lets the water push him toward the edge, then over he goes. He does the same thing in the next, hotter pool, going with the flow instead of fighting it.

Jonah goes over the last waterfall, a twenty-foot drop, and enters the river feet first. He bobs in the current for a moment with his head above water, trying to catch his bearings while the birds circle above him. Several of them dive into the river just in front of his face and he finally gets a good look at them—they're no bigger than his feet, shiny with short, waxy wings and the curly heads of sea horses. When the birds don't resurface from their dive, Jonah panics and swims frantically downstream, worried they will attack him underwater at any second. Suddenly, an incredibly strong current pulls him downward as if anchors are tied to his ankles. Jonah swings his arms over his head, searching for anything to grab, but the pull is too strong, and he looks down just in time to see the long crack on the riverbed sucking everything down into it. His fingers scrape along the warm rocks as he is pulled through.

Jonah finds himself plunging down another waterfall, a gigantic one that empties into a lake as big as several football fields. Jonah's diving training from the academy kicks in at the very last moment, and he puts his hands over his head and straightens his leg just before hitting the surface. As soon as he enters the steaming lake, Jonah swims to the surface with an enormous gasp, but the air is musty and sulfurous.

The light is faint, but there's enough of it for Jonah to see the rocky edges of the lake. He swims with all his remaining energy, terrified that the water is swarming with the birds or other hungry creatures just below the surface, circling him, just waiting for the moment to strike. He pulls himself out of the water and collapses on his stomach. He feels the sheaf in his pocket digging into his outer thigh, relieved that it's still there.

Jonah sits up and watches the waterfall pound the lake, amazed he survived the fifty-foot drop. He sees the long crack in the ceiling he slipped through, and he also sees that the birds that dove into the river didn't disappear; they are down here now, circling the middle of the falls in a massive flock before zooming off to the far end of this enormous, underground chamber. Some of the birds break from the flock, though, rocketing straight up into the dull yellow ceiling where they cry and wiggle and push through before disappearing completely. It takes Jonah a moment to realize that they are actually pushing into the long, yellow grasses of the field on the right side of the river above. He also realizes that the field of yellow grasses isn't a field at all, but rather a thick canopy created by the long, spanning branches of the thousands of charcoal-colored trees growing all around him.

Getting to his feet takes a full minute, but eventually Jonah makes his way to one of the trees and leans against it. Its trunk is soft and mushy, and at the touch of Jonah's shoulder, the bark sheds to the ground in a watery mess.

As more and more birds pass through the chamber overhead with a cacophony of cries, Jonah pulls his sheaf out of his pocket and takes a deep breath. Slowly, he unrolls the device in front of his face, studying it for cracks or broken edges, and then gives it a slight nod. Instantly, the sheaf curls inwards and expands, doubling its size to sixteen inches. The date and time float in front of his face in three dimensional figures: 19 OCT 2221, 0108 GMT.

It's been nine days since crashing on Achilles, nine days since he's held this device in his hands. The numbers fade and disappear, instantly replaced with text scrolling at the bottom: "WELCOME BACK, JONAH. WOULD YOU LIKE ME TO SCAN YOU?"

"No," Jonah says, hanging his head. He doesn't need to be analyzed right now, to know when the last time he slept was or how his brain is functioning. He doesn't need to know if he has a cold or abnormal blood pressure. He doesn't need to know if he's in any more trouble than he already is. And most of all, he doesn't need to know right now, at this moment, if his eye disease is back.

Jonah quickly checks the battery and sees that Griffin must have charged it at some point because there's fifty-one percent left. What a relief. And then, without waiting another second, Jonah drags a tiny icon from the desktop to the center of the screen and nods again. The icon expands into a photograph, and then there is his father smiling at the camera, looking much different than he did in Jonah's twisted, verve-induced vision just an hour ago. In the photo, he leans over Jonah's exhausted mother in her hospital bed. Both of their eyes look so bright and white and happy. His mother holds baby Jonah to her chest. They all look so fresh, yet so tired. They all look ready to start their new life together as a family.

Tears fill Jonah's eyes, blurring his vision. He misses his parents so much. He's never even spoken a word to them, but he misses them incredibly. Jonah pulls the sheaf up to his face and hugs it there. The warmth of the device feels good. Knowing his mother and father are touching him, in some way, feels even better.

"I love you," he whispers, pulling the sheaf back. He stares at the photo for another few seconds before removing it from the screen. Five percentage points have already disappeared from the battery. At this rate, he'll eat up all the power in ten minutes. Knowing its light will come in handy soon, Jonah rolls the sheaf back up and shoves it into his pocket. He sits down and stares at the birds swirling overhead as they decide to either further explore the cavern or return through the canopy.

That's it, Jonah thinks. *I can get out of here by climbing through the leaves.* He gets to his feet and looks up at the charcoal-black trees that loom over him. He won't be able to wrap his arms around them; their trunks are thicker than most of the yurts back at the village. And because their bark is so mushy and slides right off, he can't just scale them. He's going to have to find another way up to the canopy, or simply another path out.

The humidity sticks to Jonah with every step as he walks back and forth along the embankment of the underground lake. To his left, down a slight decline, hundreds of crystal clusters reflect sunlight into the space, sending thousands of rainbows in every direction. A tall rock wall stands beyond the crystals with water streaming down it. Jonah sees it's impossible to climb, and so he runs back the other way, noticing for the first time that a few of the trees along the lake have gashes of their trunks missing, as if some animal tried to scale them for a few seconds and then slid back down to the ground. Whatever tried to climb these trees is large, Jonah thinks. Almost as large as he is. And it must still be in here.

A noise in the water causes Jonah to spin on his heels, and he watches in awe as a jet-black animal with a wide, pebbled head breaches the surface of the lake. It groans and flips onto its back, showing off its long belly covered in what look to be a dozen flower buds that open up to bright red and pink blossoms. The beast is as long as a great white shark or a canoe, and it floats in a quiet circle for a few seconds until several more of the beasts rise out of the water and flip over to reveal their flower-covered stomachs, too. The animals hold onto each other with alligator-like arms, and soon it looks as if there's a small island of beautiful flowers just floating in the lake. In less than ten seconds, a small flock of birds from the waterfall circle the ersatz island before landing to inspect the flowers. In unison, the beasts' belly flowers snap shut and capture the birds; more than twenty of them shriek to be let go, flapping their wings, pecking with their short beaks. But the flowers hold tight, and slowly the beasts' heads bend toward their bellies and out come long white tongues that wrap themselves around one bird at a time, pulling them into their huge mouths. In a matter of minutes, the birds have all been eaten and the beasts have flipped back over and disappeared under the surface. Jonah shudders to think that he was just in that lake with those things. What else is in there?

He jogs along the water's edge, crushing bugs that screech and release a foul odor under foot, and ducks under a pack of jumping orange discs with glowing eyes. After ten minutes, Jonah gets to the end of the space and sees it's just like the opposite side: a steep wall of wet stone. He has no other option but to see what's beyond the trees.

What little light there is dims as Jonah takes his first steps amongst the mushy, black trunks. The ground is almost as soft as the bark of the trees, and he has to march his feet high and keep moving unless he wants to get stuck in place. His shoulder brushes against a thick, spiny stalk of a large plant, and at the touch, the stalk shrinks and shrivels to the ground, no taller than a couple inches. In fact, everything he touches in the forest immediately alters its state: stalks shrink, leaves curl inwards, thick yellow vines drop to the ground and turn to ash, all mixing with the mucky ground that continues to suck on Jonah's shoes. It's as if he's a wizard controlling the area around him, creating a path with a wave of his hand.

The smells are overwhelming, and the farther he pushes into the forest, the thicker the air gets. It isn't five minutes before he finds the back wall of the space. His hopes of getting out shrink like the plants he touches. He takes a deep breath and turns right, moving quickly, his fingertips trailing along the wall's slick surface. He gets to a small clearing covered in short yellow grass, much like the leaves creating the canopy above. Is there another level below this level? If he steps into the clearing, will he fall right through?

He carefully sidesteps the grass, pressing his back into an enormous soggy tree trunk, soaking his clothes. He rounds the tree, marching his feet in and out of the muck, but when he gets to the other side, his feet stop moving. There, half covered in leaves and mud, is a human skeleton.

• • •

Jonah doesn't know if it's one of the rebel kids from a year ago—one of Tunick's friends hooked on verve who maybe got lost and fell in the waterfalls—or if it's a recent deserter from the village, but it wears a half-eaten blue jumpsuit. Above the body, Jonah sees long lines of the bark stripped away. All those marks on the trunks near the lake must be from the person trying to escape. As he watches a fat black bug with red legs crawl up the skeleton's chest and into the nasal cavity, Jonah falls to his knees in despair. If this person—perhaps a highly trained cadet or experienced soldier—couldn't get out of here, how is he supposed to?

Jonah realizes he's sinking into the ground and marches his feet out of the muck. He takes a deep breath, grabs ahold of the torn collar and pulls the body through the forest until reaching the edge of the lake. There, he lets go and falls to his hands and knees, his chest heaving in grief. The only thing that brings his breathing back to almost normal is feeling his sheaf in his pocket. He sits back and pulls the device out, brings up his family photo, and then stares into his dad's eyes until two more battery percentages disappear. And then he turns back to the skeleton and roots through its pockets with shaky hands.

Soon, Jonah finds himself holding a key ring, a small blue handgun that simply sparks instead of firing, and a rolled up mini sheaf that doesn't turn on. He shoves them all into his pockets and stands, only to pace back and forth next to the body for several minutes. Light dwindles in the cavern, yet it's somehow getting warmer and even more humid. The birds drop into the cavern at an alarming pace now, flocking together in swirling tornados, fighting, screaming, darting into the darkness. A large group of the creatures with the fake flowers on their bellies float below in the water, feasting on the birds by the dozens.

Jonah looks down at the skeleton, apologizing for dragging it out into the open like this, near so much noise and carnage, and that's when he notices the thick rectangular shape in a pocket on its right shoulder. He unbuttons the flap of the pocket and pulls out a small pad of waterproof paper. It's covered with scribbling and diagrams and lists, and most of it is crossed out or annotated with frantic notes in both Spanish and English. He closes the pad and turns it over, and that's when he reads the name "Cpt. Julia Tejas" on the back cover. He stands in disbelief; it's the original leader of the Athens colony. Mirker chased her away when he found her putting explosives around the village. And this is where she ended up?

Screams from the birds grow louder, completely filling the cavern, and Jonah looks up to see the flock has expanded into a thick black cloud hovering just over the surface of the lake. The noise is unbearable, and Jonah says a fleeting goodbye to Captain Tejas as he runs toward the clusters of crystals with his hands over his ears. He turns to look back only to catch the birds swarm Captain Tejas's body and completely cover it up. To his horror, they lift her off the ground and slowly fly her up into the canopy. The birds push her into the leaves where she sticks, her left arm dangling below her like a cutoff rescue rope. A second later, the canopy glows with long electrical creatures racing to the captain's body. They light the woman up like a Christmas tree, and a few seconds later, the snakes or insects or whatever they are, wrap her up and pulse as one. The cavern brightens and brightens until a flash of light blasts from the woman's body, sending Jonah running down the hill toward the crystals for cover.

He dives into the clusters, worried the birds are following him, worried they're going to sweep him up and feed him to whatever consumed the captain. But he's all alone, and the ground beneath him is dry and sandy and cool to the touch, unlike anything else in the cavern. All around him, the crystals emit a low hum, radiating the final rainbow shards of sunlight shining through the opaque rocks above. Some of the crystals are as thick as the trees on the other side of the hill, while others are the size of baseball bats, and some smaller formations look like patches of grass just breaking from their seeds. Jonah slowly sets his back against a large crystal and is surprised by how cool it is; it's a nice relief from the sweltering cavern darkening around him. He starts to flip through the small notepad.

Captain Tejas's handwriting is legible and coherent on the first dozen pages, mapping out the village, writing about plants and animals, drawing their pictures with great detail. On one page, there's a sketch of a small bear-like animal with a see-through belly with what looks like another bear inside. "Kangaroo Grizzly?" is written next to it with a smiling face. He flips through more and more drawings and field notes, all the while wondering why she didn't just draw them on her sheaf so it could be shared with everyone in the village and back on Earth.

Halfway through the pad, though, Jonah sees why she didn't want to share her notes. Mirker's name starts popping up. Often. Captain Tejas started to watch Mirker closely, writing on a crinkled piece, "Mirker getting aggressive with others. Spent several minutes berating the purple team. Pushed Lt. Freeman to the ground. Time for him to go. But mutiny?"

Jonah thinks back to his first conversation with Mirker while he lay in the hospital bed, how he said she went crazy right after the kids left with the ship, but these notes are months before that happened.

He flips farther into the notepad until reading, in all capital letters: "MIRKER PLANNING ON GOING TO ZION. MUST STOP HIM BY ANY MEANS NECESSARY. DON'T TRUST KIP ANYMORE."

Mirker wanted to leave for Zion? The planet Jonah saw through the telescope? To Jonah, it seemed like Mirker wanted nothing more than to be the leader here on Thetis. To become its dictator. He wants to leave? Does he want to take others with him, or will they all just stay here and breathe Thetis's poisonous air? And how can she not trust Kip anymore when she never even got a chance to meet him? Kip was on the *Mayflower 2*. Was she in communication with him while he was on the ship?

The last third of the notepad is barely legible, covered in doodles and words scratched out and a few thoughts that go nowhere like: "Achilles moon dark like" and "Food must be tasted for food" and "New gloves that hurt." And then, on the second to last page, are several of the Cs with the three circles inside. They're drawn perfectly with sharp edges and the right proportions. Every time. And then under one of the symbols, written so small that Jonah has to squint and hold the page up against the nearest crystal, he reads: "Jonah Lincoln."

Jonah stares at his name, and then his eyes crawl over the captain's symbols. He flips the page over, looking for more, looking for anything. And then, Jonah sees an indentation in the paper where the ink stopped working. It's a short arrow pointing to Jonah's name, and at its beginning, it says, "Sacrifice."

Jonah shoots to his feet and shoves the pad into his pocket with trembling fingers. Mirker and Tejas had planned to sacrifice him? Did the alien ghosts tell her to do that? But in his vision, the aliens—or whatever he wanted to call them—need him to get to Zion. They didn't seem to want him sacrificed. They appear to want him alive.

There's a noise on the other side of the hill. Jonah ducks behind a large cluster of crystals, ready to run from whatever creature is about to appear with a dozen birds in its mouth, but to his surprise it's not one of the beasts from the lake looking for dessert. He sees the top of someone's head. Seconds later, he sees it's the tall Module Eight boy with the long, uneven hair. He's hunched over, no doubt ruined by Jonah's fists. Next to him walks the small girl with the space between her teeth. They both went over the waterfalls before him. Have they been down here this whole time? They stand at the top of the hill motionless, their eyes and mouths closed. Jonah holds his breath and ducks down even farther, waiting for them to charge toward him screaming. But instead, they slowly reach for each other's hands and then march down toward the crystals together.

He thinks he can get the drop on them, taking at least one of them down. But with what? The commander's gun is useless. But they don't know that. Jonah slips the gun into his hand and continues to move between the crystals, his reflection multiplying a hundredfold. But as he's backing through a grouping, he steps right in the middle of a low-lying cluster, breaking several of the crystals off at the base. The boy and girl turn their heads and open their milky eyes.

They release hands and the girl steps forward. "Enter through the exit. Exit through the entrance."

Jonah whips his head up at the water falling from the crack above. Is that what she means? To go back through the crack in the riverbed that brought him down here?

He aims the gun at her face. "What do you want from me? What the *fuck* do you want me to do? I've done everything they've asked me to."

The boy lurches forward with his cracked sternum and bloody face. "It's my turn now. You will now follow me."

Jonah aims the gun at him. Then her. Then him. Neither flinch. The boy straightens his back with a series of disgusting cracks coming from his chest, raises his arms to his sides and stretches them out wide to touch a cluster of crystals on either side of him; his wingspan is enormous. The only other person he knows with that kind of wingspan is…himself. For the first time, Jonah notices just how similar their bodies are. Jonah has maybe a couple of inches on him, but other than that, their builds are nearly identical.

"Have your turn, I don't care," Jonah says as he begins to backpedal up the hill. "Go ahead and do what everyone wanted me to do. Be their God or whatever. Be sacrificed. Do what the voices say to do. Enter through the exit. Look for door four. Kill the red one. Let them keep your fingers. Do whatever you want because I'm just…I'm just a kid. I'm just a kid, and I just wanted to live here and not be a part of…anything like this."

The boy drops his arms and moves slowly after Jonah, stopping only to bend down and grab two broken crystals from the ground. They're the size of baseball bats and he clenches them hard in his fists. "They will only choose me if you die. So, you have to die."

Jonah reaches the peak of the hill and looks over the steaming lake barely visible in the waning light, trying to decide if he should jump in or not. When he turns back, the boy is just dozen feet away from him, the tips of the crystals dragging through the soft ground creating crooked lines in his wake.

Jonah aims the gun at the boy's broken chest and says, "This is your last chance. Leave me alone."

"You have to die."

The boy raises both crystal cudgels high above his head, their tips dripping black muck, and he strikes them down at Jonah at the same time. Jonah blocks one with his right wrist, but the other strikes him in the side of the neck, sending him to his knees. The boy whips a crystal down at his forehead, but Jonah is able to catch it inches from his temple. The moment his hand wraps around it, Jonah's thoughts and fears and anger disappear, replaced by flashing images of this boy's life: playing baseball in the rain with his sister; blowing out candles on a cake, surrounded by a dozen young faces; a woman pulling back the covers to his bed and shouting for him to get to school; kissing a girl behind a dilapidated house; hugging an older couple who hand him an envelope before walking into a white building; sitting in the dining module on the *Mayflower 2* next to a fast-talking Sean Meebs; and then a vision of the boy's hand reach for a large black rock, touching it right next to a dozen other hands. The images quickly disappear, and Jonah looks up to see the boy struggling to pull the crystal from Jonah's grip. The cadet's other hand forms a shaking fist and he rockets it up into the boy's throat. A distinct crack echoes around them, and the boy falls limply to his knees, his milky eyes rolling back into his skull, and then he tips forward, his face slamming into the wet muck.

The boy slides headfirst toward the lake, stopping just inches from the water, and when Jonah turns around, the girl with the space between her teeth stands right next to him.

"You found what you needed down here," she says. "Now you must exit through the entrance."

"What did I find?" he asks.

"What you needed."

Jonah runs his hands over his pockets, feeling each item for a second before moving to the next one. Is she talking about the gun? The ring of keys? Or is she talking about the small notebook with symbols and gibberish and his name on it? He also feels his sheaf, and for a second he thinks about showing her everything on it, photos from the ship, scenes from Earth, anything to break this spell she's been under for a week.

The girl points up at the crack in the ceiling where the water falls and the birds descend. "Go."

Jonah doesn't wait to hear anything else; he runs down the embankment, stopping at the bottom to check on the boy who still lies motionless with his face inches from the water. Carefully, he reaches for the boy's wrist and checks for a pulse. He's relieved to find a faint heartbeat. He flips the boy on his side so he can breathe, and then with the toes of his boots, Jonah kicks the two crystals out of the boy's hands. Jonah picks them up and wheels around, still unsure how he's going to get into the canopy and beyond. He sees the long marks Captain Tejas left on the tree trunks as she tried to climb them. Perhaps she was led into this cavern with a purpose, too, he thinks. He hopes she wasn't tricked into falling down here just to pass along a ring of keys or notebook to a future Jonah. They could have made that exchange over a friendly lunch in the village.

Jonah walks over to a huge tree and touches its slimy bark, which immediately falls to the ground in a pile of mush. Thinking back to how he was able to scale the fence of the village with Vespa's knives, Jonah raises one of the crystals above his head and plunges it into the exposed wood. It sticks solid. Encouraged, he jumps and plunges the other crystal into the trunk, and it sticks, too. He tests his weight, hanging by his hands, and then he yanks out the first crystal, pulls himself up by the other, and plunges it back in, higher up. This might work, he thinks, and within thirty seconds, Jonah is a third of the way up the tree. The slimy bark covers his jumpsuit, weighing him down, dripping off his boots, but he keeps going.

The birds notice his ascension and swoop over his head, shrieking and spitting at him. He swings the crystals at them as he moves upwards, but they aren't scared off. In fact, more flock to him with every swing, and when he's over halfway up the trunk and can actually start to see tiny slivers of the sunset through the yellow leaves above, the birds begin to slam themselves into his sides. One of the crystals cracks and then shatters in his palm, and for a second Jonah hangs from just one hand. The birds continue to pelt him, pushing him sideways on the tree, and he finally can't hold on any longer. He falls, only to wrap his arms around the trunk where he slides straight down, pulling sheets of bark with him. He thinks about Captain Tejas and her broken neck and how he's about to meet a similar fate, but he lands in a pile of the stripped-off bark and rolls right onto his knees. Thirty yards above his head, the birds circle rapidly, churning into a thick tornado.

Jonah covers his head and runs for the hill. The girl no longer stands there, but the tall boy still lies unconscious near the water. Jonah leaps over his body just as the tornado of birds slam against his back, and he falls right next to the boy's side. Frantic, Jonah digs into the soft ground and throws handfuls of muck at the birds, and soon he begins to sink into the hole he's creating. The tall boy's body eventually rolls over the hole's edge and falls right on top of Jonah, blocking him from the onslaught. Jonah catches his breath, his head swimming with options. Should he dive into the lake and face whatever is under the water instead? Should he run back up the hill and find the girl and shake her until she tells him what to do? Should he break off new crystals and start his tree climb all over again? Just as he decides on looking for the girl and grabbing some crystals at the same time, Jonah feels the weight of the boy disappear. He uncovers his head to see the birds lifting the boy off the ground, just as they did with Captain Tejas's body. Jonah gets to his feet and jumps, grabbing ahold of the boy's ankle. The birds struggle at first to keep rising, but they recover and keep going, bringing Jonah with them. As he rises over the steaming lake, Jonah looks for the girl, but she's nowhere to be found. It isn't until they are just about to reach the canopy when Jonah locates her: she's rotating slowly, face down in the water, until a giant pink bubble rising to the surface opens up, sucking her inside. The bubble glows bright and then it opens back up with a sickening noise, releasing the girl's bones and clothes.

Jonah keeps rising, tightening his grip on the boy's ankle. As soon as the birds shove the boy's body into the yellow leaves, Jonah watches the electric creatures race in like little lightning bolts along the underbelly of a cloud. It's only a matter of seconds before they reach the boy and consume him, and then they'll move right on to Jonah. With his free hand, Jonah punches upward with all his strength, busting a hole through the canopy, sending several of the birds diving out of the way. He lets go of the boy's ankle and grabs the yellow leaves just as the electric creatures reach the boy, immediately melting his skin.

He punches and punches at the leaves, his knuckles bleeding against the tiny branches, and as soon as the hole is big enough, he pulls himself through and rolls onto his back in relief, sinking a few inches before holding still. A hundred birds escape right after him, exploding from the canopy with a deafening collective cry. Jonah hears the electric creatures buzzing right below him, so he quickly finds the strength to get to his hands and knees and crawl toward the river. When he gets to the stone embankment, he sits and pulls his knees up to his chest, rocking back and forth as the waterfall roars behind him. The sun is almost gone. With shaking hands, he empties his pockets and spreads the items out next to him: his sheaf, the captain's sheaf, a ring of keys, the tiny notebook, a couple of crystal shards, the unusable blue handgun, and one small verve seed. Jonah picks up the seed and holds it up to his face, examining its ridges, and then he tosses it in the river hoping to never see another one. He knows he could use the type of energy boost a seed would give him at that moment, but he doesn't want that type of help ever again. If he's going to get back to his friends and get rid of Mirker and stop Dr. Z from killing again, he's going to do it alone.

He unfurls his sheaf and nods at its screen. It comes to life, practically blinding him in the evening light. Jonah steals a few moments with his family photo, gaining an ounce of strength from his mother's eyes, and then flips through the applications until he finds the *Thetis Bible*. He hasn't looked at it since the week before entering the wormhole, and he immediately scrolls for the map section. The map of Thetis is anything but complete, but it covers thousands of miles in every direction outside of the village. The drones have been busy, Jonah sees.

Jonah is tempted to search the map for alien spheres and caves and symbols, but the battery drains quickly, so he finds his exact spot on the map—the bottom of the multi-tiered waterfall—and zooms in. His fingers spin the map around, scanning for a way up the mountainside and back to the village. He looks for worn paths, creature trails, anything, but finds nothing. His fingers pinch and swipe, covering so many different angles of his surroundings, that he grows dizzy with frustration. Suddenly, though, his sheaf connects to the village's communication system; the Thetis document begins to update, and when the status bar completes, the map refreshes with that day's date: 29 OCT 2221.

And then there Jonah is, an image of him standing on a cliff just hours ago, surrounded by the Module Eight kids and Dr. Z. And there's a frozen image of Mirker climbing up the backside of the mountain. Jonah moves the map around, finding the incomplete sphere with Everett inside. He spins the landscape here and there on his sheaf until he sees it: a narrow path through the vegetation, just on the other side of the river bank. Captain Tejas. She must not have gone over the waterfalls. She hacked her way down here.

Jonah gathers his things and then leaps, launching himself over halfway across the river. As soon as he hits the water, he swims with all his might, knowing there could be something waiting for a meal, or a crack in the riverbed that leads to another underground canyon. He makes it to the other side and then walks carefully along the bank until meeting the mist of the waterfall. Jonah takes another look at the map on his sheaf, finds a few markers in the nearby jungle, and then jogs along the stones to find path.

The jungle sings and growls as Jonah sprints through it, his broad shoulders banging against black trees covered in thick brown leaves that shatter when touched. He jumps over trickling red streams and scurrying herds of fuzzy black rodents, pushing himself as fast as he can go, but after a half hour, his empty stomach drops him to the sideline. *When was the last time I ate?* he wonders.

There's a sudden series of cracking noises far off on his left, and Jonah holds his breath. The cracking gets louder and louder, and Jonah doesn't waste another second; he bolts up the path, ignoring his shrinking stomach as he plows through branch after branch, brown dust exploding behind him in thick clouds. Finally, the path ends with a black wall of rock. Out of habit, Jonah looks for an alien symbol to manipulate and separate the rock like curtains, but it's just a flat wall of disappointment. The cracking noise reappears, and Jonah pulls the broken gun out of his pocket and flattens his back against the wall. Sweat beads down his arm and slips between his fingers and the gun handle. He raises the gun and waits for Dr. Z or Mirker or a herd of mimics to appear. He waits. And waits. But the noises stop. He looks to his left for a way out, then to his right, and there he sees a trampled section of black dirt at the base of the wall. He reaches the climbable section of the wall and up he goes. The sun sets behind him, and Jonah never looks back.

CHAPTER THIRTEEN

Jonah crouches just twenty feet from the village fence. He listens for the buzzing of drones and the voices of patrol units, but all he hears is his own heaving breath and growling stomach. A soft white glow rises above the fence where two small drones circle the middle of the village. With the gun in hand, he sprints to the hole in the fence he and Griffin made, but finds it blocked with a freshly cut log. He moves swiftly along the perimeter, stopping only to check the trap door he escaped through the day before when the Module Eight kids were hot on his trail. When he finds it locked, he keeps running until reaching the closed gate. How is he going to get inside this time?

While he paces next to the gate, there's an uproar on the other side of the fence. A few seconds pass before Jonah hears the distinct, amplified voice of Commander Mirker: "Never again. We said never again would we let our community be taken over by the insolent and unruly who choose selfishness over the whole. Have you forgotten? Have you all forgotten?" Cheers and boos answer Mirker's booming voice before he continues, "And so we have a choice, to banish these three traitors—they are *not* children, they are *not*; they are full-grown traitors—who can just come back in here to ruin us, who can just sneak up on us when we least expect it to sabotage what we came here to accomplish like Captain Tejas. Or, we can end their acts of terrorism right here and now, taking them down to the pit where I will personally pull the trigger. Because we have so much more to accomplish here."

As the villagers inside yell and bicker, as some decry Mirker's suggestion while others cheer it on, Jonah knows who Mirker is talking about. He pictures the man standing over Paul, Vespa, and Brooklyn, their hands bound behind their backs while bags cover their heads. Jonah's skin blisters with rage. He has to get inside. He has to save his friends. He has to take down Mirker before it's too late.

Jonah shoves his fingers in between the gate doors and pulls, but they don't give an inch. He runs over to the keypad and rips the keychain from his pocket, but there's nowhere to stick a key.

Mirker's voice booms: "So, I will be taking them down to the pit, or perhaps we should do this right here, in front of everyone, so that you all can witness what happens when you don't follow the rules here."

There's a gunshot, a sudden cracking pop that causes Jonah's knees to give. He falls to all fours and sucks wind, his vision tunneling to the black soil squeezing through his fingers. Vespa? Brooklyn? Paul? Which one went first? Which one was punished for Jonah's actions? He scrambles back over to the gate and presses his eyes into the door cracks, desperately trying to see what happened, to see which friend is slumped over on a stage, but there's no one in sight. The congregation must be closer to the middle of the village. Everyone must be there. Even the guards must be watching.

Jonah pounds his fist on the gate in frustration. He backs up and kicks the door with his heel. He doesn't care if they hear him. He just wants inside. He takes the gun out of his pocket and whips it against the wood, the small weapon bouncing with a quiet thud. Desperate, Jonah reaches into his pocket to throw something, anything, else—and he finds his sheaf. Jonah holds it over his shoulder to launch it into the gate, hoping to watch it shatter like his heart just did thinking about Vespa's hooded body taking a bullet to the back of the head, but at the last second, he stops from throwing it. Instead, he lets it fall to the ground where it unfurls at his feet.

Mirker shouts something and people shout back. Jonah can't tell if they agree with what's happening or not. Everyone seems angry. No one seems satisfied.

With a tear crawling down his cheek, Jonah falls to his knees and nods at his sheaf. He'll run through its remaining battery by staring at his parents. And then the sheaf will die. And then his friends will die. And then he will die attacking Mirker.

But before he can open up the photo, he sees an icon reminding him the sheaf is on the village network, connected to the main server. Jonah immediately gestures at the icon and then blows through the folders until finding one titled *SECURITY.* The battery is at four percent. The screen fades in brightness. Jonah finds a folder for the front gate and opens the utilities and applications inside, hoping to find the right button to separate the doors above him. What he wouldn't give to have Kip with him at that moment. Or Richter or Hopper, any hacker that could easily infiltrate the system. He clicks on each icon, popping up screens asking for codes and commands he'll never know.

In anguish, Jonah closes his trembling fingers in front of the screen, bringing him back to the server's top folder. The battery is at three percent. The screen dims some more. He points at the folder and sits back on his heels, seeing an icon for the village's drones. Jonah opens the folder and scrolls through them without thought until seeing which ones are active and outlined in green. The first one he opens brings up a video, streaming a drone's live view. In less than a second, he sees Mirker standing on top of a rover, a handgun pointed in the air. People circle all around. And sitting in the rover's seats with gags over their mouths are Paul and Vespa, with Brooklyn's head resting on Vespa's arm.

Jonah watches for a few seconds, and when Brooklyn sits up straight before leaning back on Vespa, relief melts his shoulders.

They're all still alive. His friends are still alive. Mirker must have fired a warning shot. The drone then circles around for a different angle, and twenty feet away, several people kneel and rush around a body lying in a pool of blood. Jonah tilts his head in front of the screen, unconsciously urging the drone to get a better view, and that's when he sees the controls in the bottom corner of the video. Jonah nods and opens the controls and tries one of the green arrows, and immediately the drone shoots forward and away from the gathering. He's steering it. The screen dims and goes black for a second, but when it pops back up, Jonah finds the drone still moving under his command. He turns the drone around until it's heading straight for the gate, the video swaying high above the fence.

When he pictures the inside of the gate and its surroundings, it hits him: He knows what he can do with the final moments of his sheaf. The red button halfway up the wall enters the drone's video feed, and he aims right for it. It slams into the button, and then the screen goes black and the sheaf dies, curling up in his hand and shrinking. Jonah covers his face in anguish, knowing this was his only shot, but then there's a low whirring noise in front of him: the gate doors begin to separate. The drone landed a direct hit. He shoves the sheaf into his pocket and runs.

As soon as there's enough room between the doors, Jonah dashes inside the village and turns sharply to his right, hiding behind a row of tents. Finally, he peeks around the corner of the farm building and sees the gathering. Mirker stands on the rover, his friends sit in the seats. A group of men and women point fingers at Mirker, shouting for him to stop. Several villagers surround a body on the ground. And that's when he sees who's been shot: Freeman.

The man huffs for air while holding a woman's hand. A tall bald man applies pressure to Freeman's side, which spills more and more blood into the growing pool beneath him.

"You had us! You had our loyalty!" Freeman yells. "What more did you want?"

Mirker points his gun at Freeman's face. "I wanted your trust, not your loyalty. I want all of your trust!"

Jonah watches Freeman take his final breaths, desperately reaching his other arm at those around him until it falls across his chest and slides to the ground.

The bald man jumps to his feet and shouts, "You killed him! You son of a bitch! He was just... You're out of control and we're not going to take it anymore. Put down your gun, let go of these kids, and get your ass to—"

The bullet rips through the man's chest, spraying red on those standing behind him. He falls backward, dead before hitting the ground. Everyone stays silent for a second, whipping their heads back and forth from the dead bodies to Mirker, who stands on top of the rover and shrugs before reaching down and grabbing Brooklyn by the collar. He lifts the small demic up to his face, whispers in her ear, and then holds the gun up to her temple.

Jonah bolts out from behind the farm building, and when Mirker catches sight of the cadet, he drops Brooklyn onto Vespa's lap. Mirker snarls and aims his gun at him, but Jonah changes direction, diving behind a clay barrel of water just as Mirker fires. The barrel shatters and collapses, soaking Jonah, who lies on his chest with nothing between him and the commander. Mirker smiles and takes aim again, but then the rover jumps under his feet, causing the man to stumble over the roof and land on his back. Paul, with his hands tied behind his back and gag in his mouth, has his foot on the accelerator and his eyes on Jonah.

Paul can't get his hands under his legs in time to grab the wheel and the villagers scatter as the rover gathers speed. Jonah gets to his feet and runs behind the nearest tent. And from there, he zigzags his way toward the back of the village, hands covering his head, knowing that Mirker is probably right behind him, waiting to get the shot. Jonah locks his eyes on the Woesner Telescope rising out of the sea of tents, and he picks up speed. He skids to a stop in front of its door and immediately shoves each key from Tejas's key ring into the lock until one finally clicks. As soon as he's inside, he dives under the desk and pulls the chair in front of him.

Now what? he thinks. Surely, the villagers will revolt now, but will they stop Mirker from hunting Jonah down in cold blood? Jonah thinks about Tunick, Mirker's son, sitting cross-legged in front of the purple fire, his body splitting into two as the verve entered Jonah's mind. He sees the same madness in Mirker, the same God complex. Jonah and Vespa were able to get the upper hand on Tunick, so he knows it's possible to take down his father, too.

Next to the door, Jonah spies a charging station blinking with tiny green lights. He quickly pushes himself forward and pulls out his sheaf, and in one quick motion, he wings it toward the tiny lights. The station and sheaf communicate midflight, and the sheaf takes the perfect turn and slaps itself against the station where it immediately begins to glow with an incoming charge. He sits back under the desk and hugs his knees to his chest.

The room hums from the monitors above him and beeps from the telescope that shifts slightly every ten seconds. Jonah continues to hold his breath, losing himself in the sounds, wracking his brain for what to do next. If he had a working gun, he could scale the lens of the telescope again and take Mirker down from the roof. He pictures the villagers helping his friends off the rover which has crashed into the fence, untying their hands, hiding them from Mirker who stalks the grounds searching for Jonah.

The beeping from the telescope grows louder. The bottom of the lens protracts, lighting up, as the tube shifts up another few inches. With his eyes on the window in the door, Jonah pushes aside the chair and crawls to the telescope lens. He presses his face up against the eyepiece. The Silver Foot Galaxy glows in his eyes, its stars bright and ghostly, surrounded by the moving lines and numbers in the telescope's field. It takes Jonah a few seconds to recognize that one of the stars is moving. Jonah cups the lens with his huge hands and zooms in. The numbers on the screen rise, and the lines from the edges of the screen come together to form a square around the moving star, which Jonah now sees isn't a star at all. It's as clear as day. What he's looking at is the ship that once sat at the bottom of the cavern on Achilles. And it's heading toward Thetis.

Jonah watches the ship for a full thirty seconds, forgetting to breathe, forgetting that Mirker could be right on the other side of the door with his gun aimed at Jonah's head. Faces of those who boarded the ship a week ago flash through his mind: Lark, Krev, Camilla, Hopper, Hess, Aussie, Malix, Christina. Vespa said others ran up the ramp at the last second, too, other runaways from Thetis. They did everything they could to steal the ship and get away, and now here they are, coming back. Or, at least one of them is coming back.

The telescope continues to track the ship, and Jonah continues to battle his thoughts. He needs to warn Vespa and Brooklyn. He needs to know who is on board and what they want. He needs to get out of this building to save his friends before he finds out what "Sacrifice Jonah Lincoln" means on Tejas's notebook in his pocket. He looks over at his sheaf, hoping its battery fills up quickly.

The door suddenly slams open, its lock ripping out of the frame, and there stands Mirker with his right foot extended, dust billowing between him and Jonah.

"There you are, boy."

Jonah's eyes dart from the man entering the room to his sheaf near the doorframe and up to the space in the roof where he escaped before.

Mirker flexes his jaw. "I'm going to need you to come with me. There's some *activity* that you need to be accountable for. And I want everyone to watch."

Jonah pulls out the handgun and aims it at Mirker's chest. "Back off. Now. Or, I swear I'll blow your head off."

The man chuckles and raises his huge hands. "You're going to blow my head off? Where did you even get that gun? Because to me it looks...kind of broken."

Jonah rubs the trigger with his sweaty index finger. *Don't let him know he's right*, Jonah thinks. *Stay strong.*

Mirker takes another step forward, his hands still up. "So, where did you find her? I know that's the captain's gun because of the markings on the barrel there. See those three scrapes going down the side of it? She put those on there after shooting three ribbers who flew into the village and attacked us during our first month here. Tejas showed a lot of muster that day. A lot of leadership. Took three of those fuckers down with a shot apiece. It was quite the spectacle. So, where is she? She dead? Hiding in some cave talking gibberish like that Everett boy when he showed up a couple days ago in the sphere we were building for you?"

"I killed her," Jonah says as he takes a step back. "I shot her after she told me everything that you guys were up to. About the other planet, all the stuff you're hiding from Earth. She told me what you guys were going to do with Zion. She told me you were going to sacrifice me. And that's when I shot her with her own gun."

Mirker keeps moving forward until he stands next to the telescope lens. "You don't have the balls, kid. You found that gun. And maybe you found her dead somewhere, but this one is for sure: you're no killer."

"She wasn't on your side, you know," Jonah says. All of these lies come to him as he opens his mouth, no real plans developing in his head aside from biding his time. "She was communicating with the kids on Achilles the whole time. She told me she was talking to your sons. And if you want to know what they were planning together… Well, look into the telescope right now. Look into it and you'll see exactly what I mean."

Mirker squints at Jonah and cocks his head; it looks like Jonah has told him enough things close to the truth that Mirker seems to take him seriously. The man looks down at the moving telescope lens and then back at Jonah. "Promise not to shoot me with your broken gun when I take a look? And if you even *think* about coming at me, well, kid, I'll put you down faster than you can say your dead mother's name."

That makes Jonah take a step closer and raise the gun to the man's smiling mouth. If he can't shoot it off, he's willing to try to punch right through it.

"Hold that thought," Mirker says. And then he quickly dips his face into the eyepiece. After just a second, the man presses his hands on either side of the eyepiece and pushes his face harder into the machine. "Holy shit. They're coming back. Those little fuckers are coming back. My boys."

Mirker stands up straight, and the look in his eyes is that of both rage and excitement. It's possible he thinks his sons are alive and well and coming to see him, or it's possible that when they arrive he knows the chaos they will bring. After all, the ship could be filled with a dozen kids high on verve, raving mad with superhuman strength. The man's eyes shift to the monitors behind Jonah. Jonah twists his head to take a quick look at the screens, and there it is, the ship that once sat at the bottom of the cavern on Achilles—the prize that everyone was trying to win—enters Thetis's atmosphere with streaks of blue fire speeding off its nose.

"They'll be here in a few minutes," Jonah whispers. He finds that he's terrified at the news himself. There's enough going on here already. Enough madness. Enough mystery. Enough people to defeat to bring order to the colony. He can only imagine what a verved-out Krev, the towering wolfish boy, will do once the ship's doors open.

Mirker squints at the screens and grinds his teeth so hard that Jonah can hear the enamel crack. The man twists around and takes a step toward the door, but then turns back at once to snatch Jonah by the neck single-handedly. His grip is incredible; Jonah slams the butt of his gun down on the man's wrist, but it only makes him squeeze harder. As he's pulled through the door, Jonah whips his hands at his sheaf stuck to the charging station at the doorframe, but he can't reach it in time. Mirker pulls him into the bright sunlight and tosses him forward with such strength that Jonah stumbles and falls face first into the ground. The cadet pushes himself up and tries to scramble away, but Mirker's grip finds the back of his skull and squeezes.

"You try to run, I don't care if you're supposed to be sacrificed or whatever, I'll kill you like a street dog, and we'll all eat you for dinner."

The pressure on the back of his head is debilitating; he feels like a basketball with the air being squeezed out. Jonah can't focus his eyes anywhere, sees blurs of villagers' feet jumping out of his way. He hears people shout at Mirker to stop, to stand down or face the consequences, and then Jonah hears Mirker laugh and tell them to follow him, that there's something everyone needs to see.

Finally, Mirker tosses Jonah onto his stomach and slams a boot down onto his back, pinning him helplessly to the ground.

"Someone help me!" Jonah shouts. "Get him off of me!"

Ariel Abbasi's mother in the blue and yellow headscarf pushes through the crowd, shouting, "Mirker, just stop! These are our children! These are our own!"

"Shut the fuck up about this kid!" Mirker barks. "You have bigger things to worry about. I was just in the observatory, tracking down this piece of shit here, and right there on the monitors and in the telescope, I saw our stolen ship coming this way. The kids are back. The same kids who almost took this colony down with their addiction and recklessness, they've just entered our atmosphere and they're coming back right now. Who knows who they'll kill this time."

Jonah strains his head to look at the crowd around him. He looks for Vespa and Paul and Brooklyn, but they're not there. That means they've escaped, or they're already dead.

"Don't believe me? Look up!" Mirker yells. "Look right there!"

There's a resounding gasp from the crowd. One man says, "I can see it. Look."

Ms. Abbasi raises her arms over head. "Ariel! She's coming home!"

"She's not coming home. It's Armitage and the whole lot of them. So, I suggest you arm yourselves with whatever you can find, and hide," Mirker says. "I'll take care of this. And *nobody* touches my boys. Nobody touches Sean and Tunick. I'll handle them." He then points to several men in the crowd, including the man with the red cap and the bald man with the scar on his face Jonah met in the first rover exploration. "You guys are coming with me."

The bald man practically bounces on his feet in excitement. "Good. Because I've got some unfinished business with a couple of those kids. That Lark girl better not be on that ship. Not after what she did to me."

"She's all yours," Mirker says.

The man rubs the scar on his face and laughs.

CHAPTER FOURTEEN

The crowd scatters in every direction—some waving down the ship, hoping their children or friends have been rescued from Achilles, others disappearing in tents or running for the far corners of the village. Mirker rips Jonah up to his feet and then shoves his lips into Jonah's ear and says, "You're coming with me, too. Maybe we won't have to sacrifice little Jonah Lincoln after all. But I still may need you for something special."

Jonah stumbles forward just as the ship's thrusters pierce the air. He twists around trying to locate it, and then there it is—coming from beyond the southern mountains—a black speck with red lights blinking on its wings. The blinking speck turns into a small blinking triangle, and then the small triangle grows bigger and bigger as it swoops toward the ground, barreling right through the black smoke of the modules.

Jonah tries to run, but Mirker snatches him by the wrist and wrenches it behind his back. "Just wait, just wait."

The ship comes right toward the village, its long silver nose shining in the sunlight. Jonah shields his eyes and remembers when he spotted the ship in the canyon back on Achilles. It was one of the last things he saw before he went blind. And then he and Vespa battled Tunick amongst the fire and spider carcasses until Vespa finally plunged a knife into Tunick's side, killing him. How is Mirker going to react when the ship opens and they tell him his sons are officially dead? Then again, they may not even know.

Mirker grabs a rifle from one of his men and presses its scope up to his eye. The ship's wings wobble as it comes closer and closer to the ground. At first, Jonah thinks it's going to zip right by and land near the forest and they'll have to chase it in the rovers, but it looks like the ship is headed right for them, aimed directly at the village.

"They fucking better pull up soon," Mirker says.

But the ship keeps growing and growing in the sky until Jonah thinks he can see the windows in the front. It's slowing down, but not fast enough. It's supposed to hover and land standing straight up, but the pilot doesn't seem to have that in mind. It's going to try to land on its belly.

"Holy shit," the bald man whispers. "They're going to crash right into us."

"Move!" Mirker shouts. He turns and runs, pulling Jonah toward the western fence. His men follow close behind, covering their heads as the ship screams straight toward the village. Its nose blasts right through the top of the northern fence, knocking the black logs down like toys. The ship sways and skims over a row of tents and the hospital building before banking to the left. The right wing clips the top of the Woesner Telescope, flinging the huge tube out of its building, sending it spinning end over end across the village. The ship's nose finally hits the ground and grinds along, taking out dozens of yurts and two water wells.

The ship's tail swings to the right, and the ship grinds to a stop just before hitting the southern fence. A huge cloud of dust sweeps through the village, the wake of the ship covering everything in dirt and smoke and noise. Jonah can't even see the spacecraft for a few moments, but when the air finally settles, shadows dart out of its open tail.

"Go, go, go!" Mirker screams.

Jonah doesn't need to be pulled along; he runs right with the men, pulling ahead of the bunch. He has no idea who he's about to encounter—Hess, Christina, Aussie, Hopper—but he wants to get a look at the ship. He wants to see if it's still usable after a crash like that.

He sprints around the vegetable garden, sticking his hand into the rows of corn stalks as he zips by. Mirker is right behind him, shouting his sons' names, for everyone to hurry, to not shoot until he says they can shoot. They speed past the farm building and its pens empty of animals. And then there's the ship, fifty yards long, dented and blinking and sputtering smoke from its thrusters. Thick dust fills the area as two slow-moving shadows descend the ramp's tail, leaning on each other until they make it to the ground where they both fall to their hands and knees.

"Sean? That you, Sean?" Mirker yells as he sprints past Jonah. When he reaches them, the man slides on his knees and immediately pushes both figures over onto their backs to see their faces, and then runs up the ramp shouting for his sons.

Jonah reaches the two shadows lying on their back, squinting through the dust until seeing the withered bodies of Lark and Camilla, the two girls who found Brooklyn and Vespa on Achilles. The two girls who double-crossed him and left him for dead.

Camilla, the once stoic and muscular young woman with dark skin and a cloud of beautiful black hair, looks nearly green with sickness. Her arms are thin and bony, her face bloated and lined with deep purple veins. The girl's cloud of hair is now half missing, patches of her raw scalp blanketed with dust. She's barely breathing.

Next to her, Lark slowly moves her hand from her side until she finds Camilla's leg, resting it there while she tries to catch her breath. She no longer has the thick band of purple running across her temple and over her eyes and nose like a superhero mask. The large silver circle still hangs around her neck on a rope, though, its greenish brown metal dull in the dust cloud. Her braid of long brown hair lies above her head on the ground like a dead snake.

"Who's with you?" Jonah asks. "What are you doing here?"

It takes Lark a moment to recognize him, and when she does, her eyes widen and she lets out a short chuckle that turns into a hoarse cough. "Jonah Lincoln. We're here…we're here for you, Jonah."

The rest of Mirker's men run by and scramble up the ramp. Jonah hears them argue and scream, and then metal hits metal. Something falls and shatters. Someone fires a rifle and Jonah sees its blue beam in the ship's window.

"You have to listen to Hopper. Find him," Lark says as she reaches for Jonah's hand. "We went back for you, but you were gone."

"Hopper's here? You went back for me?"

"I can't believe we actually made it." Lark smiles and then rolls onto her side and pulls herself up to Camilla. She rests her head on the girl's chest and interlaces her fingers with her girlfriend's.

Mirker's voice bellows from inside the ship: "Where are my sons? Fucking tell me!"

Jonah jumps over Camilla's body and puts his face inches from Lark's. "Where's Hopper? Hey? Lark?"

Lark doesn't answer him; she lets out a huge sigh of relief and hugs Camilla tighter. Camilla's head rolls on the ground toward Jonah, her eyelids fluttering before finding his face.

"You weren't supposed to leave yet," she says.

"Leave Achilles yet? Why?"

"We saw it, Jonah. We saw *you*, what you're supposed to do. Now you have go to the pyramids on the other place. Or Earth dies…everything dies."

Jonah falls back onto his heels. After taking the verve, in his visions inside the tip of the pyramid, Jonah saw a picture of Earth get cut in half and then explode. After a second, though, the picture moved in reverse, the pieces of the planet coming back together.

"What exactly did you see?" Jonah asks.

She gives him a weak smile and then closes her eyes, rolling her head back the other way and appears to fall asleep. Jonah places a hand on her bony shoulder to wake her up but immediately pulls it back; her skin is freezing to the touch. Behind him, Mirker's voice continues to echo in the belly of the ship, demanding answers and barking orders. Jonah stands and can't decide where to go next, to check out the ship himself or to run and find Vespa and the others or to hunt down Hopper, when he sees several small shadows run toward the farm building. He takes one step toward the ship, hears another round of rifle fire, and then runs for the building.

He reaches the door just after it clicks shut. He rips it open and charges inside and practically runs right into the end of a long wooden black table, one of dozens in a row spanning the entire length of the building. The tables are topped with monitors and medical equipment and dissected carcasses of alien creatures enclosed by containers. Dozens of doors line the left and right sides of the room, some with windows, others with bright yellow warnings scrawled across their wood. A door closes somewhere halfway down the building, but Jonah can't tell which one. He races along the tables, knocking over a tall bottle of blue liquid containing a six-legged, owllike creature stripped of its feathers and beak. The glass shatters on the floor, and the owl creature immediately begins to move, scraping its sharp feet along the slippery concrete until it meets the wall and flips onto its back.

Jonah twists around to see a door far down on the left crack open an inch and then close. He runs straight for it, peering in the window only to see the yellow capstones sprinting back and forth in their pen, their long arms dragging limply behind them as they search for rocks. Jonah is about to check the next door over when he sees a black shoe pull out of sight. The person must be right next to the door on the other side of the wall.

He knocks softly. Again. And then, "That you in there, Hopper? It's me, Jonah. Camilla said I'm supposed to—"

The door opens quickly, and a hand grabs Jonah by the collar, pulling him inside. Jonah suddenly stands face-to-face with Jules Hopper, the hacker who betrayed him and his friends on Achilles and joined forces with Tunick. Days ago, Jonah would have attacked him on sight, but now he needs him for answers. The boy looks haggard, as if he's been lost underground for a week with no food or sunlight. Dark bags hang under his eyes like half-moons and several layers of sweat cake his cheeks and wispy black mustache. He stands over a huddled and silent Michael, the demic with long brown hair who once was Hopper's main target. The boy hugs his knees to his chest and rocks back and forth with his eyes focused on the floor in front of him. The sour smells wafting off of their skin make Jonah take a step back and cover his nose with his arm.

"Can't believe we actually found you, ya freak," Hopper whispers. "The man of the hour. We went back to the crash site looking for your ass, but apparently you were already here doing your thing. Hell of a hitchhiking move."

Jonah doesn't know what to say. He just stares at him in disbelief, and then looks down at the huddled demic at his feet and asks, "Hey, Michael? Are you okay? Did Hopper do anything to you? Did he hurt you? Where's Aussie? Is Portis still alive?"

Michael doesn't respond; he just keeps rocking back and forth until reaching out and setting a limp hand on Hopper's pant leg.

"He's just going through it. We all are," Hopper says as he easily steps out of Michael's grip. "Coming down off this verve crap is fucking brutal, man. The fucking worst. And some of us," he nods at Michael, "are huge pussies and are taking it a *little* worse than others."

"I just saw Camilla and Lark and they're all messed up," Jonah whispers. "They might be dying. But Camilla says you have something that you want to tell me, some information or something for me. Hurry up and tell me before Mirker finds us. They're going to kill you if they find you."

Hopper bends down to pet one of the capstones, only to have the creature speed off the moment his hand touches its head. "I'm doing well, Jonah. Thanks for asking. *Jesus.*"

"Shut the hell up and tell me. You have *no idea* what's been happening here."

"And you have *no idea* what's been happening with us up

there!" Hopper shouts. The capstones start to chirp and sprint along the walls, their long skinny arms flailing, leaving claw marks along the wood. "We came all this way for you, you ungrateful piece of shit. We're here right now *for you*. We never went to Peleus. Krev and the others beat the shit out of me and Michael and Aussie and everyone else, and then they flew us to the other side of Achilles where we did shit but find more verve and run around like savages. And that was all fine and dandy for a few days, and we stuffed our faces with it and flipped out and had some fun, but then, dude, we had too much. All of us did. Like, all at the same time and the hallucinations were bonkers and everyone freaked out—including yours truly—and the next thing you know we're all sitting in one of those portal cave rooms. But without a portal and just the hieroglyphics. And that's when the freaky monsters showed up…and they put on a real show for us."

Jonah is scared to ask, but has to. "They have two heads? And they're yellow and like ghosts, and when they talk they sound like robots in your head?"

"So, you're old friends? Interesting."

Something crashes to the floor in the main room, stopping both boys from saying another word. Jonah slowly peeks through the door window, but all he sees is one of the tables covered with empty cages and a few tools lying on towels. His fingers find the door latch to make sure it's locked.

"Hurry up. Tell me what you saw," Jonah whispers.

A devilish smile creeps across Hopper's face. "You don't even know, do you? You don't even know what they want from you. Guess you're not *that* good of friends, huh?"

"I'm going to kill you if you don't hurry up and tell me."

"Ah ha. *There's* the aggro Jonah I know and don't love. Okay, well I hate to be the bearer of such good and bad news, but those alien guys showed up while we were sitting in that cave verving the shit out of ourselves, and they start circling around the room faster and faster and the hieroglyphics on the walls start to glow, and the room like, starts to blur—and we're *all* seeing the same thing because we're all asking each other if they're seeing the same crazy shit and we're all freaking out—and then *boom*, we see you, cool guy cadet Jonah Lincoln, the blind dickhead who punched me in the face, and you're just floating over our heads. Your eyes look good now, by the way. Real pretty. I like what you've done with them. But so, we see you hovering over the room just standing there, and then you start to run, and then you're on some ship flying somewhere, and you're *with me*. I'm on the ship, too. And then the movie we're watching, like, cuts to these two-headed alien monsters walking around on what we think is here, Thetis, because Lark and Camilla recognize some of the landscape. But the monster guys aren't yellow and not looking like ghosts or whatever; they're like living beings, and they're kind of pink with gross skin and everything. They're alive. And they're doing their thing or whatever on Thetis when there's a light in the sky above them and all these ships arrive. Our two-headed guys are like 'What's up?' and these ships land, and then these short gray guys with horns on their faces come out of the ships."

A shiver runs over Jonah's spine; he saw the same gray beings in his vision from the verve. They were on Zion. They're the beings that built the pyramids and the giant symbol on the side of the mountain.

"So, these gray guys just straight up start slaughtering the two-headed things. They round them up and shoot the hell out of them and pretty much murder them into extinction. Killed them all."

A low, sickly moan comes out of Michael. He finally stops rocking back and forth to look up at Jonah with bloodshot eyes. "You have to kill them before they kill us. You have to kill them before they kill us. But in the past for the future. In the past. For the future. Do you understand? Does that make sense?"

Hopper pats Michael on the shoulder and continues: "What my esteemed colleague is trying to say here, Mr. Lincoln, is that in this movie, they show you flying to the gray people's planet and you're an alien, and they're all impressed and scared as hell and start to worship you, and you like, become their God."

Become their God? That's what Dr. Z said, too. When he visited her in the jail cell the first time, she said he was long enough and smart enough "to be their God." It meshes with his other visions, too, how he descended to their planet and some of the gray beings immediately began to worship him. Even so, Jonah shakes his head and says, "That's so…stupid. That's ridiculous."

"I one hundred percent agree," Hopper says. "If anyone is godlike around here, it's me. You know it, and I know it. I'm definitely the smartest kid here. I can fix anything. But you? You're simply the *tallest.* The reason you're so hot on their charts is because of your height, dude. And your wing span."

Again, Jonah is amazed that more of Dr. Z's gibberish actually had some meaning. "Why? Who cares?"

"Because you can reach shit other humans here can't. That's what they need. They showed you standing in some room and you're reaching your arms out wide and touching these controls on two walls at the same time. I think you can reach out as far as the two-headed guys can, but they can't do that anymore because they're stupid friggin' ghosts now."

Jonah thinks back to the tall Module Eight boy with the uneven hair. He had almost an identical stature. That's why he was next in line.

"Is that it?" Jonah whispers. "Anything else? Because we need to move. They find us and we're dead."

"'Is that it?' You just heard you're going to be a God and you want to know if that's it? But no, man. There's definitely more. *Jesus Christ*, listen to me. There's a whole time jump thing happening with all this shit. It's fucking crazy, but here's what we think is going on: These monsters were wiped out by the gray guys, okay, but if you travel to the gray guys' planet or moon or whatever from here with me on some ship and we go through this blue wormhole or portal first, you are somehow in the past, and you can derail the whole freaking thing before it starts. You become their God or leader or whatever, and you gain their trust, and then you lead them astray, and you stop them from advancing their civilization so that they don't evolve to build spaceships and then kill the two-headed guys here on Thetis. Because if you don't do this, then these gray guys end up making the trip to the Milky Way and destroying Earth. And then like, humanity is fucking done and shit."

Several pairs of boots run by in the main room, and they're the only thing keeping Jonah from shouting how ridiculous this all is, how stupid Hopper and the others are for believing it. They were all just high, stoned on an alien seed, hallucinating. Yes, most of what Hopper says fits together with Dr. Z's warnings and what the Module Eight kids seemed to be after, but they're all just having psychotic breakdowns at the same time. *They're all just messed up from the initial wormhole jump into the Silver Foot Galaxy*, Jonah thinks. *It's the radiation from the wormhole.*

"Why should I trust you anyways?" Jonah whispers. "You've lied to me so many times. You hid the homing device, you backstabbed us all in Tunick's cave. You turned on us."

Hopper leans forward with fire in his eyes and his neck muscles flaring. "I just flew a spaceship from Achilles to Thetis to find you here to tell you all of this, and you're wondering if I'm lying to you? This isn't bullshit; I believe everything we saw. And you were supposed to stay on Achilles and go to this new planet from there."

"Zion," Jonah says. "The planet is called Zion."

"I don't give a shit what it's called, but I'm going to take you there. It's like my mission or whatever. I think if I don't, I get eaten or something."

"I'll come with you, but you have to take everyone," Jonah says. He can't believe he's starting to see this as a viable option. "The air here is poison. Everyone is slowly dying, and they need to get off Thetis soon."

Hopper smiles. "No, they're aren't. Because I found the terraformer from the *Mayflower 2*, brah. It was smashed up a bit, but I think I know how to fix it."

"What? How did you even know about that? They never told the public. People on Earth don't know about it."

"Dude, I'm godlike, remember? Or, I'm the next best thing:

I'm a fucking hacker. I hacked into the ship's mainframe on the very first day of the trip and read all about the terraformer. Read the schematics, about what was happening on Thetis, how fucking important it was. It was going to be the ace up my sleeve when we landed here, but then, you know, there was a little detour-slash-crash on Achilles. But when we went back looking for you after our little vision quest, I found the thing all smashed up and didn't think anything about it, because fuck Thetis for how they treated Tunick and the other kids, but then who comes out of the trees all half dead to say you got picked up and flown back to Thetis? Little hacker Kip Kipperson who got zapped up in that first portal."

"Now I know you're making stuff up," Jonah says. "Kip is here right now on Thetis. I just saw him a few hours ago."

"He's on Achilles, brah."

"He still is," Michael whispers.

"Totally," Hopper says. "Kip popped out of the trees, told us where you were, and then he booked it right out of there. We yelled for him to come back get on our ship, but the little bastard ran off."

Jonah shakes his head. They were obviously hallucinating from the verve. Kip got picked up on the island days ago, just like him.

"Anyhow," Hopper says. "I brought the terraformer because I'm not coming down here to save the freaking day just to be poisoned by a shitty atmosphere. Plus, it's our little peace offering to the colony. Welcome us home because, hey, we have your life force."

Michael suddenly sits up straight and vomits all over himself, retching an explosive red and white mess that keeps coming and coming. Jonah and Hopper jump to their feet, sending the two capstones into a loud chirping fit. A second later, a shadow appears in the door window and the latch rattles. And then something bangs against the door, splintering the wood. Another bang and another. And with the fourth bang, the door falls from its hinges. Standing in its place is the bald man with the scar going down his face. He points a LZR-rifle at Jonah's chest and steps inside.

"There you are, big guy. And who are your friends here?"

A capstone runs right into the man's leg, buckling him at the knee. Jonah doesn't hesitate; he leaps and tackles the man to the ground. As they wrestle for the rifle, Hopper jumps in between the man's legs and raises his foot.

"I'm your new neighbor," Hopper says before stomping down on the man's groin. "Nice to meet you."

The man cries and curls up into a ball, but as soon as Jonah gets off of him, the man kicks Hopper's legs out from underneath him and the hacker falls flat on his back, right into the vomit.

"Fucking gross, man," Hopper whines.

Jonah dives for the rifle, but the man rolls over and gets to it first. The capstones continue to chirp and run back and forth, and then one leaps over Hopper and speeds off into the main room, dragging its arms through the mess.

The man gets to his feet and spits over his shoulder. With the barrel of the rifle aimed at Jonah, he places his boot on top of Hopper's face and slowly puts his weight on it. "Welcome to the neighborhood, kid."

Hopper groans and grabs at the man's ankle, gasping for air. Jonah takes a step forward and the rifle barrel rises up to his nose, stopping him.

The man coughs several times and then brings his wrist up to his mouth and speaks into his watch: "Commander Mirker, I've got Cadet Lincoln pinned down in here. We're in the farm building. Room number..." He looks down at the broken door next to Hopper. "Room number fifteen."

Mirker answers back: "Good work. Is Tunick in there with you? What about Sean?"

"Negative. Just the cadet and two other kids."

"Be there in five. Don't you fucking lose him."

"You better get off of him," Jonah says, nodding at Hopper. "If you want to live, you need to let him up."

"And why's that?"

"Because he brought the terraformer back from Achilles and

only he knows how to fix it. He can save the whole colony; no one will get sick and die."

Hopper struggles to move his head enough to the side to say, "It's true. I'm here to save everyone. So, get the fuck off me before you ruin my brain."

The man thinks it over before slowly removing his boot from Hopper's face. "Get up."

Jonah offers Hopper his hand and pulls him to his feet, vomit dripping off every inch of the hacker's clothing.

"And you," the man says, pointing at Michael in the corner. "You get up, too."

"He's too sick," Jonah says.

"I don't give a shit. Get. Up."

Jonah grabs Michael by the elbow, bringing the nearly comatose boy to his feet, and then he's standing there holding both demics upright, unsure of how he's going to escape before Mirker arrives. Just then the other capstone wanders up to the man with a flat rock balanced on top of its yellow head. Annoyed, the man backhands the rock right off, sending it ricocheting into the dark corner of the pen. "Get the hell out of here."

The animal twists its long neck all the way around to watch the rock spin on the ground, and then it turns back to the man and emits a low, devilish growl. It crouches and then springs up, attacking the man's chest with its long arms whipping in a blur. The man yells and spins around, and Jonah immediately flings Hopper forward into the chaos, then he lands two good punches to the man's chin, knocking him to his knees while the capstone continues to thrash at his chest and neck. Hopper bounces off the doorframe and then wheels to deliver another kick to the man's groin, sending the man face first into the pool of vomit.

"Drink that shit up," the hacker says.

The capstone turns its head to look at the three boys, and then it scurries into the corner, puts the flat rock back on its head, and then jogs out of the room.

Jonah grabs the rifle and peeks inside the main room, seeing only the backside of the capstone as it rounds the end of a table. No Mirker. No kids from Module Eight or Kip. But no Vespa, Paul, or Brooklyn, either. He looks back at Michael who lies on his side near the man, and then at Hopper. "You guys stay here or maybe go get help. Hopper, tell them you brought back the terraformer and get people to listen to you and stop all this stuff."

Hopper places his foot on top of the man's scarred face and steps up and over him. "Screw that. I think I'm going to follow the God kid with the gun. Besides, Michael has this under control." He then drags and drops Michael on top of the man's back. "I mean, just look at him. Number one security agent in the galaxy."

Jonah doesn't want to leave Michael alone like this, but he doesn't have time. He crouches down and enters the main room, passing empty cages and jar after jar holding creatures suspended in liquid. He sees a baby mimic bobbing up and down in one large jar, its red feathers floating all around it. Hopper is right behind him, mumbling about the vomit dripping into his underwear. When they get to the end of the last table, Jonah peers around to see dozens of doors and the capstones feasting on the owl creature.

A door bursts open on the other end of the room and Hopper and Jonah hide behind the end of the table. Above the thunder of boots running down the room, Mirker shouts, "Room fifteen! Down there!"

Jonah swings the rifle onto his back and army crawls toward the closest door. He looks up to see that it has the number three painted above its window, and he's about to try to duck inside when he sees next to it, marked with a big yellow hazard sign, is door number four. He pauses, remembering how a few of the Module Eights repeated the phrase, "Door four," how Dr. Z said the same thing on top of the cliff.

"Go already," Hopper whispers behind him.

"What the fuck happened in here?" Mirker shouts on the other side of the tables, his voice echoing in the capstone's room. "Where is he?"

Jonah crawls to door four and reaches up for the latch, and to his surprise, it's unlocked. He cracks it open and squirms inside the pitch-black room. Hopper follows right behind, and as soon as he's inside, the hacker locks the door.

It's silent inside save for Hopper's heavy breathing. The stench from the boy's clothes immediately overtakes the room; the smell is so strong that Jonah gags quietly into his shoulder and considers pushing the hacker back outside.

"Christ, that you?" Hopper whispers.

"That smell is coming from you," Jonah whispers back.

"That shit is not from me."

Jonah swings the rifle around to his chest and finds its spotlight, clicking it on. There, sitting cross-legged in the middle of the room is Dr. Z with her milky eyes staring right into the light. Her hands are caked with black dirt, and they slowly open and close on her knees. And right next to her sits Kip with his faded pink hair. His jumpsuit is in tatters, ripped completely across the chest so that his collar floats around his neck like a broken halo. With trembling hands, Jonah shines the light directly in his face, but he has no reaction.

"Kip?" Hopper whispers. "What the hell are you doing here? We left you on Achilles."

Kip's upper lip twitches once, and then the young boy slowly twists around to face the other direction. All across his exposed upper back are fresh, bleeding carvings of the three circles in the "C." And in the middle, between his shoulder blades, bleeds the name, "Jonah."

CHAPTER FIFTEEN

Jonah gasps at the sight of his own name on the boy's skin. He moves the light back to Dr. Z, and the woman's yellow teeth glisten as a wide smile grows across her face.

The words stick in Jonah's clenched throat before he's able to say, "Let him go."

She doesn't respond; she simply turns around to face the other direction, too. And that's when Jonah sweeps the light across the back of the room only to find it lined with dozens of shelves holding the same giant alien skulls he found after escaping the mimics the first time. The wire thin, mesh bones are a dull white, standing three-feet high with no eye sockets or ear holes, and they're in pairs, connected by thick vertebrae in the back. Shiny black numbers are stamped onto each of their pointed beaks, the digits reflecting the gun's light like tiny mirrors all over the room.

"Um, I think we should leave," Hopper whispers.

Dr. Z and Kip slowly stand up at the same time and walk to the bottom shelf in front of them. They both pick up a skull—a pair connected by vertebrae—and they raise them high in the air before pushing them down over their own heads. Kip reaches for Dr. Z's hand, and then they turn around to face the boys. The giant skulls begin to emit a slight glow.

"Nope. Nope, nope, nope. Fuck this," Hopper says, reaching for the door latch.

Jonah stares in horror at the huge glowing skulls on top of the small human bodies, their distended shadows looming larger than life in the spotlight. He backpedals until he's right next to Hopper, his back pushing hard against the door. On the other side of it, Mirker wants to sacrifice him, presumably to the same beings these skulls once belonged to. In front of him, he believes he's about to be eaten alive or forced to put on a skull himself, maybe with Hopper as his partner. He rubs the trigger with his finger, whipping the barrel of the gun back and forth between Kip and Dr. Z.

Hopper suddenly opens the door and darts out, shouting, "It's just me, it's just me!" leaving Jonah to fall flat on his back into the main room. His finger pulls back on the trigger, sending a flash of blue into the room. The laser hits the beak of the skull on top of Dr. Z, spinning it completely around her neck and sending Dr. Z and Kip crashing into the shelves. The bottom shelf buckles and breaks, dropping a dozen skulls all around the perimeter of the room, sending bone shards in every direction.

Jonah pushes himself away from the door frame with his heels, only to have his shoulders run into a pair of legs. Gasping for air, he looks up to find the man with the red ball cap standing above him with a handgun aimed at his nose. The man takes a quick look through the door in front of him, watching the giant alien skulls crash to the floor, and to Jonah's surprise, it doesn't seem to faze him.

"That room is off limits," Mirker says.

Jonah looks to his left to see the commander holding Hopper by his bicep. The hacker tries to rip himself away from his grip, but Mirker whips him right into the wall, denting the black wood. Hopper crumples to the floor, shouting, "I brought back the terraformer, you assholes! I can fix it! I can fix it here, so we can all live!"

"That true?" the man in the red cap asks.

"Yeah, it's true," Hopper says, rubbing his shoulder. "I'm here to help if you all will just let me. I found the terraformer. I'm saving the fucking day, man."

"Bullshit," Mirker says.

"It's true." Jonah tries to get to his feet, but the man kicks his hands out from underneath him. Inside the room, Dr. Z stumbles forward, pulling Kip behind her like a dog on a leash. The skulls on their heads begin to glow brighter than before. And all around them, the other skulls on the shelves and those broken on the floor begin to light up, too. Jonah needs to close the door before whatever is about to happen happens. He's not going to be a part of Dr. Z's plans anymore.

"Um, Commander," the man in the red cap says. "You should probably see what's going on in here."

Mirker drags Hopper along the floor and throws him on top of Jonah's legs. The commander, along with three other soldiers, stare into the room. Finally, Mirker clears his throat and says, "Throw them in there and lock the door. We're going to check the ship and see if what this little prick says is true."

"No way," Hopper says. "I'm not going in there."

Before he can say another word, one of the other soldiers grabs Hopper by the back of the neck and shoves him into the room. He immediately slips on a bone shard and falls onto his side. Dr. Z and Kip walk over to him and both extend their free hand to him.

"Hopper, don't touch their hands," Jonah says.

Mirker winds his fist into Jonah's collar and yanks the boy into the air, holding him up so that Jonah's boots hover inches over the ground. "Where are my sons? I know they're here somewhere."

"I don't know," Jonah lies. "Maybe you should go in there and look for yourself. They could be behind the door."

Mirker laughs and pulls Jonah's face down to his. "Nice try. Now, do you want to go in there yourself so that we can finally start up the sacrifice they've been asking us for, so that these fucking alien things will leave us all alone like they said they would when we handed you over, or do you want to come with me to the ship and look for my boys?"

The door at the far end of the room swings open, and in come several Module Eights, holding hands, marching quickly toward them in a tight huddle.

"These freaks again," Mirker mumbles.

"Get lost!" yells the man with the red cap. He aims his gun at a lanky teenage girl in the front of the huddle that moves faster and faster down the hall.

Another soldier, a pale woman with a long black braid falling down her back, raises her rifle. She looks nervous, sweat pouring down her temples. Jonah knows she's about to shoot. They're all about to shoot.

"Jonah!" Hopper yells as he crawls all around the room, desperately trying to avoid the two outstretched hands that follow him.

Another door slams open, this one at the other end of the building. Jonah peeks his head over Mirker's shoulder to see Vespa and Brooklyn standing in the doorway, LZR-rifles in their hands. Brooklyn's eyes are open, and they're not blue anymore. And her face is twisted into the angriest scowl Jonah has ever seen.

The soldier with the braid spins around and immediately fires two shots as the girls dive into the room. They fire back, blasting a stack of empty cages off a nearby table. Bottles shatter on the floor. Hopper shouts from inside the room. The Module Eight kids reach the soldier and the teenage girl grabs her wrist, sending the woman into a seizure just as a capstone appears underfoot, chirping and whipping its claws in a tornado above its head. Jonah wraps his hands around Mirker's fist and pulls with all his strength, wrenching himself free only to fall flat on the ground.

Mirker remains calm amid the chaos, kneeling on one knee, pressing his eye slowly into the scope of his rifle. His first shot hits the Module Eight girl touching his soldier, blowing a hole right through her gut. The capstone shrieks and runs in the opposite direction with its claws whirling above its head, coming straight at Mirker, and he simply reaches down and snatches it by its arms.

With one quick swing, he smashes the creature against the floor then tosses it into the room with Hopper. He quickly picks it up and swings it at the skull on Kip's head.

The air above Jonah turns into a light show of blue lasers zipping in every direction. He thinks he hears his name, but he's not sure where it's coming from. He needs to get to Vespa and Brooklyn and then to the ship to show everyone Hopper brought the terraformer to end Mirker's dictatorship. The colony can survive. It can thrive.

"Vespa!" Jonah yells.

Mirker shoots at the table where Vespa and Brooklyn disappeared. The man with the red cap jumps on top of the table behind Jonah and fires at the Module Eights, hitting a small boy in the leg, knocking him into a wall. A second later, a laser blows through the man's shoulder, spinning him on the table like a top until another laser hits his stomach. He falls off the table, landing right next to Jonah. The cadet wrenches the handgun out of his fingers and immediately aims it at Mirker's back, but then Hopper bursts out of the room still holding the capstone in his hand, knocking Jonah off balance. Hopper leaps on top of a table and then jumps off the other side, disappearing from view.

Mirker sees the gun in Jonah's hand and dives on top of him. The man's weight is suffocating and Jonah struggles to hold onto the weapon. A soldier's boot comes out of nowhere to kick the gun out of his hand, sending it into room four just as Dr. Z and Kip exit, their giant alien skulls pulsing light on top of their shoulders. Jonah twists onto his stomach and attempts to crawl away, but the rest of the Module Eight kids are right there, blocking his path. Mirker's hand wraps around the back of his neck and pulls him up just as Kip's fingers touch the commander's arm. A wave of electricity shoots through Mirker and into Jonah, bringing a series of flashing images into his head: Jonah landing on Zion, Brooklyn drowning in a sea of red sand, a gray being setting its strange hand on Jonah's forehead, a pyramid imploding with a cloud of dust, Jonah pulling a spear out of his bloody gut.

And then just as quickly, the images disappear, and Jonah's eyes focus on a fresh wound on Kip's thigh. The boy leans against the wall, still holding Dr. Z's hand as the woman soldier stands in front of him and yells things that Jonah's mind can't pick up. Everything sounds muffled. Things seem to move in slow motion. He wants to turn and run, but his body still shakes from the Module Eight connection. Mirker is on his knees, his head down, hands planted on his thighs, trying to make his own recovery. Finally, Jonah's legs catch up to his brain, and he scrambles on top of the table behind him and tumbles over to the other side.

He lies on the floor and looks up and down the long room for his friends. "Vespa! Brooklyn!"

The top of Mirker's head appears on the other side of the tables, his gray hair moving in one direction for a second before turning and going the other way. He's either looking for Jonah or trying to get away from the Module Eights and Dr. Z who must be closing in on him. Jonah army crawls to the nearest door and pushes his way inside.

He's in a room with the three frosties, the fuzzy green round creatures who hop around on their one thick leg. The creatures immediately surround Jonah, their big yellow eyes staring at him through green fur, and the boy prays they remain quiet. He reaches up to be sure the door is locked, but that's when Mirker dives inside and lands on his side, his rifle rocking against his bloody shoulder as it unleashes a barrage into the main room. Jonah crawls to the far corner of the room, covering his head, trying to hide in shadows, but the frosties squawk and hop after him.

"There you are," Mirker says. He pushes himself up onto his elbow, wincing in pain. "You ready to get out of here? You need me to carry your skinny ass?"

"You don't need to sacrifice me; I know what the aliens want now. And it doesn't involve you."

Mirker sits up and presses his back up against the wall, keeping his gun trained on the doorway. A bloodstain appears and expands on his jumpsuit at his right knee. "They talked to me, kid. They talked to a lot of us, even though a lot of us don't want to admit it. And if we don't sacrifice your ass in that sphere down in the jungle soon, then they're going to kill us all. And that's a fact. We tried using Everett instead, but they only want you."

Two Module Eight kids, a boy and a girl, shuffle into the doorway holding hands. Mirker mows them down before Jonah can say a word.

"You don't have to kill them!" Jonah yells. "It's not their fault they're like this. They're just kids. And Hopper really did fix the terraformer. He brought it back. It's on the ship and if you help bring it out, everyone will think you're a hero and you can stop all this."

"I'll stop all this when my boys show up safe and sound and you're sitting in that sphere."

Jonah gets to his feet. "They're dead. Tunick and Sean are both dead. I watched them die right before I went blind. They're not going to show up."

Mirker's face tightens, his jaw pulsing rapidly. He takes a deep breath and then jumps to his feet with a guttural roar. He charges at Jonah, scattering the frosties, but his bleeding leg gives out, and he falls flat on his stomach. His rifle skids across the floor and right to Jonah's feet. The nearest frosty immediately hops on top of Mirker's head and digs its claws into the man's skull. Mirker howls and bats at the creature while the other two frosties time their jumps perfectly, landing on top of the first. Mirker struggles to his feet and spins furiously, bouncing off the walls, desperately trying to knock the stack of frosties off his head. A ring of blood drips down his face as the first frosty tightens its grip. Mirker falls to his knees and wraps his fist around the creature's foot, but he can't match the animal's strength.

Jonah picks up the gun and aims it at the man's chest. He knows it's time for this to stop. It's time for Mirker's reign to end, to bring peace back to the colony. Hopper is going to fix the air, yes, but Jonah is going to fix the rest.

"Don't," Mirker says between cries when he sees Jonah holding the gun. "Don't kill me. Shoot them off and I'll make you my number two. No sacrifices, okay? Fuck the aliens. I'll take care of you."

Jonah takes a deep breath and keeps his finger on the trigger. When he first met the man, lying in the hospital bed, Mirker seemed empathetic and kind, saving him from Dr. Z's first attack. He gave him medicine to see again, caring for him almost like a father would for his own son—a feeling Jonah has desperately wanted in his life. But the truth slowly unspooled: the man was fully prepared to kill Jonah to save himself. But isn't that what Jonah is about to do? Kill Mirker to save himself?

Mirker moans and falls onto his hands and begins to sob, his blood dripping onto the ground in a thick stream. The frosties lean forward with him, perched in a perfectly straight line, sticking out over the floor like a diving board over a swimming pool. The man then leans back and sits against the wall, painfully bringing the creatures with him.

"Shoot them," he begs. "And I swear I'll treat you just like a son."

Jonah opens his mouth to respond, to say he simply wants to be treated like a person—a person worthy of respect and dignity for just being who he is—but then two blue lasers zip in the room through the doorway, one hitting Mirker in the chest, the other shooting right through his neck. The man's head spins away from his sitting body with the frosties still holding on.

Trembling at the sight, Jonah whips his gun at the doorway, only to find Brooklyn slowly march in with an LZR-rifle smoking in her small hands. She raises her foot and places it on Mirker's seated, headless body, and shoves it over.

"Your sons were assholes," the girl says. "No one wants to be like them."

"Brooklyn!" Jonah yells, dropping his gun to the floor. He runs up to her and drops to his knees, wrapping his long arms around her tiny frame. He then pulls back and stares into her eyes. The blue is almost completely gone. And she has corneas and pupils and Jonah just can't believe it. "You're okay. You're okay?"

"It's really good to see you."

He wraps her up again, looking over her shoulder to see Vespa standing there with a smile on her face, her arms crossed over her chest. She lets them have their moment.

"I'm sorry I haven't been around to help. Thing's here have been a little crazy around here," Jonah says.

"It's all good, cadet," Brooklyn whispers. "I'm just happy I could get in a couple good shots."

Jonah looks back at Mirker's body and shudders at all the blood. The frosties have jumped off the man's severed head, leaning over to taste the puddle. It didn't have to be this way. He didn't want this. He should have been able to convince the man that he was worth more to the community than just as a sacrifice. That he could have been an integral figure here, someone who made the community better through his addition, not subtraction. After all, it's because of him that Hopper came to Thetis, and he brought the terraformer.

"Okay, you guys good?" Vespa asks.

Jonah pulls back and sets his hands on Brooklyn's shoulders. "Yeah, we're—"

Dr. Z stands wavering behind Vespa, the giant alien skull over her head now nothing more than a crooked necklace of sharp bones. Her eyes are milky white, and in her hand held high over her head is a sharp metal tool.

Jonah grabs Brooklyn's rifle that hangs off her shoulder and spins the girl around as he fires. The lasers zip past Vespa and hits the doctor's outstretched arm, blasting the woman into the table behind her, knocking it completely over. Vespa ducks and runs into the room just as Jonah runs out of it. He looks both ways, making sure there aren't any last surprises, and then steps up to Dr. Z who lies still with her mouth moving, repeating something that Jonah can't hear.

This isn't fair, he thinks. Dr. Z was a good person. When all he's ever felt is insignificant and invisible, she had actually treated him as a person worthy of respect and dignity for just being himself. He can still feel her fingers on his face after blacking out from the crash, how gentle they were as she cleaned his eyes and checked his broken nose. And now, he looks down at her milky white eyes and broken arm, wondering if he can somehow help her—be it saving her life or ending it without further pain.

Her mouth keeps moving and moving and Jonah aims the rifle right at it as he bends down to hear what she's saying. Maybe she's asking for help. Maybe it's one last set of instructions she needs to relay. He gets close enough to smell her rancid breath, to hear her throat softly click as she tries to speak. And then there's a hand on his shoulder, pulling him back.

"Jesus, dude. Are you really going to put your face down next to hers and give her one last chance to kill you?" Vespa asks. "Come on, Firstie. That's like, rule number one."

Dr. Z's head rolls toward Vespa's voice, still repeating the same word or phrase, but now with a slight smile.

"Speak the fuck up, lady," Vespa says.

Brooklyn joins the huddle, stepping on the doctor's left wrist and holding it there. "What already?"

Dr. Z's head rolls back and forth until she stares straight up at the ceiling. Her neck suddenly strains as if an invisible hand chokes it, trying to get her to stop talking. But her voice finally becomes clear: "They're not pyramids. They're not pyramids. They're not pyramids."

"What aren't pyramids?" Vespa asks.

Those things on Zion aren't pyramids? Jonah thinks. *Then what else could they be?*

"What is she talking about?" Vespa asks.

"I've seen them. They're on another planet in the galaxy," Jonah says. "I think...the ghosts that I've been seeing, the ghosts that a lot of people have been seeing, they say I need to go to this other planet called Zion, and I'm supposed to go inside the pyramids there and do something. I saw it when I ate the verve and when one the Module Eight kids touched me. If I don't go, then Earth is going to be destroyed. Everyone is going to die."

"They're not pyramids," Dr. Z says one more time. And then, as the middle of her neck magically twists and narrows until it's the size of her wrist, she whispers, "I'm sorry, Jonah."

The woman's eyes clear up, turning back to their shade of

green. She takes one last short breath and then her body twitches and rises a few inches off the ground before she goes rigid and quiet and falls back to the floor. Dr. Z is dead. Whoever was inside of her, possessing her to attack and lie and dig up dead bodies and mutilate people's skin, has left.

"Good," Brooklyn says.

Jonah wipes a tear running down his cheek. "It's not her fault."

Far off on their right, the woman soldier limps toward the exit with her head down. Behind her, the frosties teeter back and forth stacked on top of each other, slowly following a capstone that stops every few seconds to put a shard of shattered glass or a piece of broken wood on its head. And huddled in front of room four's doorway are the last three Module Eight kids and Kip, all holding hands, all humming softly.

Brooklyn gently takes the rifle out of Jonah's hand and aims it at the kids, but Jonah pushes the barrel toward the ground and shakes his head.

"Jonah, they'll kill us the first chance they get," Brooklyn whispers.

"They're just kids. Mirker's dead. Dr. Z's dead and lots of those Module Eight kids died. Griffin died out there. Can we just take a break shooting and killing each other and instead try to figure out what we do next?" Jonah asks.

"What we do next is we all slowly die from the air here," Vespa adds.

Kip and the three Module Eight kids sit down simultaneously and let go of each other's hands. This is the first time Jonah's ever seen one of them sit.

"No, we don't. I think that's about to change, too," Jonah says.

The door on their far left creaks opens slightly, bringing in a narrow slice of sunshine. Brooklyn whips her gun toward it, only to have Paul and Hopper peek their heads into view.

"Vespa?" Paul shouts. "Firstie, you guys good?"

Vespa hugs Jonah's arm and shouts back, "Yeah, no thanks to you!"

Her warmth brings a moment of peace to Jonah. And a moment of clarity. He said he wanted to take a break and figure out what they do next, but he knows what he's doing next. He makes eye contact with Hopper and nods and the boy smiles. Nothing is going to change here—the ghosts will keep trying to communicate with him, people will continue to be possessed and be killed—unless he leaves to fix things. He's not going to be someone's God, but he will be someone's hope.

• • •

Jonah sits between Vespa and Brooklyn, his spoon carving a trail through his mashed potatoes. Across from him, Paul stuffs a cold pile of corn nibs into his face while telling the table about new insects he saw that morning: "It was like a spider meets caterpillar meets mosquito, and they fly around in fours and each hold a corner of a web like a net, and they just buzzed around catching other insects in the net until they had enough for a feast." He guides the last remaining noodles on his plate onto his fork. "Then they'd land and just go to town."

"How were they like caterpillars, though?" Vespa asks.

"They had these fat, chubby long bodies," Paul says. "Kind of what like Firstie here would look like if he ever ate his fucking food."

Jonah stops playing with his mashed potatoes and pushes his plate toward Paul who digs right in.

"I'll take the bar," Brooklyn says, reaching over to stab a crumbly white square with her fork. A bag of medicine sits slumped on her shoulder, slowly dripping into the tube attached to her forearm.

Paul grabs Brooklyn's wrist. "Like hell you will."

"*Paul*," Vespa says.

"Fine."

Brooklyn drops the square onto her empty plate and cuts it into fours. Without saying anything, she sets a piece in front of each of them just as Aussie, the redheaded demic with a constellation of freckles on her face, enters the dining tent with a tray of food shaking in her hands. It's the second time he's seen the girl since the ship arrived over a week ago, and Jonah waves her over to join them.

"Hey," she whispers as she sits down.

"How are you feeling?" Jonah asks.

"I don't know. Every day is a little better, I guess. Having a hard time breathing. Feeling nauseous a lot. Don't really feel like eating."

Paul quickly reaches his fork toward the girl's plate when Vespa shakes her head. "Come on, dude."

"Well, you sound like everyone else here, then," Jonah says to Aussie. "But Hopper and the others are supposed to launch the terraformer today. Then, hopefully everyone will start feeling better. If it works."

Aussie nods and picks at her rice.

"It'll take months, maybe years for it to make a difference, though," Brooklyn says. "You don't just change a planet's atmosphere overnight. So, get used to feeling like shit for awhile, is what I'm saying."

Everyone falls quiet. A few people come and go from the tent—original settlers of the colony—and Jonah can't help but notice their heads are held a little higher than they used to be. He even sees a few smiles and hears someone laugh. A man and a woman in matching gray jumpsuits hold hands at a table in the corner. The woman leans over and gives the man a kiss on the cheek, and he leans into her with his eyes closed.

Aussie clears her throat again. "Jonah, look, I'm really sorry we...I'm really sorry about what happened on Achilles and how we left you behind and for what happened in Tunick's cave and everything. I don't know, I just couldn't control my—"

"Your burning desire to see me again?" Paul interrupts. "I totally get that."

"*Jesus,*" Vespa says.

Aussie opens her mouth to continue, but then she shuts down and slumps over her tray. Jonah can feel her guilt hovering over the whole table. It hangs just over his own cloud of guilt and shame and sadness. He never thought so many people would die around him. He never thought that so many people would die because of him.

"It's okay," he says. "I know that wasn't you. I'm just glad you're okay. And that Portis and Christina made it, too. And that Michael is getting better."

Matteo enters the tent, quickly making eye contact with Jonah, hesitating in the doorway about where he should sit. Jonah immediately empathizes with the situation; he used to be the one wondering if it was okay to join a group of people before eventually finding an empty table to eat by himself. But now, he's somehow surrounded by kids who aren't disgusted at the sight of him. He's surrounded by friends. And Paul. Matteo walks in his direction, but instead of inviting him over and welcoming him into his crowd, something no one ever did for him, Jonah looks away. Ever since he moved out of Matteo's yurt and got his own private place, the two boys have stopped speaking. Matteo sets his tray down at the end of a nearly empty table in the back corner and gets out his sheaf to read while he eats alone, but then a second later, he picks up his tray and leaves the tent with his shoulders low, his sheaf stuck under his arm.

Jonah's own sheaf is curled up in his pocket, fully charged, updated with the latest findings on Thetis and what's happening back on Earth. The war rages on in England, spilling over into Ireland and France. Thousands continue to die every week. Canada tested another nuclear weapon, its third in the last month. More of Florida and Georgia are underwater, and California continues to burn. Mexico has reached its limit on accepting Americans fleeing both the draft and their destroyed states, and now there's a lottery system in place.

"You guys hear about that volcano erupting in Bali?" Vespa asks.

"Fuck Earth," Paul says, jabbing a fork full of mashed potatoes in her direction. "I don't want to hear about it. We're on this shitty planet now. And this shitty planet has spider caterpillar mosquitoes with cool flying nets. And I get to name the bastards."

The door opens again, and two women enter with their food,

and before the door closes behind them, Jonah sees Matteo sitting outside on the ground, his tray resting in his lap.

"I'm going to go check on Hopper, see if it's ready to go," Jonah says, standing. He pats his pocket to make sure his sheaf is still there, a new routine he follows every few minutes.

"I still hate that kid," Vespa says.

"Ditto," adds Brooklyn.

In walk Krev and Hess, and then Portis with a severe limp. It's the first time Jonah has seen any of them outside of the hospital tent. As Jonah crosses paths with them, Portis gives him a sarcastic salute, and Krev purposefully rams his shoulder into Jonah's, knocking the cadet off balance and into a table. The whole dining room grows silent.

"Touch him again and I'll fuck you up," Paul says matter-of-factly from his seat. "For real."

Jonah takes a deep breath and stands up straight, staring the huge boy right in his wolfish eyes. The old Jonah would sheepishly turn and walk out the door without speaking. The Jonah from Achilles would walk right up to the boy and smash his nose into Krev's, daring the kid to take the first punch so he would feel good about unloading on him until his arms grew tired. But this Jonah, the one who knows he won't be around much longer, says, "I'm sorry about Camilla."

Krev doesn't know how to respond, and so he just grunts and turns around to find a table, immediately digging into his food. Portis joins him.

"Lark isn't taking it well," Hess says.

"I bet."

"Everyone says you saved the day here. Took down Mirker and everything."

"It was a joint effort," Jonah says with a shrug, stealing a glance at Vespa and Brooklyn who shake their heads at something Paul has just said. "But I do think people might be a little happier around here now."

"I hope so.

Jonah turns to leave, but Hess grabs his wrist. Her eyes suddenly brim with tears. "I saw it, too, you know. We all saw what they want you to do, Jonah. It's messed up. Are you going to... What are you going to do?"

He wants to tell her the truth, that he and Hopper have been meeting every night to go over their plan, that they've been putting together a list of people who they want to ask to join them. Hess isn't on it, and neither is Krev or Portis or Matteo, although Matteo did corner him to say he knew what he was up to.

"Did you know that Everett was here when we arrived? Mirker had him chained up in a sphere they built in the jungle. I guess it was for me. I was supposed to go through that portal we found and get here sooner. And then I was supposed to be sacrificed, whatever that means."

Hess lets go of his wrist. "Seems like everyone has a plan for you."

Jonah reaches for the door, but then stops himself and moves toward a small table sitting against the wall. He pours hot water from a pitcher into two cups and then drops in some loose orange tea leaves. He then backpedals out of the door and into the afternoon light. A drone zips by before sweeping over a line of yurts and circling the villagers trying to fix the telescope before it rises and disappears over the wall.

Matteo sits there with his tray of food on his lap watching the drone, too, and Jonah surprises him by handing him a cup of tea.

"Hey, thanks," he says, taking a sip. "What kind is it?"

"You're sitting out here all alone and the village is in shambles and you're being picky right now about what kind of tea it is? That's the funniest shit I've ever heard."

"Touché."

"Come on," Jonah says. "Let's go see how they're doing with the terraformer."

The two boys walk silently toward the ship that's still on its belly in the northwest corner in the village. Hopper and a few others circle the satellite near the tail of the ship, performing their final inspections on the car-sized terraformer with sheafs in their hands. A crowd has started to form.

Matteo takes a long sip from his cup. "So, what do you think?"

"Well, I think it's probably a huge mistake for me to leave Thetis now that things are going to be better," Jonah says. "I think what I'm going to be doing and where I'm going in the next week is either going to be the stupidest thing I've ever done, or the best. I'm pretty sure it's going to be stupidest, but honestly, man, I still hear them. They're still in my head, telling me what to do. And if I don't go, they'll never stop. And I can't live like that. They won't let me."

"I was talking about the tea."

"Yeah, I know."

Brooklyn and Vespa suddenly appear by his side and Vespa gives him a playful shove in the back. Jonah spills the hot tea over his fingers. "Dude."

"Relax, Firstie," Vespa says. "Drink your tea, and let's go give Hopper some shit and tell him he doesn't know what he's doing."

Brooklyn laughs and readjusts the medicine bag on her shoulder. "Cool, I've been doing that all morning."

The four of them walk together for a few steps, but then Jonah slows down and lets them get ahead. He watches them move forward without him, thinking about what he's about to do, where he's about to go. He's still torn about asking a few of them to come with him. He just doesn't know how he could go without his friends by his side, watching his back. How is he going to show up on a new planet that's still in the stone age, not speak their language, and then somehow change the course of their history so they don't wipe out alien civilizations in the future, all by himself? But then again, how's he even going to do it with anyone's help?

"Fucking wait up!" Paul shouts.

Jonah turns to see the cadet speed walking out of the dining tent, shoveling food into his mouth. His freshly shaved head shines in the sunlight.

"Hurry up, ya pig!" Vespa yells back.

They join the crowd around the satellite, Jonah's head sticking high over everyone else's, a buoy bobbing in a sea of hope. He listens to their coughs and wheezes, knowing how much rests on Hopper's shoulders. More and more villagers gather, including Krev and the other Splitters, plus Aussie who pushes Michael in a wheelchair. Kip and the few remaining Module Eight kids are nowhere to be found, most likely still in the hospital, strapped to their beds.

One of the scientists asks everyone to back up, back up, back up, and when everyone is at a safe distance, Hopper follows the other engineers and scientists up the ramp of the ship. Moments later, his face appears in one of the windows, his sheaf blinking red under his chin. The boy circles his index finger over the device several times with a goofy smile on his face, and then he presses it.

Smoke appears in the satellite's thrusters and the silver and blue cylinder starts to shake. A hand slips into Jonah's, and he doesn't need to look down to know it's Vespa's. When the satellite begins to lift off the ground, she squeezes his fingers and he squeezes back, and when the boosters ignite and blast the machine into the sky where it will orbit Thetis to release nitrogen and carbon dioxide into the atmosphere, Jonah pulls the girl into his side and kisses the top of her head. Vespa looks up in surprise, and then she pulls him down to press her lips into his.

The satellite gets smaller and smaller, and soon the only evidence of its arrival is the column of smoke marking its departure. Hopper and the others descend the ship's ramp to applause, and then the hacker finds Jonah's head above the crowd and points to him.

Jonah nods and his shoulders stiffen. He looks down at Vespa and searches her eyes for comfort. "Hey, this is hard for me to ask, but I wanted to know if you—"

"Yeah, Firstie, I'll come with you."

"Me, too," Brooklyn adds, giving her medicine bag a slight squeeze. "I mean, who doesn't want to travel back in time and take down an entire evil civilization?"

Jonah shakes his head and watches a drone zip through the satellite's column of smoke. He reaches into his pocket and makes sure his sheaf is still there, and then he heads for his yurt to finish making his plans for departure.

END OF BOOK TWO

ACKNOWLEDGMENTS

Ah, the second book of a trilogy, the one where you try to answer just enough questions from the first book to keep readers from grumbling and then ask crazier questions and plant seeds for the third book to keep readers still interested. The middle child of trilogies. The one unfavorably compared to the oldest and then later overshadowed by the youngest. But even if *Thetis* is the Jan Brady of The Deep Sky Saga, I hope you enjoyed reading it just as much as I enjoyed writing it. (And remember that Jan ended up being the fan favorite.)

I'm assuming you already read *Achilles* (thank you!), so all those fine people I mentioned in those acknowledgements pretty much apply here, too. But I'd like to put a spotlight on a few of those people and add a few more:

To my literary agent, Wendy Sherman, thank you again for getting this ball rolling and then for giving it a push when it got stuck. Let's keep this momentum going.

To Keith Wallman, Kayla Park, Alexandra Israel, Erin Mitchell, and everyone at Diversion Books, thank you for helping me get this story out there. Your notes and direction have been invaluable. And a special thank you to Jaime Levine for bringing the series to Diversion in 2016.

To my family and friends, thank you for helping me promote my work and giving me a pat on the top of my head when I needed it. I want to add Justin Kinney for encouraging me to keep going and helping me with last-second editing questions (on many different projects) and Jeremy Bell for reading the very first draft of *Thetis* and giving his much-needed advice. Oh, and Joe Andosca's brain proved to be helpful again. Thanks, Joe's brain.

To Veronica and Juliette, my brilliant daughters, thank you for not burning down the apartment whenever I ducked into my room to write something down real quick. Oh, and for your endless love and all that stuff.

And again, to you, the reader: I know there are a lot of books out there, so thank you for spending some time with mine. Truly appreciated.

ABOUT THE AUTHOR

The fourth of six kids, Greg Boose grew up on a large produce farm in northeast Ohio. He received his undergraduate degree from Miami University, and then later received his M.F.A. at Minnesota State University Moorhead where he focused on screenwriting and fiction. He lives in Santa Monica with his two young daughters.

Printed in the United States
by Baker & Taylor Publisher Services